Atlantis: Order of the Librarians

IRWIN GLENN

Atlantis – Order of the Librarian

2nd Edition
Copyright © 2022 Irwin Glenn
All rights reserved.
ISBN: 9798359256285

DEDICATION

To Dad.

ACKNOWLEDGEMENTS

Thanks go to my friends and family who provided support and
encouragement in bringing this story to the printed page

GLOSSARY

Aps is a title of a child selected into the Order of the Librarians
Councillors of Atlantis have the title Con and are also known as
Elders

Characters of Note
Dels – Empsar
Dwig, Con – Empsar
Fras, Con
Grote, Birtek – Master of Selection and Grandfather of Utek
Grote, Utek – Master of Selection
Hootas, Toc Circ – Soldier of Atlantis
Hort – Master Teacher
Pars, Devas – Assistant Master Stonemason
Pars, Ro Con
Postet, Stivus
Pras, Con
Strevs, Toc – Soldier of Atlantis
Stu, Toc – Soldier of Atlantis
Sua – Daughter of Ela
Trun – Councillor
Trun – Old Man
Voret, Gamute – Master Stonemason
Voret, Givas – Son of Gamute
Voret, Jonas – Son of Gamute and Brother of Givas

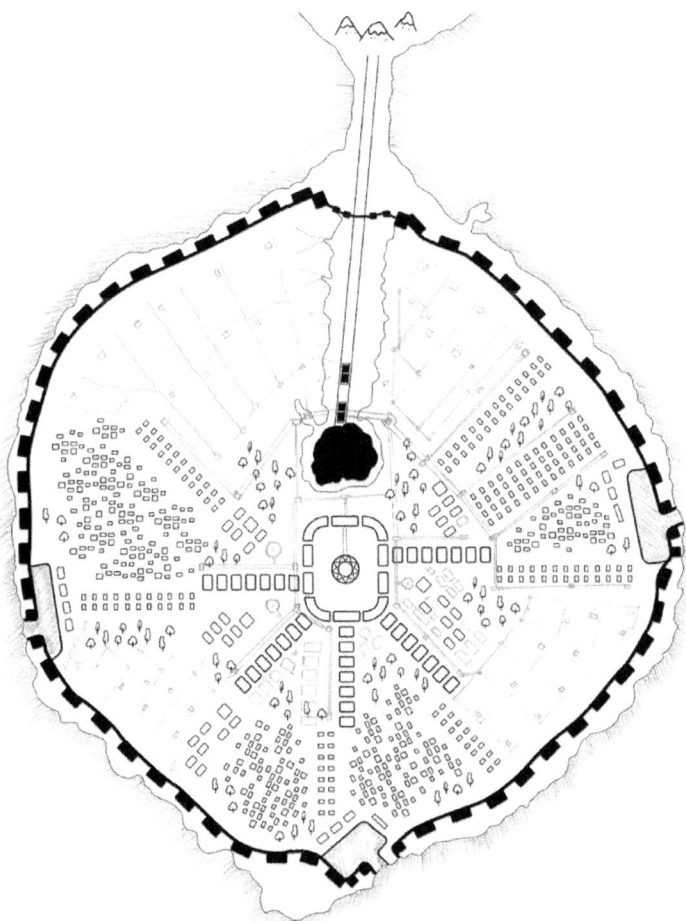

Atlantis

Prologue

The young librarian cleaned the statue with a rag.

"Of all the duties I could have been given," he hissed. "Cleaning and looking after the statues of the past old gods. I would have been better as an assistant to an Elder! Even the assistant to the empsar herself. I would do a much better job than Occa. She is past it now anyways. Empsar Dels needs a younger assistant!"

The gigantic statue looked down upon his ranting without judgement.

The tanned teenager had a full head of shoulder-length jet-black hair. Although not overly muscled the young man's wiry frame had little body fat.

He remembered as a child breaking into the museum at night and glancing through the low light in the direction of the doors. The museum was silent as dust motes drifted in the air. Even the dust was caught in the few rays of sunlight beaming from the windows up high.

The librarian was bored with his duties and wandered between the stone statues of historical figures and fables of the past. It was all lost on the eighteen-year-old. Although he didn't appreciate the gigantic beings under his care, he carefully avoided touching them. He did not want to have an accident and topple one of the beings, certainly not on his first day.

They would probably shatter anyway!

The junior librarian spied a door at the back of the cavernous hall.

What is this? I wasn't told about any room!

The door squealed as he pushed it open. One small gap in the wall above his head allowed the light to trickle in.

On walking into the room, he breathed in a lungful of dusty air and coughed explosively. Then he sneezed. The young man cupped a hand to an ear and listened out for Master of Selection Birtek Grote. He did not want to experience the wrath of the ancient man again. Even though the master of selection was his grandfather he had not been treated any better than any of the other junior librarians.

Phew! He relaxed and moved deeper into the room. The young librarian lifted his stubbed toe. He accidentally knocked the table again. A stone tablet fell and landed with a thud. The young man screamed.

He hobbled and hopped, alternating his weight between two injured feet.

"What are you doing?" The master of selection yelled from the front of the hall.

"Nothing, Grandfather!" Tears were at the corners of his eyes as he grabbed the offending stone tablet and placed it back on top of the table whilst snorting in derision.

Lost of family a man is
With no idea of future
Gifted beyond others
Will put into action
Annihilation of our life
Foundations and all

Unless the past can
Be forgiven and
Living starts anew
Time will be changed forever
Except for the few

He draped a cloth over the offending article, trying to ignore the jagged broken edge where a piece had broken off, and left the room.

"Where are you, young man?"

"I am here, Grandfather!"

The master of selection opened the doors wide letting in the afternoon sun.

The young man raised a hand to shield the blinding light and bumped into a smaller statue.

"Watch what you are doing," the master of selection barked.

"Yes, Grandfather!" He grappled with the statue until it was once again standing still.

"It is the end of your first day as a junior librarian. Let us go home before you damage anything!"

"Too late," Junior Librarian Utek Grote whispered and glanced back at the door to the room at the back of the hall.

1

Decades later Utek Grote had become a seer and one of the best masters of selection that Atlantis had ever experienced. He held the annual selection process and assessed children on whether they had the qualities to become librarians of the future.

"Stivs!"

Stivus Postet ignored his mother's call. The build-up of excitement over the long hours in the baking sun could no longer be suppressed.

Stivs reached the door and was knocked flying to the ground as the door opened suddenly.

A young girl with a big grin held the door open. She turned and looked back inside the gloomy room.

Stivs followed her gaze and he saw the master of selection holding a man's hand. Master of Selection Utek Grote's hood had slipped off. The greasy silver hair was pulled back, away from the wrinkled ancient face. Utek Grote's eyes were without pupils and irises. The orbs glowed a bluish white.

Stivs was mesmerised.

"Assistant Stonemason Devas Pars," the voice of the master of selection sounded out.

Stivs held his breath. *The master of selection is in a trance!*

"...you must look after your best friend and his second son..." Utek Grote's head lolled and his voice resonated with authority.

"What?" Stivs asked.

"...regardless of how you are perceived... look after your friend and his son when you can and as long as needed..."

"My friend and his second son?"

"...as he will be the one..."

"Father?" The girl at the door had her hands on her hips.

Devas Pars looked at his daughter. "One moment!"

"He will be the one? Who will? The father or the son?"

The master of selection dropped his head, wiped the spittle from his lips with the back of his hand, and raised his head back up.

"Are you still here, Assistant Stonemason Devas Pars?"

"Master Grote... I... you..."

"Do not argue with the decisions in this room of selection! Now leave! I have many more children to assess."

"Father!"

Stivs Postet watched, still sitting on the ground as the girl's father walked out of the hut shaking his head.

"Next!"

The assistant to the master of selection must have been undergoing her vow of silence as she waved Stivs in without a word.

"And who are you, young man?"

"Stivs... Stivus Postet," Stivs replied staring at the blind man.

"And what do you want to be when you are older?"

Stivs stared at the old man's leathery face as the blind man stared blankly back.

"Well?"

"Uhhh... master of selection or empsar."

The master of selection cackled. "You do, do you?"

Stivs nodded.

The master of selection grabbed his hand.

"Master of selection... mmm... I don't think you will outlive the likes of me."

Stivs stared at the old man with his mouth agape.

"Empsar?" The old man's white wispy eyebrows furrowed together in concentration. "So much potential... so much ability." The sentence trailed off.

Stivs' eyebrows raised.

"You must follow your heart and not your head!" The head of the master of selection had tilted back as though he was staring at the roof of the hut. "Do not be fooled by old beliefs of the past but trust the young!"

The female librarian who was acting as the master of selection's assistant placed a hand on the man's back to prevent him from falling off his stool. The brief touch broke the master of selection's connection to the energies.

"Well then, young boy; not master of selection in my time, but maybe empsar one day." He turned his head to his assistant and nodded. "This boy is to be an aps."

The young woman scribbled Stivus Postet on her list and the selection process was over, for Stivs at least.

Stivs was led back home by his mother. He was stupefied as they passed the Fountain of Albacas and still silent as they passed the School of the Aps and he only returned to the present when they passed the Hall of the Querks.

The Querks were chanting as the mother and son walked past outside. They were raising the vibration through the use of sound and intention. Stivs felt peals of joy bubble in his belly. He turned and smiled up at his mother.

"So, what do you think of that? You may be an empsar in the future."

"Whatever will be, will be."

His mother smiled at him and the farther away from the Hall of the Querks they were the less they felt the joy.

Stivs kicked a lonely pebble along the pathway in front of him and he saw a puff of dust rise in annoyance at his passing.

The heat of the day quietened the chatter between mother and son to a languid silence.

"What would Father have thought?" he finally uttered with emotions bare.

His mother glanced down at him and saw tears at the corners of his eyes.

"Do you need to ask?"

Stivs nodded.

"He would have been so proud."

Stivs smiled and kicked the pebble once more. His mind, now satisfied, was flickering onto other topics once more.

2

"What are the three of us like?" Devas asked himself. "I am unable to give my beloved another child. My friend Gamute has two boys but his wife is ill and Oran and his wife have lost a boy in childbirth."

He glanced at Gamute Voret who had recently been appointed master stonemason. Devas, also a stonemason, was overlooked for the role but knew that they had selected the right man.

Gamute looked up and saw Devas looking at him. His eyebrows arched in question above his piercing blue eyes. Devas raised his cup and saw a silent nod given in response. Devas downed his cup again and felt the alcohol settle the anxiety and buoy him on a wave of contentedness. He waved his empty cup and pointed for all three cups to be filled.

"You have been drinking far too late, husband," Ro mumbled, half asleep on his return.

"I am not in the mood anymore, darling," he whispered.

Ro raised her head off of the bed and her eyes opened wide. "What has happened?"

"Oran and his wife… their second son died in childbirth."

Ro raised a hand to her mouth and tears welled in her eyes.

"It answers one question though," he said sombrely.

Ro leant back from his embrace and stared at him. "What?"

"It means that I have to look after Gamute… that is when Givas, his second son is inducted into the Order of the Librarians and becomes an aps." Devas hugged his wife again and stared over her shoulder into the distance, lost in thought.

As the months rolled into years, Devas saw his friend lose his air of calmness and confidence as his wife's health continued to go downhill. Smudges of anxiety-filled sleepless nights hung from his eyes giving Gamute a haunted look.

Until one day Devas found his best friend staggering drunkenly to the stone works project mid-morning with no apology or excuse.

"Gamute have you been celebrating again?" Devas joked.

Gamute looked at him and Devas' heart dropped as he saw the pain in the man's soul.

"She has... gone."

"Who?"

"Ellie, she has gone."

Devas hugged his friend, ignoring the gazes of curiosity and interest from the labourers and young boys on the stone works project.

"You know what everyone should be doing, Durp?" Devas asked.

Durp was a squat solid rock of a man without a strand of hair on his head. He nodded after seeing that something was happening and waved Devas away.

"I can look after this!"

Devas nodded once and grabbed Gamute's shoulder directing him away from the stone works.

Devas took Gamute into town and stopped at the Fountain of Albacas. He glanced at the position of the sun and realised the drinking room had yet to open.

He grabbed a ladle of water and offered it to Gamute.

Gamute stared into the water of the fountain and gave no reaction.

"Gamute? You need some water."

Gamute grabbed the ladle, drank the contents and handed it back without a word.

"Where are Givas and Jonas?" Devas looked at Gamute's bowed head. "Gamute! Where are your sons?"

Devas cringed when Gamute looked up at him with bloodshot eyes and tears streaming down his cheeks; his friend was close to falling apart.

"Jonas is looking after his younger brother."

Devas guided Gamute through the city. The heat of the late morning sun bounced off the walls and any conversation evaporated in the dry air.

The pair of stonemasons automatically checked the harbour walls as they reached the western coastline. Devas noted one or two points that needed further investigation and potentially repair.

Standing on the wall looking westwards the fresh sea-laden air invigorated him and he glanced at his friend processing his grief.

"What am I to do?"

Devas kept silent.

"I have two sons. Jonas can look after himself but Givas...?"

Gamute was struggling. "I wonder… could he be selected for the Order of the Librarians? Could he become an aps?"

"Well, there is a selection day tomorrow. Didn't Ellie want Givas to be an aps?"

Gamute nodded. "Is it too soon though? Too soon after this afternoon?"

Devas looked out at the water and saw a man at the edge of his vision. The man paused, waiting for the right moment, as he knew from experience not to interrupt conversations amongst friends. Gamute saw the man too and nodded.

"Stonemason Voret?" The man asking had the flat eyes of a person who has worked with the dead all his life.

"This afternoon?" Givas asked.

"This afternoon."

Devas looked at the keeper of the dead and raised an eyebrow. The man's face was untouched by the sun and wrinkled. With no hair on his head, only the thick wiry eyebrows hinted at the colour of the night his hair would have once been. The coarse, brown shirt and shorts highlighted his pale skin even more.

"From where?" the keeper of the dead asked Devas.

"The Healing Hut." Devas glanced at Gamute who nodded before turning to the horizon as a tear slipped down his face.

"Where are the boys?" Devas asked, looking back at the city.

Gamute, standing at the farthest wall of the harbour dropped his gaze. "They should be at home. Jonas is looking after Givas again." His mouth tightened

"Is he alright?"

"He doesn't understand, but I haven't got time for his childish demands."

Devas raised his eyebrows but said nothing further. Any conversation was cut short as they heard the flaming arrows fly through the air and light the small boat. The two stonemasons watched as the flaming pyre floated out towards the horizon and they only moved once it was no longer distinguishable in the sunset.

They walked back in silence through the growing shadows in the myriad of alleyways. The walk was quicker as there was drinking time dripping away.

Devas heard the raised voices as he waited outside the house. He

6

scratched his nose absentmindedly, knowing that his wife Ro would be happy enough looking after their daughter as he looked after his friend even if it meant a late drunken night again.

"I hate you!"

Devas was startled as Jonas burst out of the building and sprinted away. Gamute came to the door, again with tears in his eyes.

"No drinking tonight."

Devas nodded and only walked away when Gamute went back inside shutting the door behind him.

3

The four-year-old boy stood uncertain and alone. Looking back with disbelief emanating from him, he turned and walked away. Givas strode across the marble floor to the library entrance and left them.

The boy could not see the tears streaming down his father's face which was melting in utter desolation. The boy's mother had died the previous summer, and Gamute had lived his life protecting his son ever since.

"I hope he grows up to realise the sacrifice I have made for his security and future," Gamute whispered.

Devas nodded but kept quiet.

Devas could see the loneliness in his friend that grief brought on. Gamute pulled the rough cloak tighter, hunched over in an attempt to avoid the energy-sapping chill, and the two friends walked to the drinking room.

"Ah, you've done the right thing," Oran said before taking another mouthful of vine wine.

"But I miss him so much," Gamute choked out then took a long draught from his cup.

"Yes, but you did say he was difficult," Oran offered from the other side of Devas and avoided looking at the tears at the corners of Gamute's eyes.

"No! He wasn't that bad. Losing Ellie... losing Ellie so suddenly... and Jonas." Pretending to scratch the bridge of his nose, he wiped his eyes. "He will be happier within the order and find some stability. I hope and pray to the old gods that he does. I miss him so much."

His two drinking companions said nothing further. All three of them finished the topic of conversation with a swig from their cups. Devas lifted his empty cup and made a silent toast then let out a long and proud belch.

Devas pushed open the door and wobbled inside whilst his wife watched, stifling a smile.

"How is he?" she asked.

"Gamute is as expected. But we celebrated Givas being inducted."

"So, his second son is now in the order?" Ro asked.

"Yes," Devas replied with glassy eyes.

"And you will need to look after him as well?"

"Yes."

"How will you do both?"

"I don't know. Maybe I shall just say that I am drinking."

Ro smiled. "I am sure everybody will believe you."

4

The young boy thrived within the security and routine of school. The more he enjoyed the security the more he craved the attention of the adults. It appeared that the more secure he felt the more he was fearful of losing it.

Back in his small room, Givas kept himself busy. He had charmed a young librarian to give him two candles and he was fascinated as the librarian showed him how to use a flintstone.

The librarian put a finger to his lips and the young boy nodded. His eyes were glued on the flintstone as he didn't want to miss a thing.

The young man swiped the flint against the stone and inclined his head. The boy took the flint and struck the stone, gasping in amazement as sparks flew into the air.

The young librarian took the flintstone back and with a smile prepared a fire. He grabbed a handful of wood shavings and placed them in the centre of the floor in front of them. With one deft motion, he struck sparks into the shavings. A wisp of smoke snaked upwards as the shavings caught alight. Givas grinned and tried to grab the stones from the man.

The young librarian raised a finger in caution. He tipped a candle above the lick of flames and the wick smouldered before it caught alight. Satisfied, he passed the stone back to Givas. Givas struck sparks immediately. The young man tut-tutted at the haste of the boy and held up a hand for Givas to stop.

The librarian cleared the burnt shavings and placed a fresh pile in front of Givas. He noted the young boy's newfound patience and nodded.

The young librarian didn't know what it was about this boy but he was different to the rest. Givas was special. He held a small canvas bag out to the boy.

"You will need these."

The boy snatched the bag and shoved a hand into it. A grin spread across Givas' face as he found the striking stones and a couple of candles.

"You will need to get yourself a supply of shavings."

Givas nodded smiling.

5

Teacher Hort took his duties very seriously. He cared for the clutch of aps as if they were his own children. The teacher of future librarians knew that every child in this intake was special. They had all been offered up by their parents for selection. The children had been scrutinised, sensed, and considered before selection and entry into the Order of the Librarians. Only one child in a hundred had been granted a place. Some years it was not even half that and some years, not one child was selected.

Hort nodded. 'Numbers never affect the outcome! It is the master of selection who makes the ultimate decision.'

He often wondered about the venerable master. Was he wise, insane or was he just fooling everyone? Hort remembered the first time he had visited the museum.

The uncaring smell of age surrounded the figure like a swarm of bees around a hive. A mottled hand pulled back the hood of the cream-coloured cloak. Silver-white hair, brushed back to form a ponytail, revealed eyes of a shocking blue-white. It was obvious the man was blind. The eyes glowed out of a wrinkled ancient face that was untouched by the sun.

Hort wondered how many summers this wise old man had experienced so far.

The man was smiling at an unsaid joke.

"It could be over one hundred!"

Hort was shocked into rigidity.

"How did you know what I was thinking?"

"I may be blind but I am not ignorant."

Hort stood there non-plussed.

"Well? What do you want?"

"I… I am looking for the master of selection. Do you know where he is?"

"What do you want of him?" the old man demanded.

"I would speak to him about a matter and not with an old bag of bones such as you!"

"So you don't want to speak to the master of selection then?"

Hort looked again at the man in front of him. His irritation faded into scepticism. The man wore long flowing robes that had yellowed with age. Could these robes be on the man who was once Empsar of Atlantis?

The wizened face, crisscrossed with so many lines, stared at him without emotion.

Could this be the master of selection?

"Pass me that stick," the old man commanded pointing a long bony finger at a walking stick in the corner.

Automatically obeying, Hort grabbed the stick only to breathe in a nose full of dust. A loud sneeze echoed through the museum.

"That reminds me to do some cleaning," the old man chuckled.

Hort wiped his streaming eyes and saw the glint of light reflecting off the stick he was holding. He lifted it to the light and was amazed at what he saw.

"You have got my stick!"

Hort's eyes caressed the gem-encrusted golden walking stick. He placed it carefully and with reverence into the impatient outstretched hands.

The old man raised himself from his seat. Leaning on the Staff of Atlantis, he stood up beside the open-mouthed teacher.

"Now what did you want to discuss with me?" the master of selection enquired.

Since that meeting, he often wondered if the master of selection was fooling everyone or was very perceptive and had abilities beyond anything he could imagine.

Hort had never married. Of course, he could never marry now, being a teacher. Hort snorted. Being a eunuch, he would be no use to a woman apart from for doing work. He had known the conditions and requirements of his appointment before agreeing. Still, he'd made that fateful decision twenty-five summers ago. His parents had been confused initially but were ultimately glad that he was happy. They, in time, became the proudest parents they could be. Their son was a teacher. Not only a teacher, but their son could also end up being the master teacher. The only more trusted positions were the master of selection and beyond that the reigning Empsar of Atlantis.

Hort smiled to himself before refocusing his attention on the brood. He surreptitiously watched Givas Voret.

He sensed the young son of Gamute Voret, the stonemason, was different, but he couldn't quite put his finger on how or why he was different. The boy was certainly bright and despite the tragedy in his life to date was seemingly emotionally unscarred.

How would I have been if my mother had died and an older brother had disappeared, seemingly lost at sea? Hort mused. Ah well! Time will tell all!

"I don't want to go to the beach," Givas whined.

Hort looked at the boy and saw tears in his eyes. Glancing at the rest of the class he could see that the other aps were excited at the prospect of an afternoon out.

"Would you like to help the stablemaster look after the horses instead?"

A few other children perked up at the suggestion.

"It won't be easy!" Hort quickly covered. "It will be work that will make you sweat. You may have to clean out the horses' dung!" Hort sensed the other children's diminishing interest in going to the stables.

Givas still nodded enthusiastically.

"Good! That is settled then. Givas, go to the stables and tell the stablemaster you are there to help him with his duties. I will check up on you by the end of the day."

Givas ambled through the alleys with his favourite dog Ua. Although they weren't supposed to have pets, a ratter dog had managed to get treats from Givas and ever since had followed the young boy whenever he was out of school.

The dog was a small bitch with tight black and brown fur and four white socks. When she wasn't hunting rats, it was at Givas' ankles with a tail constantly whipping back and forth.

Ua darted off into the shadows and Givas heard a squeal and a yelp followed by a growl. Moments later Ua brought over a dead rat and dropped it at Givas' feet.

Givas toed the carcass with the end of his leather sandal and pushed it back until the dog bit into it.

"Stablemaster!"

Goras turned to face the boy.

"Oh! It's you again!" Goras turned back to face the horse and hid his smile.

The man wiped beads of sweat from his brow and breathed out. The heat of the day was overpowering and Goras realised the horses needed more water.

The stablemaster was tall and broad with a belly that pushed out his leather jerkin. With thick, tanned, muscled arms folded over his chest, he towered over the young boy.

"Master Teacher Hort told me to help you this afternoon."

"Oh, did he?"

"Yes! The other children are going to the beach."

"And why aren't you?"

"My brother went to the harbour and never came back."

Goras stopped what he was doing. He saw the fear in the boy's eyes.

"I much prefer to look after Hennie." Givas stuck a hand through a stable gate.

The horse snuffled at the hand and whickered in protest.

"Hennie is thirsty. Can you fill a bucket at the fountain and give her a drink?"

Givas darted off, armed with an empty bucket, and Goras glanced down and saw the dog.

"Well? What are you waiting for?" Goras smiled as the dog raced off after the boy.

6

Devas felt unsettled. Looking up at the sun he realised that there was still plenty of time left in the working day. The feeling grew stronger.

The image of the master of selection popped into his mind and the instructions he had been given all those years ago echoed through his head.

"Gamute!"

"Devas?"

"I need to see someone!"

Gamute Voret glanced at the position of the sun. "There is still plenty of work to do, Devas! What is this about?"

"All I can tell you is that it's important."

"If you must!"

Devas walked quickly off the site and headed to the centre of the city. He had no idea where he was going and went on instinct alone. He was surprised when he arrived at the stables.

"Stablemaster!"

"What? Who is interrupting me?"

"It is I, Devas Pars, a tired and thirsty stonemason!"

"Ah-ha, Devas Pars the stonemason! It is too early in the afternoon to be thinking about drinking."

"It is never too early! But I am not here for that. I am wondering where your young assistant is."

"What? You are not here for some witty banter and remembering how a young librarian was thrown off a horse on his first-ever ride?"

"Will that memory ever stop haunting me?" Devas laughed.

"I will never forget as it was the first time I was looking after the fresh-faced librarians before they were selected for their roles." Goras closed the gate and grinned whilst wiping perspiration from his brow.

"Givas," he yelled.

Both men looked around but did not hear a response.

"When does his school day finish?"

"Not for a while." Goras frowned. "Givas," he yelled again. After waiting a moment he secured the gate and moved off.

"Where—"

"I am going to tell Master Teacher Hort."

"I shall leave you to it."

"Thanks."

Devas ambled through the alleyways, frequently glancing upwards. The approaching dusk was a concern. Turning a corner, he was relieved to see his best friend's son in the distance.

He watched as Givas knelt down in an alleyway, darkened by growing shadows.

"What is he doing in this rough area of the city?" Devas whispered.

A flicker of movement caught his attention and he realised he wasn't the only adult watching the boy. A man in filthy rags stood just inside the shadows at the far corner of the alleyway. Devas saw the itinerant lick his lips and the hair rose on the nape of the stonemason's neck.

Devas moved quickly and quietly. He knew that, although the society of Atlantis was enlightened, there was always a small minority who slipped through the cracks and acted out of hurt, anger and evil.

Without a sound, Devas opened the tool bag that hung around his waist and lifted out a chisel. The dust-encrusted human being shuffled closer to the boy who was squatted in the middle of the alleyway.

"Grandfather, I think you should find your bed for the night!"

"What?"

Devas held his tool in a beam of sunlight causing it to glint. The old man's eyes widened. The stench of stale vine wine merged with the reek of weeks of unwashed sweat and caused Devas to gag.

The old man looked at the tool and saw the steely determination in Devas' eyes and the honed muscular physique of a stonemason in his prime.

"I am not doing anything," the man muttered. "Grandfather, ha," he grumped and sloped off along the dark alleyway away from Devas and the boy.

Devas put his tool back into his pouch and stared at Givas.

The boy was sobbing and had a motionless furry body in front of him.

"Nooooo!"

Devas watched mesmerised.

"You can't die," the boy whispered. "Not you too. Please don't die."

Devas realised that in the boy's first six summers Givas was staring another death in the face. Too much death for one so young, he opined.

Givas' hands were planted on the bloody chest of the dog and his eyes were screwed tight. His face frowned in total concentration.

"You must live," Givas whispered over and over.

Devas felt his world shift. Time billowed and warped, flowed and ebbed with the only sound being the susurration of Givas' mantra.

Nobody else passed the alleyway. They would have seen a young boy cradling a blood-soaked dog. Curiously, the flies stayed away Devas noticed.

'Were they for once being respectful?'

Devas was startled out of his reverie just before sundown. Goras appeared and by the look of him the stablemaster had almost given up hope of finding the boy. Devas was motionless and watched Goras empty a feedbag and place the bloody dog inside. Devas saw the care the man showed in easing the sleeping form of Givas over his shoulder before heading off towards the stables.

Devas followed at a distance, not wanting it to be known that he had been checking up on the boy.

Goras met Teacher Hort who was apoplectic with a mixture of fear and anger.

"What happened? Where was he?" Hort saw the blood. "Is he injured? By the old gods! What happened?"

"The boy is asleep and breathing well." Goras gently rested the boy against the stable door.

Devas saw both men look on with paternal concern as Givas' head lolled to one side. Goras brushed a lock of hair out of his cherubic face before standing up. The stablemaster winced as he opened his bag and saw the blood-soaked dog.

Devas saw the men look at each other and shake their heads.

"His dog may not survive." Goras placed the bag on the ground beside Givas.

Hort had his head bowed and was wringing his hands.

"The boy is safe, Master Teacher."

"Yes."

"Let us not make this into anything bigger than it is."

The stablemaster moved a bucket of water to the dog's side and Devas' eyes widened as the two men jumped in alarm. He heard the dog whimper and then pant. Miraculously the dog had awoken and bounded over to Givas before licking the boy's face.

Givas came to, spluttering in protest before realising what was in his face.

"Ua!" The boy held the dog against his chest with delight lighting his face.

Goras the stablemaster shrugged his shoulders and Master Teacher Hort scratched his head.

Devas needed a drink. When he got to the drinking hut he sat alone in silence. The wine stood on the table untouched.

What did Ro say? Devas' eyes narrowed in concentration. *A prophecy... that was it! She mentioned there were rumours that someone special would be responsible for the destruction of civilisation!*

Devas shook his head slowly. *Could the second son of my friend ...someone who I have been tasked with keeping an eye on, could Givas be the special one?*

"Devas Pars! My fellow stonemason! Is this where you had something to attend to?"

Devas' eyes widened. He instinctively grabbed his cup and took his first mouthful of wine.

"Master of Wine! Has my friend been here long?"

The pot-bellied man glanced across to the table. "Are you asking about today, this week or since the last full moon?"

Gamute laughed then signalled for a drink.

19

7

Devas looked at Gamute and frowned. His friend's shoulders were slumped, and the man's eyes were red-rimmed. An oppressive cloud of grief hung over him and saturated his soul.

They stood at the front of the crowd of onlookers. Devas didn't think they were all mourners. After all, it was only the stoneworkers and the Council of Elders that had really known the deceased. The ex-master stonemason's body floated away from them on the tide.

Devas glanced at the young archer at the end of the pier and frowned again. The youth could barely have finished training and was blushing furiously as he struggled to notch a flaming arrow.

The first arrow landed at the front of the small boat which carried the mortal remains of the ex-master stonemason. The crowd tittered as the flame fizzled out and Devas felt compassion for the mortified young archer.

The second attempt lit the oil-soaked wood, and the crowd made a sound of impressed appreciation. The body was quickly indistinguishable in the flames.

Devas felt the stare of the empsar and gave a half bow. The empsar glanced at Gamute then looked back at Devas and raised his eyebrows in silent question. The two youngest councillors, Con Pras and Con Fras, were on either side of the leader of Atlantis and were oblivious to the silent question, and missed Devas' smile and brief nod in response.

Devas remembered back to the choosing of the replacement of Master Stonemason Harcute. It had taken place in the empsar's chambers. Devas had nodded quietly for Gamute to be chosen and the empsar had selected the shocked and equally baffled Gamute Voret as the new master stonemason. Gamute had assumed that Devas would have been the obvious choice. Devas had the words of the master of selection ringing in his ears to look after his best friend and the second son.

"You deserve it more than I," Gamute said sheepishly.

"You are more imaginative!"

"As long as you keep helping me. I cannot do it without you."

Devas had nodded.

Gamute clapped Devas on the back. "Come on, I shall treat you to an urn of vine wine!"

"Where have you been?" Devas asked Gamute who had a strange look on his face.

"I have been away thinking."

"Why?"

Gamute laughed. "I have an audacious plan!"

Devas shook his head in mock disapproval. "Nothing good ever comes from thinking too much!" He sighed and looked at Gamute with a resigned smile. "So, what is your audacious plan then?"

"Well, you know how the new western settlement means a greater demand for fresh water on the aqueduct system as we will have to add another spur."

"Yes."

"And you know that adding another spur onto the aqueduct system will lessen the amount of water across the system."

"Yes."

"What about an additional supply?"

Devas scratched his head. "More water? From where? The sky?"

Gamute grinned. "Not quite." He nodded towards the side of the volcanic crater.

"The Big Deep?" Devas asked.

"Yes."

"How?"

"Tunnels."

"Tunnels?"

"Two or three tunnels that will come out there, there and there."

"You're serious!"

"Yes. Think about it. Another constant supply of fresh water onto the aqueduct system will improve the pressure and allow us to add more spurs to supply all the new housing districts."

Devas stood with his mouth open.

"I am sure the councillors will agree to it."

Devas nodded dumbly.

"Audacious!"

"Yes!"

Devas saw the sparkle in his best friend's eyes. The sparkle that had been missing for some time had once again returned. He nodded again slowly. "Yes, I am sure the Council of Twelve will approve it."

This time it was Gamute nodding.

"If you focus on describing the benefits."

"Yes, the benefits."

"Reducing the effects of the dry season. Maybe even stopping shortages once and for all. Water security! With a constant supply of water all year round there will be no more need for a guard force to patrol the fountains."

"Yes, no need for security."

"And it will supply water to the whole city throughout its growth."

"Yes! Right, let's go then."

"Go? Go where?"

"To petition the empsar and the Council of Twelve of course!"

Devas shook his head and tried to clear his confusion.

"Master Stonemason Voret and Stonemason Pars to propose plans for an additional water supply," Gamute told the guard.

Devas watched the guard eye them up and down once before opening the door behind him and shouting the same words down the corridor to his comrade who stood outside the chambers.

Devas tried to look over the guard's shoulder into the corridor, but the soldier turned, and the door closed.

Gamute sighed and pointed at the wall. "Shall we?"

Devas laughed. "A good idea!" He sat in the shade of the wall and faced the council building as Gamute sat down next to him.

Despite their best efforts to stay awake the soporific heat, even at dusk had its way.

They were awoken by the shout of the guard.

"The Council of Elders will see you now!"

Devas and Gamute stood up groaning and stretched out their limbs to ease their muscles. They looked at each other and Devas saw the flicker of excitement in Gamute's eyes.

"Shall we?"

Devas nodded and followed the master stonemason into the cool corridor.

The guard at the door to the chambers opened it for Gamute. As Devas moved to follow, the guard closed the door.

"The empsar wants to speak with you alone afterwards."

Devas stood, uncertain of what to do. The guard indicated down the corridor.

"Master Teacher Hort is to speak to the council about Givas Voret being the one!" The guard at the front door shouted down the corridor.

Devas raised his eyebrows in surprise then slowly walked down the corridor to stand outside the empsar's chambers.

Givas Voret… the one. Givas, the second son of Gamute Voret is the one?

Devas remembered again the words of the master of selection.

Am I to look after the one? Am I to look out for someone that will be the cause of the downfall of Atlantis? That means I will be helping with the downfall of the city, doesn't it?

The silence of the empsar's room was deafening.

"Stonemason Pars! Thank you for waiting for me." The empsar saw Devas' face. "What is the trouble, Devas Pars?"

"Gamute Voret. His son is the one?"

The empsar frowned. "That is only a prophecy of old. Someone else's opinion from so long ago that has no bearing on now."

"But Master Teacher Hort believes it!"

"The only certainty that Master Teacher Hort believes is that young Givas Voret may be special."

"But that's why he came to speak to the council! He came to speak about Givas Voret being the one!"

"Stonemason Devas Pars!" the empsar snapped. "Breathe deeply!" His gaze softened.

Devas breathed way down into the depths of his stomach and felt the calming influence of the empsar.

"That is good. Now, when you look at a stone how many potential shapes and uses do you see?"

Devas was momentarily confused. "What?"

"When you look at a rock do you see one or more uses?"

"What… a rock?" Devas scratched his head.

"One or more uses?"

"Many uses of course," he said at last.

"Just like an untouched rock, everyone has many potential futures. Only when it is the end of their life is their place in history set in stone is it not?"

"Yes."

"Every moment there are multiple pathways, decisions and choices to be taken."

"I understand now, Empsar." Devas relaxed.

"I suppose you are curious as to why I asked to speak to you." Devas smiled. "Yes, Empsar."

"It is about our friend Master Stonemason Gamute Voret."

"Gamute?"

"Yes, and his plan for adding another water source."

"Yes."

"How is he?"

"How is he?"

"I sense he is tainted with grief. Grief can flatten a person and weigh them down in life."

Devas felt the full scrutiny of the empsar on him.

"Gamute… he has found his sparkle. This idea, this plan has relit his fire. For the first time in a long while I have heard him laugh and seen him smile."

"That is a relief."

"Oh?"

"The council and I unanimously approved the Big Deep project to start forthwith."

"Oh." Devas frowned.

"Is something wrong?"

"When I took my daughter to see the master of selection he instructed me—"

The empsar held up his hands. "Stop! I do not need to know what Utek Grote said to you!"

"But?"

"That is between you and him." The empsar tilted his head at the doorway. "Thank you for your time, Devas Pars."

"Thank you, Empsar."

Devas walked out into the corridor and then out of the council building. Gamute was nowhere to be seen. Devas, still in a daze, staggered to the drinking hall.

8

"Stivs!"

"Shhh!" the master historian hissed.

Stivs looked up and saw a guard from the Council of Elders building. The logo of Atlantis gleamed golden from the chain around his neck.

Stivs placed the carved stone back down and saw the master historian nod and wave an ancient bony hand towards the door.

"What is it, Toc?"

The soldier pulled him away from the archives' doorway. "The empsar wants you!"

"The empsar wants me?"

"Yes! Now move!"

"What does he want me for?"

"The leader of the Council of Twelve does not find it necessary to give a mere guard that information."

Stivs hurried after the guard.

Stivs stood waiting behind the guard. He smoothed his thick hair flat before brushing down his pale brown tunic and shorts with both hands. He didn't want to be in front of the empsar, filthy with stone tablet dust from the archives. Lastly, he raised a sandalled foot and rubbed it against the back of his calf before switching legs and cleaning his other sandal.

"Stivus Postet, Empsar!" The guard shoved Stivs into the empsar's chambers and withdrew.

"You wanted to see me, Empsar?"

"Librarian Stivus Postet, you come highly recommended." The empsar looked for any reaction. "Do you enjoy working in the archives?"

Stivs automatically felt the callouses on his hands. "It is what it is."

"And what is that?"

"Keeping the order of the tablets so the historic records are easily accessed at all times."

"And how are your hands?"

"Empsar?"

"When I worked in the archives it took years before my hands were tough enough."

"You, Empsar? You worked in the archives?"

"It was many years ago." The empsar grinned. "So, you and I are quite similar."

Stivs' eyebrows raised in surprise but he did not say anything.

"My assistant has had to retire."

"Retire?"

"Yes, his father is ill, and he has felt the need to look after him himself."

"Oh, I see."

"So, you are my selection to replace him." The empsar stared at Stivs.

Stivs felt a wave of energy wash through him, and he looked into the empsar's piercing eyes.

"It would be my honour, Empsar."

"Indeed!" The empsar's bushy eyebrows narrowed. "You won't have much to do for me, just the usual energetic safety when the council and I meditate and look at the councillors on my behalf."

"You want me to look at the councillors? To stare at them?"

"Yes."

"But... is that not rude?"

"You will be stood behind me back in the shadows."

"But why?"

The empsar stared at him.

"Of course. If you want me to, I shall look at them."

"Good, I shall see you in the morning then." The empsar nodded at the doorway and Stivs left.

Stivs finished his breakfast and tidied away the dish and spoon before wiping down his best clothes. The sun had yet to move across his window and show any offending dust.

He pushed his dark chestnut hair away from his face and behind his ears. Being tall for an Atlantean, his athletic frame allowed him to get away with drinking much vine wine and eating many sweetened breads, not that he did. He found the alcohol and sweet treats clouded his mind and made him want his bed on the rare occasion he partook.

Stepping out into the alley, he felt the warmth of the morning sun as it bounced off the facing wall, and he was pleased to note no dust remained on his clothes.

The soldier barely glanced as the young man passed him as he guarded the council building.

Stivs saw the logo of Atlantis marked into the wooden door. The three overlapping triangles within the circle had been etched by a craftsman. Time and care had gone into creating the logo on the door of one of the most important rooms in the city.

"Good morning, Empsar!"

The empsar was sat cross-legged on the floor, eyes closed and motionless.

Stivs waited patiently, looking at the old man. Despite the empsar's advancing years, the man had a strong angular nose and a firm jawline. The pale cream cloak with its hood down hid the empsar's burgeoning girth. Only the man's pale white toes peeked out from underneath the hem of the fabric.

The empsar's eyes opened and Stivs was momentarily startled.

Was that a hint of anguish I saw?

"Good morning, Stivus Postet. It is good that you are early."

Stivs raised his eyebrows yet said nothing.

"I feel this is going to be a challenging day." The empsar smiled. "Challenging for me, not you."

Stivs followed the empsar into the council chambers and was surprised that the councillors continued talking despite the empsar's arrival.

Regardless of his nerves, not a single councillor looked at him and when the empsar sat down, Stivs stepped back into the shadows. The other assistants did not seek his guidance before going into their meditative states.

"Empsar, when are you going to admit that there is a child in Atlantis that is the one of the myth?"

Stivs stared at the councillor. The Elder he was looking at must have been one of the oldest of the Council of Twelve.

"Con Trun, what do you know of this myth you speak of?" The empsar had raised one of his eyebrows.

"Yes, Con Trun?" another Elder asked.

"Yes, what is this myth?" Con Hrap asked.

To Stivs' unpractised eye it was only in Con Trun that he detected something deeper. In the other Elders, he only sensed interest and mild curiosity.

Con Trun straightened his posture and tilted his head patronisingly. "Empsar, a young talented future librarian who will be the reason for the downfall of our civilisation of course."

"Con Trun, may I suggest you accept the loss of your son so that your beliefs in the future of our civilisation are not tainted."

Con Trun's face burned with embarrassment.

"But, Empsar, what is this myth?" Con Hrap pressed.

The empsar looked at Con Hrap and saw the man's jowls quiver. The Elder's beady eyes were sunken deep into his florid face and were wide with fear.

"My fellow Elders… it need not hold our attention any longer."

"But—"

"But I feel your interest would continue to be piqued if I did not address the topic."

Stivs saw the empsar cover the room with a roving imperious glare.

"Many lifetimes ago a librarian etched a tablet with his belief of the downfall of Atlantis."

Con Hrap's hand went to his mouth and he sat down.

Despite Stivs' interest in the empsar's words he continued to focus his attention on the Council of Twelve one at a time.

"And this does not deserve our attention?" Con Hrap spat out.

"You are correct! It is one man's perception and the more we focus on it the greater the chance of it happening will increase."

"Do not treat us like aps," Con Trun snapped. "Does that mean if we focus on a tablet that records the annual harvest do we get a bigger harvest?" he sneered.

"Councillors, let us meditate on what to focus on that will serve us best."

Stivs saw that Con Hrap and Con Trun were the last of the Council of Twelve to close their eyes.

The empsar turned, winked at Stivs then nodded. Stivs bowed his head slowly and only after the empsar began the meditation did he close his own eyes.

Stivs sensed fear, annoyance and anger in the room which was interspersed with calm and peace emanating from most of the councillors. He focused on his task and surrounded the group with a protective shield of energy.

Stivs saw Con Pras and Con Fras whispering as they stood in the shelter outside the council buildings. Con Pras had stuffed something in his cloak. And Con Fras had pulled the cloak of Con Pras to cover whatever it was.

As Stivs neared the building's entrance they noticed his arrival and stepped into the shadows out of his view.

"Toc?" Stivs noticed the guard's bored look and did not finish his question.

"Yes, Librarian?"

"I hope your day is enjoyable."

"As enjoyable as the next," the soldier agreed automatically.

Stivs knocked once and pushed open the empsar's door.

"Good morning, Empsar," Stivs said seeing the tense features of the leader of the Council of Twelve.

"Stivs," the empsar replied simply.

Without a further word, he followed the empsar into the hall and then stepped once again into the shadows.

"Let us go through the harvest reports first," the empsar said looking towards Con Hrap.

As Con Hrap monotonously went through his report on the harvest of each field of each farm of Atlantis, Stivs saw the disinterest shown by the lolling heads as many Elders struggled to stay awake. The morning sun heated the eastern side of the building which warmed the air in the hall.

A shaft of light was hitting Con Trun squarely in the chest. Trun, the eldest councillor, was visibly slumped and snoring in his chair.

"Con Trun," the empsar said sharply, both cutting off Con Hrap's monologue and waking the old councillor from his slumber.

"Empsar?" Con Trun asked acidly.

"I understand that the grain count of Atlantis is not the most exciting information but please show some respect to your fellow Elders!"

All eyes swivelled towards a reddening Con Trun.

"At least I am here today!" Con Trun nodded to the empty chairs of Con Pras and Con Fras.

Stivs saw the empsar frown as all eyes focused on him.

"As long as you are here mentally as well as physically," the empsar retorted. "We still appreciate your focus and attention even if you don't." The empsar nodded to Con Hrap who, after a pause, once again began his soporific report.

9

Devas looked at the structure then back at Gamute. His friend's face was drawn and gaunt. Despite the stress and strain the master stonemason was putting himself through, Gamute still managed to smile.

"So, someone has to swim in the Big Deep and ensure the foundation blocks are flush." Devas stared into the depths.

The inky black waters could be hiding frightening monsters.

"The monsters of the deep are only out at sea," Gamute continued.

Devas grunted. He remembered the instructions of the master of selection.

"I shall do it," Devas said and noticed his friend relaxing as the fear left him.

"Are you sure?"

"You know I can place your stones exactly, even with my eyes closed."

Gamute grinned.

"Anyway, I shall be helped by Tuve. He swims so well I am sure his mother must have been a fish!" Devas looked at the youth a few paces away.

Tuve was bobbing with enthusiastic energy. His thin frame was at the growth spurt stage of adolescence. Devas could see Gamute's reservations. "We will be fine. The water is warmer than the seas in the Atlantean western harbour."

Gamute, after some thought, nodded. "It is agreed then. Tomorrow at high noon when the sun hits the water here, Tuve shall help you place the barrier stones." The master stonemason looked at Devas. "Until then relax! I shall treat you to an urn of the finest vine wine."

"Tuve is a bit young for vine wine, isn't he?"

"Master Stonemason, I have supped wine before," Tuve protested.

"So be it. I shall treat both of you this night!" Gamute scratched behind his ear. "Do you need to tell Ro of your whereabouts?"

Devas laughed. "We have an understanding. She will know where I am."

Devas was clapped on the back and they began the climb up the inside of the Big Deep. Both men watched the youngster speed upwards, streaking ahead of them easily.

Devas looked sceptically at the base of the barrier that he and Tuve had constructed. He knew from the minute gaps where his work finished and Tuve's work began.

He looked up the slope and saw Gamute on the ridge waving down at the workforce at the side nearest the city.

With a frown, Devas saw some water trickle through the tiny gaps of the fitting stones.

All three channels were almost complete. With two workers tunnelling towards the outside of the Big Deep's hillside, Gamute was directing the inbound tunnellers from above.

All the birds went quiet and Devas looked towards the innards of the ancient volcano. He felt the ground tremble. Wide-eyed, he waved at Gamute above. Gamute staggered but did not see his friend's alarm.

Devas watched in horror as the trickling water turned into spurts and then poured through the gaps.

"No!" he yelled. "Everyone get out!" he screamed at the entrances of the tunnels. Two workers in the tunnels nearest him could be seen struggling. Their heads were bobbing in the torrent as the water poured into the tunnel over them.

Devas ran along and lay down on his stomach, reaching his arms out. The second worker managed to hold up a hand. He grabbed him by the wrists and pulled him up to safety. As the two soaked workers recovered, Devas dashed the few yards over the stand above the second channel.

No worker was visible.

"No!" Devas cried. "Tuve! Where are you?"

Devas heard a sound. Again, he dropped to the ground and hung out over the tunnel.

Tuve's hands were gripping the edge of the tunnel. His whole body was stretched out into the depths as the water poured in over him.

Devas grabbed a wrist. "Help me! Somebody help me!" Devas

cried.

He heard Gamute stumbling at speed down from the escarpment as one of the first channel's workers rushed over.

Gamute finally reached the pair of them, and they all pulled Tuve out of the tunnel. The force of the water battered the youth and slowed their attempts. Once Tuve's head was out of the water he managed to help himself and after one final heave, they landed him like a fish.

Devas sprinted over to the third channel. There was no worker visible. The water flowed into the tunnel smoothly. Gamute stood by his side.

"For the love of the old gods," he breathed in horror.

"Is that—?"

"Yes, that must be the one tunnel that has been opened at the other side." Gamute finished. "I killed them," he muttered with eyes glazed.

"No! The earth bellowed. The ground shook."

"I am responsible! I am the master stonemason!"

"No! It's not your fault."

"Three workers missing, and it is my project."

Devas put a hand on his friend's shoulder. "It was the ground shaking. It was not your fault."

By the time Devas and Gamute had walked up the inside of the crater and down the outside, two bodies were laid out next to the first section of the aqueduct. The workers were attacking the entrance to the second channel with fury.

"Here it comes!" someone yelled as water shot out into the air.

Eager hands tore at the hole, widening it and they only slowed when a white-faced corpse slipped out of the aperture.

"Grab him!"

Hands grabbed the body before it dropped into the aqueduct section. The body was gently lowered onto the dry bank away from the manmade scree.

"I need to tell the parents," a white-faced Gamute said.

"Do you know who they are?" Devas got out.

"Yes!" Gamute cut him off. "Of course. I know the names of all the boys on the project."

"I am sorry. Of course." Devas looked away from his grief-stricken friend. "I shall inform the council."

"It should be me."

"You are best to inform the parents." Tears were at the corners of

Devas' eyes. "I will inform the empsar."

Devas followed the stumbling figure of the master stonemason of Atlantis. The man was once more weighed down with grief.

Glancing back, Devas saw three groups of men carrying the bodies down the hillside.

One of the men saw Devas, the assistant to the master stonemason's stare.

"We are taking them to the room of resting."

Devas nodded and felt a tear slip down his face and drip off of his chin.

The guard outside the council building saw Devas' face and did not ask his usual question but simply pushed open the door.

Similarly, the second guard saw Devas' tormented countenance and rapped twice on the door to the council chambers then pushed wide the door for Devas to enter.

The empsar and the Council of Twelve quietened with every step Devas took toward the empsar.

As the empsar nodded to Devas Pars the dreaded melancholic Chant of Passing by the Querks could be heard.

"How many?" the empsar asked.

"Three youngsters, Empsar." Devas wiped his eyes. "Gamute Voret the master stonemason is informing the families as we speak."

"Thank you for informing the council, Devas Pars."

"How?" Con Hrap blurted.

Devas glanced around the council and then back at the empsar.

"The ground shook the barrier loose and drowned three of them in the tunnels before they were complete. We—"

"They drowned?"

"Yes, Councillor. We managed to save three, but couldn't save the others." Devas' words trailed off and he hung his head.

The empsar saw Devas' damp and muddy clothes.

"The council thank you for saving as many as you could."

Devas nodded once and saw the empsar indicating he should leave the chambers. He bowed to the empsar and then to the twelve councillors before leaving the hall without a further word.

Devas found Gamute already drinking when he walked in. Other men were also drinking but were silent, and studiously avoiding looking at the heartbroken master stonemason.

"May their souls be enlightened and rest in peace." Devas lifted his cup heavenwards and closed his eyes in a brief prayer.

Gamute raised his cup also, before downing the contents in one swig.

10

Stivs felt the energy in the room drop. The empsar had slumped with the news and looked suddenly haggard. The room was silent as the assistant to the master stonemason left the hall. All eyes swivelled towards Empsar Con Dwig when the door closed.

"Whose idea was it to agree to the Big Deep project?" Con Trun asked with venom.

"It was a unanimous vote of approval," Con Ro Pars snapped as a tear slid down her cheek.

"You would say that," Con Hrap piped up.

"Although Con Pars is correct, I put master stonemason's proposal forward for consideration," Empsar Con Dwig acknowledged quietly. "I take full responsibility for the deaths."

"But, Empsar, Devas Pars said the ground moved. You cannot blame yourself for such an event," offered another Elder.

"If it wasn't for my recommendation, the works would not have gone forward. If the works had not been started three youngsters would still be alive."

The Council of Twelve went quiet and Stivs sensed into each Elder one by one. Most of the councillors were a mix of shock and sadness.

"The Big Deep project should be cancelled immediately," Con Hrap blurted out.

"No!" Con Ro Pars yelled.

Her natural good looks were heightened with eyes glistening with tears. All blood had left her face adding to her beauty. Everyone in the hall was staring at her.

A delicate flick of her wrist wiped one last tear from her cheek.

"We shall not let these three boys die in vain!"

The Council of Twelve nodded, all except Con Trun.

The empsar looked at Con Trun, waiting, and only when all other Elders were looking at him, did he nod once.

The empsar sat staring at the floor.

"Can I get you anything, Empsar?" Stivs asked.

The empsar did not react.

"Empsar," Stivs said loudly. "Can I get you anything?"

"What?" The empsar looked up and recognised him. "No... no thank you, Stivs. That will be all this evening.

11

S tivs had returned from a walk through the parks and caught sight of her eyes, the flash of them catching his attention. That was all it took to quicken his pulse. What was her name?

He lengthened his stride. Stivs pushed amongst the throng of people jostling in the marketplace. He couldn't see the woman's headdress. It was lost in the many cream and brown fabrics common in Atlantis.

Stivs growled in frustration. Back to his humdrum life he thought.

Doing a mental double-take he accepted, not humdrum. He was a librarian. Maybe one day he would become a historian. It didn't matter to him. He had learnt how to be happy with his life regardless of title, label, or name. Some of his colleagues had been selected or declined positions. Some had shown delight. Some had shown envy and some had shown self-importance. Few had become historians. Stivs did not even know how one became a historian. He only knew that they were selected. Nobody knew what the selection criterion was.

Stivs was happy being laid back, allowing everything to be easy. Things happen and life flows from one moment to the next. Like a twig or a stone in the river. A twig goes with the water, fast in the rapids and slows in the shallows with minimal crashing. A stone stays in the same spot. It gets battered continuously by water, very rarely moves, and gets crapped on by animals. If Stivs had a choice he would always choose being the stick. When he wanted something he would ask the universe and then focus on day-to-day living. Things always happened when he wasn't expecting them. For instance, the other day he thought about having a wife. He thought about having a soulmate. She had to have beautiful eyes. Stivs was always attracted to a woman's eyes.

Stivs had had fun with some of the baker girls in the past. But it was almost a different level of understanding, knowledge and viewpoints. How could they articulate to the same degree as a librarian from a family of librarians? No more than he understood how long a loaf of bread roasted, or was it baked, in the oven.

Stivs was never lonely, yet still sought that deeper intimate connection. His parents showed how blissful this connection was. The only arguments occurred when one of them stuck to the past. A life lesson from his parents was to live in the present moment as it was all-powerful.

The past is history
The future is a mystery
Now is a gift
That is why it is called the present

All the answers were to be found in the present. With a jolt of realisation, Stivs centred himself by breathing down into his stomach. After some time, his mind cleared and he put a question in his mind.

"What is her name?"

Aor.

It was clear as day! Stivs again continued feeling into his deep breathing allowing his mind to settle. His inner vision saw the woman Aor walking near the Museum of the Sun. The sunlight highlighted her face with a warming caress of her skin. The pale porcelain tone of her skin was a sign of her family's status. Her skin had not been browned by crop picking nor reddened through stable work.

Stivs became present once more, humming to himself as he set off towards the Museum of the Sun.

12

Ortva looked at his flock, glancing far and wide taking in the edges and, satisfied, clucked to himself. His intuition had saved many a sheep's life and he relied on it more and more with each season. The storm had passed and the damp chilled him to his bones. It was a mere inconvenience to the thirty-seven summers old shepherd.

He hadn't wanted to leave his wife at the start of the season with her having a miscarriage and all. He had known she had been reeling with the sense of total loss. She felt utter sorrow and the self-blame for losing another child. The despair was pools of liquid pain in her eyes when she insisted that he once again leave her to look after the sheep. It was only with the knowledge that death and life were in a constant natural cycle, did he return to his flock. The trek away from the city had lightened his soul with every pace.

The noises from his flock washed over him and he huddled in his leather smock. Sitting in the lee of a boulder he was up in the hills about two days' walk from Atlantis. Ortva was at the extreme of his range from the city. He was grazing the sheep on fresh spring grass. It was more nutritious than the well-trodden and overgrazed lower fields from which he had moved.

The sheep bleated incessantly as they jostled for the juiciest new shoots. Ortva took great pride in having the fattest and happiest sheep in the city. He knew that fat and happy sheep made the best harvest of wool and mouth-watering meats. The traders sought him out at every market time to see which butcher he went to.

He had always used Pet but noticed the last few times that Pet's eyes had glinted with avarice. To get the best service he may be better off striking a deal with Loj. Loj being a recently completed apprentice butcher had his youth on his side. Pet may be close to finishing his career and looking for easy options.

Ah well, a decision not to worry about now, Ortva reminded himself.

Ortva smiled at how easy life was. Deal with everything in the moment and the future takes care of itself. Put up the thought of finding an expanse of fresh untouched grass and low and behold that's what he finds. His smile slipped with a pang of guilt that bubbled up for leaving his wife.

"Oeee" Ortva heard her calling

"Over here." He shouted pleased at his guest.

The woman was of indeterminate summers. Ortva was generally a good guess of age, especially sheep but with the old woman of the hills, he had no idea. Ortva had heard the stories but took them with a pinch of salt. The magic woman of the hills was one description. The madwoman of the hills was another. He took everybody at face value and treated them with the same respect.

He recalled one story that the old woman had foretold someone's future for the price of a bag of flour. The trader had scoffed at the prediction of impending doom and refused to pay. The trader had woken up a day later on the back of his cart, not knowing what had happened. His pony had wandered away from the main path during his slumber. It had taken him the rest of the day to find his way back. He had admitted to his friends that the one bag of flour and only one bag had gone. The following season the trader experienced misfortune. His storage hut had flooded and then was plagued with rats. He dared not return to the hills since that experience and had lost much lucrative trade as a result.

The old woman had the energy of a child unfettered with judgement and she was happy whenever he saw her. Even now as she walked through a spattering of rain with a fresh wind pushing her back, she showed no sign of age. No ailment, but a wide smile at recognising him. She brought him bread and a lump of cheese plus a beautiful bright red apple. Ortva's mouth watered in anticipation. She knew him well enough to know his likes.

"I sensed you were getting thin." She chuckled looking at him maternally.

"Oh, Mother!" He used the greatest compliment he knew.

"Don't 'Oh' me young man," she snapped brusquely. Only the twinkle and gleam in her eyes gave away her pleasure at being called mother.

Get your fire going, Ortie, he commanded himself, looking forward to the delights of her energy drink. He had no idea what was in it but on the life of his prize sheep, it was delicious.

His flock edged closer, enjoying the company of the old woman too.

From within her shawl, she brought out a small bag. She extracted two round cups and a bag of magic ingredients. Ortva watched her deft and deliberate movements.

She coughed, reminding him of his duties of heating some drinking water.

When they settled back, each with a cup of steaming fruit-smelling drink, he felt her eyes on him. Her pupils expanded and opened inviting him in. She smiled and he felt the effects of the potion. He soared into euphoria. All thoughts of butchers, sheep and his wife evaporated from his mind. Joy filled him and tears rolled from the corners of his eyes.

"Oh, Mother, your fruit juice gets better each time I taste it," he said, purring with pleasure.

The old woman beamed at him in pleasure not breaking her gaze or focus.

Ortva knew not how long he had experienced those sensations but the liquid in his cup was cold and had thickened when he returned to it. He shoved a thick, rough finger into it and devoured what remained.

"Are you alright for sheep?" he asked her.

"I could do with a lamb to be company for Merely," she said, outlining her plans of fencing in a patch of land surrounding her house.

"You will have Elfy's next lamb. She is always the first in the season and gives healthy offspring," he opined.

"Sounds wonderful!"

When Ortva awoke, he was disappointed she had gone. He felt embarrassed to have dropped off in front of a visitor. But then who was visiting whom?

A lamb!

He remembered his promise. Mind you it was a small price to pay for her magic fruit juice.

The butterflies of delight fluttered throughout his insides at the wonderful memory. It was the same feelings he had during every visit. On reflection, he was uncertain whether it was the fruit juice or being in her company.

Must be the fruit juice, Ortva decided.

Dels walked back, happy that she had Ortva's promise of another lamb. She enjoyed his company, the references to the comings and goings-on in the city and hearing about his flock. Her lips puckered as she thought about his wife and their challenges to conceive. She decided to meditate on the matter at the next opportunity.

She knew that Ortva thought the fruit juice was magical. She smiled knowing he did not know what was going on.

Her focus allowed her to influence his energy. To increase his energy vibration as the more it increased in vibration the happier he felt.

Dels considered the trade and was satisfied it was fair. She did not use her work on the energy of everyone, only those who she deemed needed a boost or rebalancing. Arriving back at her cave she sensed the calm of the place. Nothing untoward had occurred, although in her absence some wildflowers had begun bursting through the topsoil.

She breathed deeply and expanded her awareness towards the city. Her energy touched that of the city as gentle as a feather falling to the earth. Dels sensed the excitement, the anguish, pain, joy and peace bubbling around and about.

She thought about Ortva's wife and her attention went to the image of a figure, her knees tucked up to the chin under a dark woollen blanket.

Dels called on the old gods, the Spirits of Nature and all beneficial energetic entities, asking them to heal the upset, and release any blockages of negative energies. That done, she drew back her attention. She sensed the usual chaotic tumultuous mix of energies of the city.

She sensed a pulse.

A different pulse was stronger than before. It was an undirected, and infrequent pulse. Youthful, but energetically strong to be so distinct.

Dels sent a loving vibration back to the individual that was the centre of the unusual pulse. She was surprised when it ceased immediately. Dels reconnected her focus and withdrew her awareness, again breathing deeply, returning her consciousness to her physical being.

"Who could it be?" she asked with a smile. "Someone young no doubt," Dels told a bird that landed on a branch a pace away.

In her recent journeys, there had been no distinct pulses of which she was aware. She momentarily doubted her previous sensitivity. Then she realised that her sensitivity had not increased nor changed for many summers.

Someone pulsing. Young and untrained. Possibly an aps. One of Hort's pride no doubt, she mused, noticing a rabbit in the distance.

Tonight I will connect with Hort and the empsar and advise them of my readiness for a new companion. A new apprentice.

With the decision made she went into her cave to make arrangements for a new companion. "Who goes there?" a voice rang out.

13

Givas was drawing on his slate whilst sitting on his bunk. He'd had a difficult day. Kors had been pestering him and being awkward. He knew that peaceful solutions worked best but every time he backed off, Kors kept asking for more. Whatever ground he gave way on, Kors seemed to take it as an invitation for more. Kors was sly and cunning, always trying to get the upper hand whereas Givas was not bothered with winning. He never wanted to fight but when he was backed into a corner with nowhere else to go he'd lashed out. Kors had been surprised by the extent of the response when it came. Givas had pushed him away and Kors had stumbled. Givas was upset and tears were streaming at having to fight back.

Hort had seen something in his peripheral vision and had heard the children were making a fuss. On arriving at the scene, Givas was standing defiantly over Kors. With eyes blazing, Givas was quivering with pent-up emotion. Kors, always one to use situations to his advantage, began crying and pretending to be the victim.

Hort grabbed the two children and moved them into the empty classroom. Upon questioning, Kors was the quickest to tell his version of events. Goras looked at Givas hoping for a denial. Givas decided to say nothing. Calling Kors a liar, when he felt guilty for fighting, he knew he would more than likely burst into tears. He would have been even more humiliated. Standing there dumb, with eyes hurling daggers at Kors, he realised he had been set up as the culprit.

Hort knew that he would have to report the situation to the council. He was mystified about why there was a change in the boy. He had treated him gently and more than fairly. He even allowed him to do as he pleased during the class expeditions to the harbour.

That will have to be different, he thought. This had changed his outlook in an instant.

Givas knew Kors was jealous of him but knew not why. He could not pinpoint a single reason. Scratching the slate he noticed he had drawn the outline of a horse. Losing himself in thought, he wished himself out of the class. But then he wanted to stay because he had always enjoyed the time spent in the stables when the class had its trips. I could run away, Givas mused.

Father wouldn't care, Givas thought. After all, he had sent him away as a child with no visits either. Givas's mood took a further downward swing into self-pity. He closed his eyes and wished he could leave. Not this summer but the summer after that he was due to finish but that was not soon enough. He could not bear it that long. He wished with all his might that something be different.

A feeling of warmth washed over him, and a calming gentle wave of energy flowed into him. Givas found it unsettling. It felt comfortable – too comfortable! For some reason, it made matters worse. He wept, feeling so alone.

He stopped thinking about leaving and the gentle energy immediately receded. Givas pulled his knees up to his chest and lay on his bunk in a foetal position, clasping his drawing slate with big fat tears rolling down his cheeks. They left drip stains through his drawing. His breathing slowed into the night. Finally, sleep embraced Givas in its forgiving unconditional acceptance.

In the morning Givas was lost in the present. The sun was warming the stone building and he knew that the relative chill in the room was in direct contrast with the air outside which was already heating up in the morning sun. The glare bouncing off the walls and the ground ensured everyone avoided looking directly at the sun.

Givas had forgotten about his emotional purge the night before and although his confidence had yet to be fully restored, he was feeling a sense of peace. The peace buoyed his returning optimism.

When he got to class, everything was surprisingly normal. Kors was keeping to himself. Apart from the occasional glance at Givas, no other indication was given that anything had occurred.

As they all started, Sua looked at him surreptitiously. Then with a flick of her hair, she focused back on the task at hand. Givas was as usual oblivious to any special attention. Kors on the other hand noticed, and, his only reaction was a narrowing of eyes and petulant puckering of lips.

During the midday break, Givas was at the water fountain about to take a cupful when Sua arrived at his side. Givas paused and with a flourish and a grin gestured for Sua to quench her thirst first. Sua smiled and as she was being given a once-over slaked her thirst.

She was slender and had luscious, thick, jet-black hair. Her short skirt showed off her honey-coloured tanned legs. The legs were finely toned and athletic.

"Sua." Kors called her away. "I have a gift for you."

As she turned to see Kors' gloating smile, she missed Givas' scowl.

Givas drank his fill and sat down in the shade of the pillars of the towering aqueduct feeding the fountain. Helpless and angry at Kors, he realised he was jealous. Jealous of Kors, for Sua's attention. He hadn't noticed any of the girls in the class before. There were a greater number of boys. Sua, he realised, was the prettiest and had been nice to him. No, not nice particularly, but she had given him some attention.

Givas sat in a meditative pose cross-legged on his bunk with his back against the wall. Eyes closed, his handsome thirteen-year-old face relaxed with an openness to it. His hair was plain and short behind his ears. A creamy white shirt covered his lightly tanned supple frame. His chest rose and fell. With each breath, he slowed into a deeply relaxed state. After years of practice, his mind let go of any particular thoughts, as he objectively noticed them singly, on his way to mental calm.

An image of Sua floated across his attention and he was shocked to feel his groin react. A memory of Kors passed through and his body experienced a pulse of anger, and then complete tranquillity.

An image appeared, indistinct and murky at first. Then, as his attention latched on to it, it became more defined. The back of a man stood at the edge of a precipice. A sense of sorrow and heartfelt regret gave Givas a feeling of sadness. He couldn't see the face but the man seemed familiar. He felt he knew him and yet he didn't. There was a separation – a distance. The back of the man was covered in dusty clothes. The man's physique was tanned and physically strong.

'Who was it?'

His mind went blank, and he felt a lightness and sense of freedom. He was floating above the city towards the hills. Givas felt interested but knew not why. The hills faded and he once again was aware of his breathing.

Feeling refreshed and relaxed, Givas wandered to the stables. Goras was not there and Hennie whickered in anticipation of a treat. Givas whispered his apology and showed his palms. Hennie snuffled them just to make sure. In the shade of the stable, the dust motes floated in the slivers of light that breached the building. The musty smell of warm straw was overladen with fresh horses. Givas felt the power of the beast as he stood next to her in the stall. Hennie's ears perked up and Givas turned to see what had alerted her.

Kors. He could see Kors's face through the gap between two beams of wood. Givas tiptoed to the wall and listened.

"Sua, I am glad I saw you!" Kors smiled.

"There is no need to follow me," Sua replied.

"What…?"

"Don't deny it, I saw you from the Albacus fountain. What do you want?" she inquired politely.

"To see if you would like to go for a walk to the harbour."

"Well…"

"That's if you have no other plans."

Sua paused.

"The harbour would be nice. What if we invite Givas?"

Givas perked up at the mention of his name with butterflies fluttering to life in his stomach.

Kors laughed with derision.

"Givas is scared of the water."

"Oh yes, I forgot."

Givas turned scarlet in the stable and looked at Hennie with despair. Hennie looked at him both challenging and encouraging at the same time.

Givas thought about his fear. Ever since the day he and Jonas, his elder brother, went fishing he couldn't face it. Jonas had dropped him off at the jetty. Being six summers older than Givas he was a leader to his younger brother.

Givas had stood at the jetty waiting for his brother's return for hours. Finally, suffering from hunger pangs, he had wandered about lost until his father, with tears in his eyes, had found him. Jonas had never come back. His father had told him simply that the sea had taken his brother.

Givas with a trembling lower lip grabbed the brush. He avoided Hennie's gaze and began brushing her chestnut mane. Working up a sweat he brushed her down and then two other horses. Hard work and exercise kept the fears and anxiety away.

He was hanging the brush back up on the wall when Goras returned.

"Hey, ya young scamp!" Goras laughed, pleased to see the boy.

"Hi."

Goras faltered and paused, checking his humour.

"What's up?"

"I could have gone with Sua to the harbour," he stated.

"That's wonderful, isn't it?"

"I hate the harbour," he replied vehemently.

"Why?"

"Nothing!" Givas could not answer. He felt it was his fault. He did not know why, but he felt the disappearance was because of him.

"Givas?"

Avoiding eye contact he made his apologies and left. He went to wander the city leaving a concerned Goras in the stable. Givas ambled past the chambers. They were filled with librarians chanting in time with a monotonous drumbeat. The vibrations and noise interrupted his reverie. He realised he was standing outside a museum. He breathed in and savoured the smell of the past. A past beyond his troubles, beyond his father's life and even past that of his father's, father's father.

Inside, massive sculptures of gods long forgotten stood forlorn and no longer idolised. The love and dedication in their creation were still clear even to the likes of Givas. Touching the nearest one, Givas felt the strength and resolve increase. He craned his neck to see the face of a half human, half lion stare back at him.

"Who is there?" a voice cried out from the back of the museum.

"Givas the aps!"

"An aps, eh? Come closer!"

"Who are you?"

"Who am I? Who do you think I am?"

"A caretaker?"

"Indeed, young Peevass."

"Givas!"

"Peevass, Geevass, Deevas, you are an aps and yet to make a name for yourself."

Givas saw the milky blue eyes of the caretaker and the tilt of the old man's head to one side and realised he must be blind.

He stuck his tongue out.

"Better use that tongue wisely." The caretaker cackled with laughter.

"How?" Givas smiled despite being caught out.

"I may not be able to see but I am more aware than you can imagine."

"What are you?"

"I live, I breathe and I appreciate."

"No, I mean apart from a caretaker."

"Besides being a caretaker I am the master of selection. An empsar of the past and probably the oldest person you have ever met twice." The caretaker stretched out a gnarled bony hand. "Give me your hand," he commanded.

Givas instinctively complied and felt his hand being held in a bony grip. A strange tingle passed up through his arm then up and down his body before disappearing out of his hand.

"Ah... Givas Voret. I met you over nine summers ago, didn't I?"

"How—"

"Don't interrupt," the master of selection gently admonished. "You have an interesting situation. Your fears are being confronted the more you want something. An open heart closed for love with powerful energy for one so young."

Givas stood surprised and pulled his hand back.

"Nothing to be afraid of, Givas. Your destiny is far-reaching. It is greater than your imaginings on your slate drawings could ever predict!" The old man grinned mischievously.

Givas was quiet as his fear and shock were replaced by curiosity.

"Please tell me more," he pleaded.

"More? I will not tell you what happens but I can advise you on what to do. When in fear do not fight it. Experience it. Treasure it. Rejoice in it. It is something that one such as me can only dream about nowadays. Forgive the past but heed it.

"How? Why? What do you mean?"

"Acting out of habit gets you what you always have. If you want something new, act in a new way. The only constant in your life is your breathing. If in doubt, breathe. If in fear, breathe. If in love, breathe. Then follow your instincts."

"So breathe?"

"Yes!"

"Breathe and I will be great?"

"Great you are now despite your fears." The old man stuck a finger up his nose, gave it a scratch and pulled something out that he did not want there.

Givas grinned as the old man wiped his finger on a sleeve of his old robes.

"You mentioned my destiny?"

"Yes."

"Could you tell me more?"

"You are big when you do things based on what you know deep down is right. You could be small if you do what is not. Breathe and feel."

"But what is going to happen to me?"

"What do you want to happen?"

"I want to be happy."

"Easy. Smile," the old man commanded. "Go on, smile."

Givas frowned. Then he intentionally smiled.

"Hold that smile and breathe."

Givas smiled and breathed and his smile widened. His eyes were twinkling.

"That's better… now what else do you want to do?"

"I want to see new places."

"You will."

"And be in love."

"Mmmm…" The old man paused. "Give me your hand again!"

Givas stuck his hand into master of selection's the grasp.

"Um, you will."

"Will I be loved in return?"

"Breathe and smile and you will get your heart's desire. Be sad, mad and all things will seem bad. Oh, and one last thing before you go."

"Yes?"

"Forget about these old gods. Look for answers in here!" The old man prodded Givas on the chest.

"Ow!"

"Now scat! Be gone. I want to sleep now, not trade knowledge with one who doesn't know how."

Givas left the museum not knowing if he had made a new friend but happier all the same. He tried out the smiling and breathing and ended up laughing out loud.

Some other Atlanteans smiled in passing, lifted by Givas' obvious happiness.

As he was walking back, even seeing Kors and Sua returning from their walk together did not dampen his mood. Kors scowled upon seeing Givas and Sua raised a hand to wave. Givas beamed and waved back before carrying on his return journey.

Kors looked confused and Sua seemed even happier looking. When Givas passed the stables he grinned at Goras and whistled to Hennie who stuck her head out and snorted back. The other horses pricked their ears up in curiosity.

14

U a came scampering round after he returned from his evening meal. Out of a leather pouch, Givas picked a choice morsel for the dog. He always filled his pouch with either some sweet bread or parts of stew that he did not eat. These treats were always devoured by Ua. Over the summers, Ua had grown plump and sleek. With attention from Givas, the dog became well-groomed.

"Ua, what am I going to do next summer?" I will be up for consideration of duties. I don't even know what I want."

Ua yapped, wagging her tail in unflinching support.

"I know… don't worry about it. It's a long time away. Part of me wants a twenty-four moon duty, and part of me doesn't want it. I will miss Hennie and Goras and you!"

Ua yapped in protest.

"I don't know if you would be allowed!"

Ua growled and then yapped.

"I suppose if you weren't allowed, nobody could stop you from following me." Givas grinned.

Ua yapped and then wagged her tail.

Givas showed the dog that the bag was empty. Satisfied that it would get nothing else; she laid her head on her paws and closed her eyes. Givas lay back on his bunk wondering about the future. He hadn't a choice in becoming an aps but he now had a choice on what to do next summer.

He knew he enjoyed the city. It was familiar and comforting and full of people he liked.

Maybe I can help the master of selection in some way, Givas mused. No, he wouldn't want that! What did he say? I would travel. Maybe I would enjoy being out in the hills. What would I have to do on the twenty-four moon duty? That is only two summers. Givas drifted off to sleep with all these questions in his mind.

He was dreaming and he knew it. He was happy enough to watch and see what happened.

High in the sky, he was moving towards the hills. He could tell they were hills, as the clouds above were dark and full of rain. They were unlike any light and fluffy clouds that passed over the city.

Then he was amongst the hills. It was raining but he wasn't wet. He passed over sheep, up a sloping valley and saw a dark entrance amongst large boulders. A candle flickered inside and he knew she was in there. He was curious. He knew that he hadn't met her but knew her all the same.

"I have been waiting for you," a hooded female said without turning. "It will be my pleasure helping you learn about focus and energy and whatever you want."

Givas awoke to find out he was still clothed and lying on his bunk with Ua lying on top of his legs. He slowly pulled his legs from under the dog and undressed before climbing under his blanket.

I must remember the dream, Givas instructed himself before slumber grabbed him back into its comfortable embrace.

He awoke to find a junior librarian had placed out fresh clothes whilst he was asleep. Luckily, Ua had disappeared, no doubt off foraging.

He breathed, smiled, and breathed again. The wonderful happiness blossomed once more and he hummed a tune that popped into his head.

After having his morning meal at the end of a table well away from everyone else, he went to school.

Hort was ever watchful of his brood of ten and Givas liked him. He seemed to know how much discipline he needed and how much fun.

"Has anyone thought of what they would like to do after school?" Hort asked them.

"Have food!" was a quick reply that was immediately followed by laughter.

"Next summer, Petr," Hort added realising some of them were still children in maturing bodies.

"Twenty-four moon duty."

"Me too!"

"Me as well!"

"Archives," suggested Sua.

Several children turned to her including Kors and Givas. Some children snorted with derision calling her a chep, a small useless fish that beached itself for no obvious reason.

"Oi, she can choose whatever she wants." Givas found himself defending her.

"Who are you? Her husband?" came back the retort.

Givas flushed, keeping quiet once more.

Both Kors and Sua looked at him with quite different feelings.

"Givas is right!" Hort continued. "But there are many enjoyable jobs in the city for those who are not selected for duty. There are councillor assistants, assistant archivists, apprentice historians and Querks."

"What do apprentice historians do?"

"What are Querks?"

"One at a time, apprentice historians learn how to record the history of what has happened in three ways."

"In which ways?"

"In the Atlantean script, in pictures, and in code. As you saw last summer in the archives."

"That's not a fun position is it?" Givas asked.

"It is! My father is a historian," Kors blurted out.

"Studying and recording events is a necessity to continue our history. To live our present and create our future," Kors told him.

"Querks become responsible for energising the city through music, tone and vibration."

"Oh, them," Petr exclaimed understanding at last.

Most of the children realised what Querks did. They had all heard them and seen them throughout the city doing odd things.

The rest of the day was spent getting a deeper understanding of the differing roles. Learning about all positions, not in the Librarian Order.

At one point, a disgruntled Kors had had enough.

"Why do we have to know about how early a baker starts work or a stonemason hitting a stone until it breaks." Kors was derisive about the latter.

Givas didn't realise at first that the jibe was at his father's expense. Then a slow burn of anger began in his depths and his eyes blazed with a searing gaze at the back of Kors's head.

"Kors, do you enjoy sweet meals?" Hort shouted out, cutting off any possible reaction from others before they started.

"Yes," he replied, focusing on a pebble on the ground.

"And do you enjoy a good meal of fish?"

"Yes!" Kors shrank further.

"And do you enjoy a drink from a fountain?"

"Yes!"

"And do you enjoy feeling safe in the city?"

"Yes!"

"Well, who do you think helps make all these possible?"

"Bakers and stonecutters," Kors offered.

"Bakers and stonemasons," Hort confirmed having had enough dissension in the class.

Givas felt justice had been done and almost felt sorry for Kors until he saw the look of compassion Sua gave him.

They were taught that as future librarians they need to understand that each role in the city is as important as theirs would be. Everyone has skills and experience to benefit all. To enable the city to function, every person had to have food and safety. Everyone had to contribute to the city. Everyone should be respected. Even the Querks.

Givas wanted to say that they were a form of a librarian. But he held back, knowing Hort was in no mood for debate on this topic.

On impulse, Givas decided to smile and breathe. He was filled with happiness and he rejoiced in it continuing to breathe deeply into his stomach. He was aware of a lightness.

Hort smiled and made a joke. It wasn't a joke, it was more of a statement with a smile. Givas continued to smile, breathe and focus on the lightness. He sensed the moods of the class lighten. It lightened until they were all beaming, laughing and smirking along with Givas.

15

Givas realised after his meal that he still didn't understand his dream. Who should I ask? The master of selection in the museum? He wouldn't be there now, Givas answered himself. Hort. His teacher?

Decision made he turned off in the direction of Hort's accommodation in the school. When he got there, the place was empty. He looked around and happy memories came flooding back. All the times playing, the adventures and stories of the past. He walked over to the nearby fountain, doused himself with water and sat down in the shade.

Moments later, Hort, the teacher walked up to the end door of the school. Givas scrambled up and rushed over to Hort.

"Master Teacher?" he asked.

Hort turned and started realising it was Givas.

"What do you want, Givas Voret?" he asked, feeling guilty and surprised.

"I had a dream this morning and I don't understand it."

"So?" Hort wanted to get rid of him.

"Can you help me?"

"No need for help," Hort said, ignoring the appeal on the boy's face. "Dreams are our heads finishing off our concerns that we have not dealt with."

"But…"

"But nothing… now go, boy!"

"But…" Givas was crestfallen.

"I said go!" Hort turned and went inside, slamming the door behind him.

Givas wandered back to his bunk confused. *What had he done wrong?' Hort the teacher hadn't listened to a word he said. He didn't even hear my dream.*

Sat on his bunk in the dark he felt his loneliness. Ua was off somewhere. His teacher didn't like him, and he was all alone.

He heard some of his classmates chattering, laughing, and whispering. They were farther alongside the building. It was something he had never been invited to nor had wanted to do before. But it would have been so nice now.

Without bothering to light a candle, as dusk settled he undressed and crawled into bed. Even being safe, and curled up in bed, did nothing for his feeling of loneliness.

His dream again… At first, he tried not to dream which was difficult in a dream so he experienced it instead.

In the cave. The woman was there and yet he saw no face. It felt familiar. Like home. She sensed his emotions and knew him. Givas saw her smile even though the critical part of him couldn't see her face.

He felt her smile. It conveyed so much compassion and acceptance the fear and anger inside him faded away. She stuck her fingers on his chest.

Givas awoke to find Ua on his chest arranging herself to get the most comfortable position. She rucked the blanket with a paw and, satisfied, settled down to sleep.

Givas smiled, refraining from laughing out loud. He could shout at the dog or push her off, but truth be told the companionship was marvellous. Givas felt loved, secure, and happy.

A smile played about his lips as he drifted back to sleep.

Givas awoke, breathed, smiled, and breathed. He felt happy being himself and happy in the moment. Ua, of course, had departed before a novice had replaced his clothes.

The morning meal consisting of sweet breads, fruit and water tasted superb. Givas savoured every mouthful, enjoying it more than ever before. The water was cool and refreshing and he sensed his body appreciated the food too.

He hummed a tune on his walk to school and only stopped when the others looked at him with curiosity.

Givas spent the day daydreaming of being in the hills with Ua running after rabbits or mice. He fantasised about the old woman looking after him.

A loud cough shattered Givas' train of thought and he looked round in irritation.

"Are you going to answer my question?"

"No." Givas being truthful, answered not realising it would cause more of a problem.

"No? And why not Givas high and mighty?"

Givas frowned. "I did not hear the question," he stated.

Hort had heard enough. "If you are not listening then you should tell us what you were thinking of whilst smiling."

Givas realised he had upset the teacher without meaning to.

"I was thinking of being away from here."

Hort scowled and his face went the colour of the blood-red flowers around the archives' garden. He was past being in control and was fuming.

"You have your wish. Go to your bunk and no evening meal!" Hort shouted.

Givas, knowing he could do nothing to change the teacher's mind and fearing causing any more upset stood up. The other children sat shocked, not knowing what had happened.

Without saying a word he made his way through the class and left.

Hort was in shock. What had happened to him? In all his years, nothing had ever come close to this. Anger had gripped him and he had assumed the worst. Looking up he saw the glaring sun on its downward arc and was thankful there was little schooling remaining in the day.

I want you all to meditate on listening and respect," Hort advised before letting the class finish and leave.

Another meeting with the Elders, Hort admitted to himself.

16

Givas felt confused. Anger was wrong, wasn't it? He was in a situation that he had no control over. A situation he could do nothing about. Even the thought of breathing and smiling held no interest at the moment.

But friends he could turn to. Goras. But... Givas reasoned Goras was a friend of Hort! Givas realised he could ask the old man in the museum. The rest of the day crept by. Givas ignored the rumbling of his stomach and went straight to the museum.

On opening the door, he heard the shuffling and tapping on the left-hand side of the hall. It was where he found the master of selection. He waited for the master's attention. Somehow, he had managed to get up onto the shoulder of a statue. It was half lion and half eagle and he was sat polishing it with an animal hide.

"What do you want boy?" The master shouted.

"Advice from one as learned as you," Givas replied in an attempt to smooth talk him with charm.

"You are not on the council so don't speak like you are," The master commanded. "What is it then; school or girls?"

"School. My teacher got angry with me for no reason."

"Anger, eh? No reason....well, there is always a reason. It means there is a conflict somewhere. Either resistance or desire that's all," the master told him matter-of-factly.

"What am I to do?"

"What do you want to do?"

"I want to leave."

"Class?"

"The city," Givas admitted for the first time.

"So be it."

"What do you mean?"

"Your wish is granted."

"But… but… I don't understand."

"Good. You don't always have to understand, do you?"

"Umm… yes…. no… I don't know."

"Do you understand what the sun is made of?"

"No."

"But it still warms you?"

"Yes."

"Trust your wish to be fulfilled."

"Are you sure?"

"Any other important matter?"

Givas paused. His confusion was being ignored. He breathed deeply.

"Can I take my dog?"

"Your dog?"

"A dog that is my friend."

"Ah… you have already decided that haven't you?"

"Yes." Givas smiled.

A few days later an apostle requested Givas to attend the Council of Elders. The rest of the class was gobsmacked. What had he done to deserve this?

Givas was neither excited nor fearful at the prospect of meeting the council again.

"Do you enjoy your job?" he asked of the apostle.

The apostle looked at Givas and smiled.

"I meet interesting people, Givas Voret." He winked.

"Anything else?"

"I hear wisdom wherever I go and observe much."

"Is it fun?"

"Fun?" The apostle mused. "Exciting at times, like today. Something new is always happening."

Givas, his curiosity sated for a while, lapsed into silence. The apostle looked at him, smiled and he too was quiet.

On arrival, another apostle told him to wait. Givas having nothing else to do did his smiling and breathing exercises.

Finally, a voice was heard inside the chamber and the door opened.

Givas was ushered in to stand in front of the Council of Elders.

"Hello, Empsar." He greeted with a smile.

"It is good to see you smiling, Givas Voret." The empsar chuckled.

"It is fun to smile!" Givas laughed.

"We have asked you here to consider and decide the matter of your future."

"Oh!" A burst of butterflies plumed in Givas' belly.

"It has been of interest to observe your innate talents and abilities grow and thrive."

"Thank you."

"With advice and recommendations from our advisers, your future has been decided. You will have an undefined duty with Dels ex-empsar in the Hills of Terzadon."

Givas blinked stupefied at what he had heard.

"But… I have still got a summer of school left," Givas stammered.

"That has been taken care of. history is secondary when dealing with the present is it not?"

Givas realised that all he would be missing out on was history. History of past beliefs, gods of old and the old religions.

"Yes."

"Any questions?"

"How long is my duty?"

"As long as is necessary."

Givas beamed. The master of selection was right. My wish has been granted.

"Thank you, Empsar."

"It pleases you this decision?"

Givas nodded several times, not trusting his voice.

The empsar looked at the Council of Elders. He had done as the majority had wanted but something felt wrong. He believed that the decision had been made for the wrong reason. They had wanted to avoid fulfilling a prophecy. Empsar Con Dwig knew deep down that avoiding fulfilling a prophecy was only keeping it in check and holding it at arm's length. It empowered the prophecy over their decisions. He believed it bound them to believe it to be true. He felt unease and helpless in that decision. The empsar knew that Givas Voret was better off with further learning in the mountains. He'd had the suggestion from the master of selection to do so, a man whose intuition and divine connection to the universe was second to none. He could sense that the request from a teacher was a way to resist feeling anger. It was a moot point if Hort had meditated on his feelings in this instance. *Let's hope he has no further instances to resist.*

The Elders were talking amongst themselves discussing whatever was in their awareness. Their purple cloaks were majestic and uniform. Their self-interests were not. Only his cloak had golden thread woven into the fabric, swirling patterns circling the cuffs and spiralling around the hooded opening. It formed a maze of circles on his chest with the symbol of Atlantis on the back.

Empsar Con Dwig fingered the pattern, feeling the raised smooth surface. He wondered how many of his predecessors had decided on such a dilemma. Had they dealt with the prophecy of the myth too? It did not matter if they had or not. The current Elders had set in motion a path by deciding the boy's future based on fear. He looked around at his fellow Elders and for the first time saw flickers of emotions showing on their faces. Traces of fear, gluttony, jealousy, covetousness and pride were evident. They were all bubbling just below the surface. He knew then that his time in position was no longer indefinite. Seeing these human and mortal character traits was a sign of his veering off his true path. The empsar role can only be effective when filled by one who remains on his or her true path.

He looked around the council with a pleasing smile. He realised that he could not see any of them remaining in truth. A sound behind him alerted Con Dwig to the presence of his assistant.

'Stivs! Could salvation be his assistant Stivs?' He breathed deeply then let his awareness concentrate and focus on his assistant. There was a slight tremble of recognition in energies before acceptance.

Stivs was a true warrior of his path he sensed. He rubbed a green gemstone set in a gold ring on his finger, deep in thought. One question remained to be answered. Could he continue in his post long enough to install an assistant? Install his nominated replacement onto the list of Elders before his deselection?

17

Givas was smiling. He was happy and full of excitement. He talked to Ua who yapped frequently, just as enthusiastic as he was.

"And they said you can come too! Givas paced his room. "And I am going tonight." Ua yapped in delight.

"We are waiting for the guards for our safety."

He remembered he had yet to say goodbye to Goras. Givas ran out at top speed to the stables and straight to Hennie. She nuzzled his neck and blew damp hot air on his forehead. Givas heard whistling from the end of the stall. Goras was there, sweating profusely in the evening heat.

"Come to help me move this hay? Well, you have timed it perfectly. I have just finished," Goras told him with a smile.

"Goras, I will miss you." Givas became tearful.

"What… where are you going?"

Givas recounted his meeting with the Council of Elders and how he was told he was going that very day.

Goras looked at the boy, at the youth. For that was what Givas was now – a youth. The well-tanned face was topped with an unkempt mop of brown hair and Givas had a pair of piercing blue eyes that seemed to absorb everything. Givas was growing fast and would be tall for an Atlantean. He was gangly and awkward looking like a newborn foal, but with a knowing and wise demeanour. He was someone who has already faced sorrow, pain, and tragedy. But one who has survived if not thrived from the experiences.

"Well done," he said at last.

"You're not sad?"

"Sadness is regret, and I do not regret having you as my friend. I have always known you would go to the mountains as you have a spirit that needs its freedom. But a year early! They must have recognised you are ready. Well done, Givas!"

Givas beamed.

A clanking sound reverberated from the alleys nearby.

"They will be for me," Givas exclaimed.

"I wish you well, young man," Goras croaked.

Givas could hold back no longer. He hugged Goras fiercely, feeling the solid dependable warmth of his old friend.

"You must go now." Goras pushed him away gently.

"I will see you when I get back," Givas promised.

"Yes, you will," Goras whispered, eyes tearing up as Givas sprinted away.

"Lucky boy," Goras said under his breath and turned back to his duties.

The soldiers were ruddy-faced and potbellied. No doubt they were in the last years of duty before retirement. Givas saw their dull rusty armour over dark sweat-stained jerkins and could smell the stale vine wine on their breaths.

"No number one uniforms out of the city," the taller soldier informed him. "I am Toc Strevius."

"Oh, very formal, Strevs." The other soldier laughed.

"Shut up, Stu!" Strevs reddened.

"And I am Toc Stueff but you can call me Stu," Stu told him in an exaggerated self-important way.

Givas smiled, instantly liking them.

Strevs looked around the room and saw the leather bag holding Givas' few possessions.

Ua yapped at their feet.

"What have we here? A ratter?" Stu enquired.

"Ua – my friend."

"No dogs allowed," Strevs stated.

"I told her not to come. She follows me everywhere."

"You'll have difficulty in stopping a dog from following us, Strevs." Stu grinned, mischievously winking at Givas.

Strevs snorted, eyeing the dog with disdain. Ua snuffled about the two soldiers' feet not sure what to make of them either.

Although it was dusk it was as good a time as any to start the journey. Givas walked through the streets that were quiet and drowsy in the warmth and dust. The blue velvet sky promised a clear starry night ahead.

Ua trotted along marking her territory, knowing that it was a token gesture. Time and other scents will have a stronger influence and control in due course.

Finally, the two world-weary soldiers, Strevs and Stu, brought up the rear. They were escorting a plucky fourteen-summer-old at the beginning of an adventure and each had a bag of essentials to make their journey easier.

When nearing the city gates, they shouted to their comrade in arms. They were let out into the big world of freedom, uncertainty, and new experiences. Stu looked at Strevs somewhat fearfully. Strevs forced a grin and winked. He only let his mask down when his friend and colleague faced the front again.

Givas marched through onto the spine as darkness descended. The evening brought with it a welcome cool breeze which freshened and revitalised their senses.

Givas breathed in the new air, savouring the scent of wildflowers. He felt the heat bouncing off the rocks which had absorbed the sun's energy all day. He sensed the openness, the unfettered life and the cycle of life lifting his energy. Breathing and smiling. Smiling and breathing. Ua made reconnaissance runs. She disappeared yapping returning to the path with only the sound of four pads drumming on the parched earth.

The two soldiers kept their pace with the boy. Tiring no one out and allowing Givas the false belief that he was in charge. Having only one path to take he was going in the right direction.

Dusk settled around them. They continued along the path under the watchful gaze of the stars. The temperature dropped and the two soldiers tied their cloaks. Givas and Ua with excitement and adventure in their veins continued onwards, ignorant of the chill in the air. The climb got steeper and steeper. Strevs constantly surveyed the ground ahead for an ideal place to spend the night.

Stu was happy with any place but was regretting the task of escorting the young pup into the mountains.

Ua and Givas stayed close and never ventured off the path, kindly lit by the myriad twinkling stars. The moon was a brilliant white with pockmarks of crystalline blue indentations.

Toc Strevious called a halt to their journey and indicated a flat section of land a few paces to one side. Ua paced the grass, checking for territorial scents before marking his own. Stu curled his nose up in disgust before biting a chunk out of some sweet bread.

Givas eyed the bread hungrily, not wanting to ask a favour.

"Junior Librarian," Strevs called out before tossing an apple to the boy.

Givas caught the apple and stared at the soldier, showing momentary confusion then accepted the new title. For ten summers he had been an aps; an apprentice librarian with no position and no duty. No responsibility but still having all his needs catered to. Givas realised that he was growing up. A junior librarian – one of the youngest to be given a duty in the mountains. His friends would be so envious and full of questions.

Strevs gave the remains of his meal to Ua much to Stu's chagrin.

"Don't waste your food on that thing," he grumbled.

"A trade for her services as a night guard." Strevs ruffled Ua's ears as she finished off the last few morsels with her tail wagging furiously.

"A traitor to our cause already." Stu snorted with derision as Ua scampered over to Givas.

Givas settled down for the night using his bag to rest his head on. Ua snuggled up to his chest keeping him company.

"We are safe," Strevs concluded before stretching and giving an almighty yawn. "Anyway, where is that vine wine?"

Stu rummaged around in his knapsack. He found the flask of the finest drink he had acquired from Atlantean stock.

"How did you get your hands on this?" Strevs asked.

"Doesn't matter nor will affect the taste."

Givas closed his eyes. He was aware of the warmth of Ua and the muted banter of the two soldiers. They were arguing over the merits of white grape or black grape. Slumber took him into its comforting hold.

Ua landed on Givas' chest, waking him.

"What?" Givas gasped

One of Strivs' eyelids raised revealing a bloodshot eye that needed a morning's more sleeping. With no obvious danger, it closed.

Givas raised himself on his elbows, watching Ua bound about randomly. He saw a vibrant flash of orange that Ua was chasing. Creeping behind the dog he saw an interesting insect with two large wings no bigger than the length of his thumb. They came together above the body of the insect and flapped as a bird does. As soon as it flew higher into the sun both he and Ua lost interest in the magical wonder of it.

"Anything to eat?" he asked Strevs.

"In my knapsack," Strevs replied without opening his eyes, still intent on making the most of his rest.

Givas looked in the bag pushing Ua's snout out of the way. He grabbed a handful of dates and the remnants of a sweet bread for Ua. The bag felt too heavy for just food and beneath the provisions, Givas felt something cold and hard. He pulled out a fighting knife. Givas admired the gold edges of the handle reflecting light into his face. The orange, brown, and amber offset the fiery blaze of sapphires. Other magnificent cooling blue-coloured stones were set in the handle. He held the knife feeling the balance and noting how protected his hand was by the design of the guard.

He swished it in front of his face, cleaving the air silently then stabbed some invisible foes. He singlehandedly defended Toc Strevius and Toc Strueff from imaginary marauding attackers.

Givas admired the beautiful fighting knife again then returned it to the knapsack. He focused once more on more important matters such as that of his growling stomach.

As the two soldiers were getting more sleep Givas went for a wander in the morning sun. Taking deep breaths in he felt calm and settled even with the pulse of excitement. Ua raced off hunting for anything moving and smaller than she was. The chirping of birds filled the air indicating that not everyone was slumbering.

Givas sat on an outcrop of rock facing the sun. He settled into the meditative state that he had learnt and quickly and easily, found that place of nothingness. He sensed her presence so fast that it was a shock.

He became aware of the sun on his face and the bumps of the rock digging into his buttocks. Unsure of what to make of the shock he ambled back. He'd had an ever-present feeling of certainty since leaving Atlantis. Up in the Hills of Terzadon was what was right. Smiling, happy and excited, Givas arrived back at the clearing.

"There you are," Strevs stated.

"Any longer and we would have been worried," Stu grumbled. He was gingerly feeling his face and head with his fingertips, making sure that despite his hangover he was still in one piece.

"I am safe," Givas told them cheerily.

"Let us be the judge of that," Strevs replied.

"Yes... what would you do if a Terzadonian marauder came at you?" Stu grumped.

"I would grab the fighting knife from the bag," Givas replied pointing to the knapsack with the knife in it.

Strevs raised his eyes in surprise.

"Would you know what to do with it, boy?" Stu barked, following it up with a hacking cough.

Strevs took out his fighting knife and turned it over in the sunlight. He admired the glint and gleam before losing himself in thought.

"Where did you get it?" Givas asked, his curiosity finally bursting through his reserve.

"In a war," Strevs answered, tight-lipped.

"What happened?" Givas asked excitedly.

"Lots of unnecessary deaths." Strevs looked at the boy and saw Givas' genuine interest. "War is unjust. As a tool, it may be the last resort but all in all, it is a waste of life and effort. The excitement of battle does not last. The regret of pain and conflict lasts far longer," Strevs told him seriously.

"Who did you fight?" Givas's enthusiasm was tempered with respect.

"Those who were jealous of our city, our way of life and our peace." Strevs had a faraway look in his eyes.

"You fought for Atlantis?"

Stu looked away.

"I was in the bloodiest battles of the Spine. The Terzadonians kept on coming. They were crazy... had no chance of winning. It was a waste... I don't know why they fought. Maybe because they had nothing else to do?" Strevs reasoned. "Boy, life is far more exciting than war. Love is far more special than territory. If you must fight for anything, fight with love in your heart and respect in your head."

The group collected their possessions and left the campsite without a further word. Stu was nursing his head. Strevs was thoughtful and reflecting. Givas was respectful and concerned with more immediate matters. He felt cold.

Slapping his arms around his torso, Givas tried to get warm. Strevs noticed and placed a blanket around his shoulders. He then pushed ahead with large strides.

Givas sensed something different. He felt more vibrant. Lightness filled him. Smiling, he looked around. The two soldiers looked more at ease if not exactly happy and Ua scampered onwards marking new territory with almost every couple of paces. Birds could be heard but were not seen. No doubt they were keeping their distance from the motley crew of interlopers.

The rise got steeper, and Stu was puffing and panting.

"Stop… rest here…" Stu gasped.

Givas was itching to carry on. He looked imploringly at Strevs who glanced at his friend and colleague.

"A moment to reflect." He grinned, sitting on a nearby rock.

Givas settled himself cross-legged in the lee of a large boulder. Closing his eyes, with deep breathing he immediately centred himself. Expanding his awareness, he swept out and over the hill. Up and over another rise he went before sensing the source. The source of the vibrancy. He recognised her energy, and she recognised his.

"Welcome!"

Opening his eyes he smiled, all doubts and fears were gone. He felt great; light of the soul, happy and carefree.

Stu began and stopped beside Strevs offering his arm. Strevs clasped his forearm and Stu clasped his then pulled him up to a standing position.

"Come on, friend. Let us deliver this boy safely!" The familiarity and friendship flashed in their eyes.

"Let us do it," Stu agreed, smiling.

The clouds continued their journey over the lands, the rain leaving the group sun-drenched and sweaty. Givas rejoiced in the change of temperature and Ua shook herself. She sprayed a fine mist of droplets off her coat in a way that only dogs know how.

As they reached the rise they marvelled at the view. A rainbow arched the horizon with flaming red, so clear that Givas reached out a hand to touch it.

"It is so real!" he whispered.

Even the hardened veteran soldiers were moved. The foliage and grasses were an amazing myriad of shades from dusky dark through to aquamarine. Moisture glinted, teasing the onlookers forward with the false promise of shiny jewels. Even the rocks they passed seemed stronger and prouder. They continued the last leg of their journey with mouths agape.

Sooner than they would have wanted, they found themselves at the top of the last hill. It faced a ragged imposing cliff on the opposite side of the next valley. The cliff was etched with slits, crevices, and caves.

Givas and Ua both burst into a run with excitement. They were full of joy at the prospect of exciting adventures to be had in the many caves.

Stu and Strevs wandered after them at a slower pace. They were relaxed and more carefree than they had been since they were children. Their shoulders straightened. All the years of training were forgotten. The back-breaking exercises were forgotten. The horrific memories of battle and bloodshed were forgotten.

"Strevs…?"

"Yes, I know!" Tears of joy were in Strevs' eyes.

The men walked straighter and taller. They were connected to the magnificent natural beauty around them. Fragrances and the perfumes of blossoming flowers intoxicated them. The buzz of bees and the constant chirping of birds prevented any thought. The sun's rays surrounded them in comforting warmth. In a daze, Stu and Strevs ensured the safe delivery of Givas to the ex-empsar old woman of the hills.

Givas saw her stand up. A creamy golden gown hung from her shoulders and she had been tending to some sheep. Her face was creased and lined from countless summers and much laughter. It was framed by striking, shimmering silver-white hair. Her movements were fluid yet measured, lying, no doubt about her true age.

"Greetings, young Givas."

"Greetings, Grand Matre." Givas smiled, using an accolade he had heard many summers ago.

"Welcome… Ua?"

"Yes, Ua." Givas looked down, surprised at Ua's sudden obedience.

"There is no right or wrong here." Dels raised a hand waving at the distant figures of the soldiers who'd realised their services were no longer needed and had turned back to Atlantis.

"But I haven't said goodbye to them," Givas lamented.

"Send them your thoughts of love."

Givas looked at her curiously.

"Can you read my mind?"

"That is neither here nor there. Remember there is no right or wrong."

"But…"

"But nothing."

"But what about history and learning?"

"What about it?"

"War is wrong, and love and acceptance are right," Givas reminded her.

"You have had none of one and too little of the other to believe that, haven't you?"

Givas took a moment to understand before tears rolled down his face as grief flowed from him.

"Do not resist your feelings yet still your choice to let it now go," she offered with compassion.

Givas thought about that whilst still crying. Moments later, with dry eyes, he eased and relaxed into calmness.

"Come let us have some food."

Givas watched Ua run around the old woman in circles, occasionally leaping to lick her hands. He smiled involuntarily, carefree and light. His chest ached and pulsed. His energy field was changing of its own accord, and he resisted no longer.

Dels saw his acceptance and moved him to a place to relax. Givas closed his eyes and went within, allowing his physical body to absorb his transformation of energies. Releasing grief so suddenly was a shock to the system.

18

G amute Voret nodded to Devas, at last answering his summons. Work was progressing swiftly under his friend's supervision. This allowed him the freedom to cut and line the workings for the most ambitious stage of the workings alone.

"Another mixed bag of volunteers to help quarry the blocks."

"Anyone standing out with potential?" he asked.

"One or two…." Devas answered cryptically.

Gamute looked into his friend's eyes catching the glint of amusement.

"We'll see!" He snorted.

The six volunteers stood out from the others immediately. Their clothes were cleaner. Less dust. Their faces didn't have the telltale streaks of perspiration.

Gamute went down the line, occasionally prodding an arm of one or the gut of the next. The fourth individual must have been stooped and checking his feet, for when he stood everyone gasped. He was a giant of a man. With a flat forehead over a pair of intelligent eyes, he had a handsome face except that one of his ears was half missing.

"Who are you known as?"

"Rat!" The crowd tittered and the giant blushed in reply.

"I asked what your name is!" Gamute shouted thinking the giant had misheard him.

"Rat," the giant replied with the same increase in volume.

"Seems strong enough," Gamute said over his shoulder to Devas.

"Pass-Round," The giant that was known as Rat challenged. The crowd inhaled in surprise.

Gamute eyed the giant up and down then grinned. The crowd cheered.

"Do you know what you are doing?" Devas hissed in Gamute's ear.

"Get the roughest rock there is," Gamute commanded, ignoring his friend's astonishment.

Although Gamute was the master stonemason, his physique was honed and chiselled as much as the rocks that he worked with. Standing at twelve hands high he was not small but, next to this man Rat, he appeared childlike.

"Where did they get this guy?" he asked.

"He has been hiding in the bakery as an apprentice," Devas informed him.

"Thought as much," he muttered under his breath.

Two men brought a roughly hewn rock over.

"Who dares to start?" Devas shouted, immediately taking control of the proceedings.

"I will," Gamute answered before Rat had a chance.

Rat the giant smiled, confident that victory would be his.

With a deep breath, Gamute took the full weight of the rock from the two assistants.

"Go," Devas shouted as the crowd cheered again.

Gamute twisted his torso, arms tight at his sides and dropped the rock into Rat's waiting hands. Rat with his back to Gamute twisted round to his left and returned the rock into Gamute's waiting hands.

The crowd shouted "ONE!". They surrounded Gamute and Rat with excited faces, all jostling for a good view.

Gamute was experienced at this challenge. The summers upon summers of working with stones had toughened him to the rigours of such a game. He had never lost and did not intend to, not even against a giant.

"TWO!"

The giant placed the rock back into his hands. Gamute twisted whilst intent on keeping as many muscles as possible relaxed. He dropped the rock from a slightly higher position this time. Rat again twisted and placed it back in Gamute's hands.

"THREE!" the crowd shouted.

Again Gamute dropped the rock into Rat's hands from a slight height. Again Rat placed the rock in Gamute's hands.

"FOUR!" The shout from the crowd was slightly quieter.

"FIVE!"

"SIX!"

Twist and drop. Twist and drop. The crowd watched with growing boredom.

Gamute kept counting in his head, focusing on nothing but the numbers. He alternated the rock's position imperceptibly so Rat would struggle for a common hand hold.

At twenty Pass-Rounds, Gamute was gritting his teeth. He knew that thirty-five had been his record to date and guessed his strength was no match for his opponent. There was only one thing that would win him the challenge and that was…

"Yes!" Gamute felt it. There was now a wet slipperiness to the grip. The crowd noticed it too. "Blood," someone shouted.

Rat's face puckered in a grimace of pain. The rough surface of the rock was biting into the skin of the man's hands. Gamute's hands, calloused and hardened through a lifetime of stonework were fine. He let go of the rock earlier and heard his opponent grunt in pain as it bit into the skin of his bloodied hands.

Again and again, he alternated position and distance but only enough to make the difference not enough to be noticed. His fingers and forearms were tiring. It needed to end quickly. Gamute focused on his breathing. They were now over thirty passes. The rock was slick with Rat's blood.

"THIRTY-TWO!" Gamute panted and Rat gasped.

"THIRTY-THREE!" Gamute gritted his teeth and Rat cried out.

"THIRTY-FOUR!" Gamute focused whilst in pain. Rat whimpered.

"THIRTY-FIVE!" Gamute struggled. Rat's hands slipped momentarily. The crowd gasped.

"THIRTY-SIX!" Gamute was in agony. Rat sobbed.

"THIRTY-SEVEN!" Gamute's muscles screamed. Rat's hands caught the rock. It slipped. The crowd held their breath. The rock carried on. Momentum and blood helped it slide out of Rat's grip. It toppled and fell with a thud.

The crowd cheered. Devas grinned and congratulated Gamute amidst the hubbub. People slapped Gamute's back in admiration and support.

Rat held his hands up, looking at the damaged palms with tears of pain at the corners of his eyes.

"Make sure he gets his hands seen to," Gamute instructed Devas.

Gamute looked into Rat the giant's eyes and saw respect and humility there. He clapped one hand on the man's shoulder before Devas could usher the giant to get some healer's attention on his wounds.

Gamute had heard about his son's early duty. He was both impressed and proud that Givas was a librarian; his decision had been sound, however painful at the time. He still felt a pang of regret that he had not seen him since putting him in the order.

He turned from the dwindling crowd and saw their handiwork, dusty trails from the quarry giving a floury covering to all of the plants up the slope. The aqueduct connecting the three reservoirs was complete. The workers were now clambering up the volcano side like a colony of active ants. Scurrying to and fro in organised mayhem.

The next stage began without a fuss; only Gamute knew the risks. The risks he didn't, sent fear crawling about inside his belly late at night but his grit and determination got him out of bed every morning to once more confront the fears.

Gamute watched as each worker went about their tasks. He also saw them as part of a collective, as one large team.

"Daydreaming again, Gamute?" Devas asked at his shoulder.

"Hmmph!"

"Using the basin in the volcano as a reservoir was inspired. When did you think of that?"

"I walk to the edge of the basin every moon. I see the reflection and guess what I thought?" Gamute stated.

"What?" Devas looked concerned at where the conversation may be going.

"I didn't realise life goes on." Gamute turned and faced his friend. "I had forgotten about living." His eyes shone brightly, wet with unshed tears. "All this time I have been flogging myself to death and missing out on living. Missing out on love and laughter." He beamed at Devas and then turned back to view the work being completed.

"I felt guilty every time I smiled. Every time joy came knocking at the door I would think of Jonas, Ellie and Givas." Gamute lowered his voice to almost a whisper.

"I have grieved for my son and my wife. My decision for my second son has been proven right. I have felt freedom again. By the gods! It feels good!" Gamute looked into the sky and laughed.

Devas looked at his friend in surprise. He placed a hand on his friend's back and chuckled.

"At last, I am happy to be me," Gamute acknowledged.

"So, where did you get the idea?"

"Ah-ha, I was staring into the water seeing the moon floating in front of me. The surface was still and quiet. And I thought – this is so much bigger than any reservoir Atlantis has seen. That was it! A reservoir bigger than any in Atlantis!"

"And the tunnels?" They both looked at the three channels that the workers were digging.

"One for the mind, one for the body and one for the soul."

Devas' eyes lit up and he grinned in agreement.

"The Council of Elders must have loved that."

"I think that is what decided it. They marvelled at the size of the plan and the statement it would make. This council would be known as the one who took the power of the lake of the devil and tamed it."

"I thought the empsar was above seeking fame and recognition?"

"He is. But he saw the practicality of having a new freshwater source that did not depend on the mountain's weather."

"So, a practical and spiritual empsar."

Gamute smiled, watching a team of carpenters dismantle the double parapet piece by piece. He remembered when they'd measured the height.

"What are you thinking about now?"

"Remember the parapet?"

"How could I forget?! Who devised that contraption?"

"You were scared! The parapet was safe!" Gamute chuckled.

"Hmm. I am sure you could have used someone else to measure the distance to the water surface."

"Yes – to the water surface. But remember we needed to measure deeper, so we have the pressure of water to move down the channel."

"True! There are few as blessed as I am with such understanding and superior intelligence." He laughed. "But the height of that thing!"

They both looked up. The parapet formed a T shape from the top of the volcano rim above them. The arms came out from the centre of the scaffolding. They stretched out over the hillside on one side and over the water basin on the other.

"You know I can't swim," Devas protested.

Neither can I, Gamute wanted to admit.

"How did you know the water was safe to drink?"

"Ah, that is another story altogether," Gamute said, smiling at the memory.

Gamute had needed solace. He had needed quiet and release from the mental turmoil he had been experiencing. He had found himself wandering out of the city, and had come across a small footpath through the vegetation. It had led him up the side of the volcano. The sun was setting, leaving growing shadows to spread a chill across the hillside. Inured to the change in temperature, Gamute had walked with no idea of direction. The path meandered high up to the ridge above where he found an old man sitting in total silence. With eyes closed facing the last rays of the sun, the old man had been as still as the volcano itself. Gamute had stopped out of consideration for the old man's peace and watched the beautiful sunset that was colouring the horizon.

"It is a joy to behold," the old man had said in a deep rich voice that resonated with truth.

"It sure is," Gamute agreed.

"So why the heavy heart?"

Gamute turned, startled at the man's insight.

"Your son is doing fine," the old man opined.

"How did you know my concerns?" Gamute gasped.

"It popped into my mind. So often the way when the quietness takes place and allows the truth to be apparent," the old man said smiling.

He stood and picked up a staff and line from which was dangling a beautiful gleaming silver fish. The fish's scales reflected light even after its demise.

Without further conversation, the old man walked back down the path that Gamute had instinctively followed.

Disconcerted, Gamute stumbled and slid down the hillside towards the water basin. He was still thinking about how easily the man had been able to see into his heart.

"So, who was the man?" Devas asked enthralled.

"You will never guess!"

"Who… who was it?"

"The empsar."

"The empsar? The current reigning empsar… leader of the Council of Elders empsar?"

"The very same."

"By the gods!" Devas exclaimed in amazement. "How did you know it was the empsar?"

"The staff that he was using to fish with."

"What about it?"

"It was the Staff of Atlantis." Gamute laughed.

"The empsar was using the Staff of Atlantis to fish with?" Devas was incredulous.

"Yes!" Gamute grinned. "He had to use something." Gamute went back to his story.

"That's how I knew about the water... that it is good for drinking."

"I don't understand."

"He had a fish. If fish can live in the basin then the water can be used as drinking water. As long as the settling sands are used to sieve the water from the channels." They both looked at the vast structures that would house the filtering section of the works. They had devised it through trial and error using a mixture of sand, plants, various-sized stones, and wool.

"A fish!" Devas shook his head in amazement.

"Yes! Do you know that all the Elders are entitled to fish in the waters?"

"I thought they were the only ones who were allowed to eat the fish from the basin. I didn't know that they fished in there."

"Yes. I have only met the empsar once and seen none other, on all my visits to the basin. But all the same, they are historically fishermen and women."

Devas chuckled. "And you met the empsar in person."

"I met him face to face all alone."

19

"What do you think about life, Givas?" she asked. Givas looked up from his task of looking at a flower.

"What do you mean, Matre?"

"What do you think about life? Your purpose and all that is." Her eyes twinkled in anticipation.

"That is a big question, Matre."

"One to which I am interested in your answer."

"My purpose is to live life."

"And?"

"All that is, is energy."

"Well done. What about energy?"

"Energy vibrating, pulsing, throbbing, flying and changing."

"Changing?"

"Changing from a seed to a shoot. A shoot to a flower. A flower to decay. Decay to soil and from soil to feeding a new flower."

"So do we feed new flowers?"

"Possibly."

"What about our energy?" She put a hand above his shoulder. Givas looked up at her in surprise. A slow heat was building on his left shoulder under her hand.

"Our energy... is it ours?"

"The energy that you are composed of... what of it?"

"My thoughts are energy."

"Yes."

"Everything is energy?"

"Well done!" Dels smiled at young Givas.

"Everything is energy and thought is energy." She stopped to see if he would take up the thread of conversation.

"So can I affect things with my thoughts?" he asked, eyes growing wide.

"If you think and believe you can," she told him. "Try it again with the flower." Dels left him to it.

Givas looked at the flower. He saw the shape, its shadows, contours, and textures. He got bored of staring at the flower and his mind wandered. He started thinking about what his classmates would be doing.

He realised with a start he was somewhere else and refocused his attention. The flower was vibrant. A pure yellow blossom, reminiscent of an autumnal sun. So delicate yet strong. The edges sharpened, shimmered, and glowed. Givas's eyes defocused yet his gaze remained. The world around him disappeared leaving only the flower's petals as his reality. There was only a bloom.

He never knew how much time had elapsed with the flower. But the sun on the back of his neck was a reminder of his physical presence in the natural flow of seasons. He shook himself out of a non-thinking serene state and felt his mind begin functioning once more.

'What had just happened?' Givas had gone to a place he had never reached before through the meditations which he had been taught at school. Those he realised, were based on letting go of attention. This he smiled, was more of an explosion of attention.

Dels smiled as if knowing what had transpired.

"Godliness," he stated.

She arched her eyes in enquiry.

"A feeling of complete certainty and connection," Givas ventured, expressing his thoughts immediately as they formed.

"Connection to what?"

"With anything and everything… not really connection… more of creation. Creation of reality in the moment."

Dels took him inside and served him a cup of stewed fruit juice, allowing him to savour time as well as a drink.

The liquid spread over his tastebuds and his senses reeled at the powerful shock of flavours. They were far beyond anything he had ever experienced. With a palate heightened to new levels he could discern each fruit that had been used, and how many. The pleasure sensors did not overload as Givas was taken far higher than ever imagined.

Dels saw the evident rapture and was patient whilst witnessing his internal journey.

"What?" he croaked.

"Beautiful is it not?"

"Beautiful," Givas agreed, closing his eyes briefly in memory.

Givas began learning about energy. First, he learnt about his own energy and how it was affected by his thoughts. How his energy was affected by his emotions and how his emotions could be chosen at will.

Dels saw him smile and raised an eyebrow.

"I just remembered the master of selectors telling me I did not need to know the history of the gods."

"Why is that?"

"Learning about my reality and how to create it is more empowering," Givas said beaming.

"It is, isn't it?"

"What about the myth?"

"What about it?"

"What does it say?"

"Does the past matter?"

"But it tells us about the future."

"Does it?"

Givas scratched his head and was suddenly confused. "Only if we believe in it?" he ventured.

"Well done."

"What about my father?"

"What about him?"

"Should he matter?"

"What are your thoughts on the matter?"

"I feel sad and confused about him," he admitted, his eyes instantly filling.

"About…?"

"He sent me away," Givas uttered his most feared thought.

"Did he?"

Givas started. "Of course he did… what else could he have done?"

"Tell me what happened in your family then."

"My father is the son of a master craftsman, from a long line of father, grandfather, and great grandfathers of master craftsmen. He married his childhood favourite. They had two sons; Jonas – " Givas clamped down on his emotion – "…and me."

"And?"

"Jonas went into the water and never came back. Then my mother died." Tears trickled down his face one after another. "Then father put me into the order when I was four years old."

"Why?"

"Because… because…" Givas struggled. "Because he didn't love me anymore." The walled-up emotion finally broke free and his sobs of pure desolation charged the air.

Dels waited patiently until the wave ended. Choosing her moment carefully she asked, "Why else could he have done it?"

"Because… because… he couldn't cope," Givas admitted.

"Cope with…?"

"Cope with me, with the emotions." Givas looked up into the old woman's face seeking confirmation and approval. Finding only unconditional acceptance he continued. "I would have been a reminder and may be difficult for a master craftsman to handle."

Givas awoke and smiled. He smiled at feeling good. With a spring in his step, he walked out of the cave and into the hills. The chill of the yet-to-be-sun-touched landscape brought goosebumps to his bare arms. His sleeveless tunic showed signs of being well-worn. Dotted with stains, the general dust and grime coloured the original light tan. It was now faded to a mottled dull brown. He wore a pair of short trousers discoloured through continued use. The sandals, although robust, rounded off his ensemble. They bore scuffs and abrasions across the leather surfaces. He had dark areas of dirt under his fingernails whilst his toes choked under their covering of dust.

He heard the plaintive cry of a lonely bird as it flew overhead, and he raised his hand in acknowledgement.

"Yes, I too am alone." He answered the call. "Growing up and learning new skills." Givas thought, Maybe I am like the caterpillar, gestating, changing, and growing. By the old gods. If I feel this good now, how will I feel when I am out of this chrysalis? Givas grinned, a glorious jolt of excitement in his stomach.

He reached a small waterfall, which fed a clear pool. The pool's surface reflected images of the cotton ball clouds above.

Givas focused on some deep breathing. Surprisingly, he felt none of the fear that the sight of water normally produced within him. Step by step he stalked the pool, ready to race away if anything untoward happened.

Closing in on the waterfall, he lifted the bottom of his tunic and was about to take it off when he noticed it was shabby. Letting it drop back down, he glanced at his shorts and sandals; they were of a similar state. He realised, that being outside the city, his attire was no longer cared for by the order. Dels had allowed him to generally do as he pleased and wear what he chose. With a snort, he walked carefully on the slippery rocks into the falling water. With a gasp, the shockingly cold water flowed over him.

Givas turned around slowly under the waterfall. He raised his arms into the downpour, revelling in the experience. The water muffled all other noises and once again he felt alone but not lonely. Opening his eyes he saw wavering images of dark and light in front of him, the flowing water distorting and changing the view giving him its impression of life.

Givas jumped into the pool with a sense of adventure and exhilaration filling him to the brim.

The water was warmer in the pool, although not by much. Sinking to the bottom, he was surprised that his sense of balance kept him upright. Using the power of his legs he shot back to the surface, a mere four or five hands above his head. He broke the relative peace with much gasping and spluttering, not knowing whether to breathe in or out.

In the shallows, Givas took time to rub his clothes in the water. His tunic scrubbed, Givas' lean frame shivered with every small puff of air touching his skin. With his tunic drying, Givas closed his eyes, faced the light, and rested back on the lush grass bank. A dragonfly hovered over the shimmering pool, a mere hand's width from Givas. It was checking out the interloper.

Givas opened one eye, and, seeing the flash of metallic green shimmering opened his other eye too.

"Hello," he breathed.

The dragonfly flew sideways a finger's width and continued its surveillance.

Givas raised a hand with the palm facing upwards offering an alternative landing site. With a final flash of wondrous colours, the dragonfly was gone, continuing its vigil from afar.

Sitting up, he looked around soaking up the tranquillity and peace of his surroundings.

Givas was far from the Order of Librarians and far from his father. His cheek twitched. He placed a hand under his eye to stop it. He tentatively moved his hand away checking if the twitch had ceased. The twitching was still in his eyelid.

Closing his eyes, Givas tried to centre himself but struggled. For the first time, he couldn't. He opened his non-twitching eye and realised his clothes were still wet. With his twitching eye closed, Givas put on his tunic and shorts Clumsily and painfully slowly, despite his pounding heart, he dressed. He was scared his body was telling him something and he couldn't find out. *What was wrong?* He didn't know! Panic set in. Skirting around the water he stumbled twice. The peace was gone. His breathing became laboured. Sprinting now. He tried his eye again. It twitched stronger than ever which spurred him on. He ran as if his life depended on it. Givas dodged a tree branch and felt his ankle twist. Gritting his teeth, he slowed now limping. He banged into a rock and fell to the ground sobbing. He sat up, and with his back to a tree, sorrow poured from him.

He didn't know how long he was like that. He only noticed when he had stopped. There was peace again. Both eyes were open. His breathing was calm, and his chest was no longer pounding.

Finally, he managed to centre himself. This time there was no difficulty. He posed the question.

Why?

His father's face appeared smiling in his mind's eye. Behind his father was an indistinct image of a woman and beside her was a young boy. They were all smiling. Givas felt calm, at peace and assured. Opening his eyes, he saw beauty in the leaves of the tree, the trunk solid behind him.

Taking his time standing up, Givas tested his injured ankle and, surprisingly it felt fine. To make sure, he put all his weight on it and raised the other off the ground. *No pain!*

With a smile, he hopped. The ultimate test. No change. Grinning, he continued to hop. He hopped all the way back and Dels saw him like that – a hopping smiling young man.

"Why are you happily hopping?" she enquired.

"Because I am." He laughed.

Over a meal beside the fire, he watched as the flames did their hypnotic dance. He told her then what had happened. Dels was silent as he talked, neither surprised nor offering sympathy.

"So?" he asked finally.

"So what do you make of it?" she countered.

Givas sat and mulled it over.

"Well… I remember thinking how far I had come. Far from the city… from my father. Then my muscle twitched. So it must be my reaction to my father." Givas hypothesised. "The image could have been my family… my past… could that be it? Accepting my past?"

"What do you think?"

"Yes… it was accepting my past," Givas answered himself.

"What now?"

"Have fun!" Givas smiled, allowing happiness to flow from within.

"Then what?"

Givas looked at the old woman and saw her looking back at him. There was a twinkle in her eye along with a steadfastness. He shrugged his shoulders.

"Have you thought about your future?"

"Yes," he admitted, finally facing the topic. "I thought about my twenty-four-moon duty."

"Then?"

"Then… well… then I was going to look into the myth."

Del's mouth tightened, preventing any judgement from bursting forth.

"Then?"

"Find someone and raise a family."

"A worthy cause. Anything else?"

"Have fun!"

Dels smiled. She knew that he was possibly selling himself short with his goal. But, as he was young, his dreams, desires and goals would change and mutate and change again as he grew.

"It is always good to have a goal," she said and left it at that.

20

S tivs stood behind the empsar, watching twinkling miniature stars of dust motes. The dust was catching the sunshine that was beaming through the east windows.

He breathed deeply and allowed all muscles to relax whilst standing still for so long. Only his eyes moved, swivelling around, scanning the room, and surveying the Council of Elders. He nodded to the assistant of the Elder to his left. He, in turn, nodded to his left, passing the nod along until it came back to Stivs from his right-hand side.

Within moments of each other, they all closed their eyes and centred themselves. Then they all put their protective energy out. Expanding out from the room in a golden spinning and glowing orb, it swept over humans, animals, buildings and plants.

The inhabitants in the city barely noticed, so used to feeling safe, that they never knew it was happening.

The energy grew and grew until it reached the city walls. It stayed there, pulsing as it kept the city safe. It was keeping the city and inhabitants protected during the meditation. The empsar led the Council of Elders in their important meditative journey.

Each Elder sat on a high-backed solid chair. The wood was ornately carved with visual representations of the gods of old. The four legs were rounded at the bottom. They curled underneath, supporting the chair frame and the incumbent. The Elders, men and women alike, wore flowing robes of various shades of white. One could guess the length of tenure of position each Elder had, by how deep a shade their robe had changed to. Some heads were bowed, whilst one or two were resting against the back support of the chair.

The soft susurration of gentle breathing quietened the hall and mesmerised the building.

The empsar felt the supporting energy of the council and visualised guiding it. It burst up through the roof and into the atmosphere. Once surpassing the height of the uppermost clouds he guided it in a shield of white peace. The shield flowed in a growing blanket extending to surround the whole planet.

Once satisfied that Earth had been encompassed, he released his consciousness from the energy and brought his focus back down assisting the Elders to do likewise.

The creaking of chairs and stretching of limbs signified the completion of the group meditation. It alerted Stivs to the next step. He passed a thought pulse to the assistant of the Elder on his left who in turn passed it on. Again, Stivs received his pulse from his right and all opened eyes simultaneously.

Looking around, Stivs noticed everything was alright. He knew that it was only a precaution sending out thoughts of peace. But who could say it did or did not work? The city was safe. The council was safe, weren't they?' Stivs smiled briefly before scanning the room once more.

The inner room that they sat in was basic, and furnished with a large circular table, around which the Elders sat in their chairs. On the surface of the table, a design was carved. It consisted of many overlapping triangles within a circle. This signified three points of harmony combining to make a whole entity: mind, body, and soul.

Three points, three triangles and one full circle was the motif of Atlantis. The symbol was to be found on every door of every building. The logo was chiselled on the pillars of each side of the harbours too.

Stivs traced the outline of his belt buckle which cinched in his robes around his stomach. Glancing up he saw the roof. Great aged timbers formed the frame for the stone blocks. He marvelled at the craftsmanship. His dwellings and that of the rest of the city, he was sure, all had wooden roofs. Some even had hay or some such material.

"Stivs?" Empsar Con Dwig motioned him to come closer.

"Yes, Empsar?" he asked quietly."

"Feel into the Elders and report to me after adjournment."

Stivs raised his eyebrow in surprise before moving back to his standing spot.

What is he up to? he thought. No need to wonder. All will become evident. With that self–rebuke, he looked at each Elder and sensed their mood.

Con Hrap was tired. But more so lethargic probably, after the meditation, still to return fully back to her body. Con Twor was happy and Stivs paused, enjoying the connection with happiness. Con Pwas was... was bored and distant. Stivs centred himself with deep breathing before sensing Con Pwas once more. Feeling in the connection, Stivs again sensed uneasy boredom. Putting any of his judgement to one side he maintained his focus. Underneath the boredom, there was something hidden. Stivs frowned and broke the connection. Con Pars was pleased with herself and so were both Con Dwart and Con Yass. Con Brar, Con Dwig, Con Vorey and Con Artis were all tainted with the same loving peace that was the thrust of the meditation. Con Fras was filled with peace and something else that Stivs initially couldn't define.

Once again, after some centring, he refocused on the Elder. At that moment Con Fras looked up and caught Stivs staring at her. Stivs smiled and inclined his head in recognition of his connection. Con Fras ignored his good intent and shielded her thoughts and feelings.

Stivs felt a wall shut down on the connection and he could sense her no more.

Odd! he mused. Two elders on the council hide or have hidden parts of themselves.

The chimes of brass bells signalled adjournment. This was followed by a scraping of chairs on the floor and shuffling of sandalled feet. All the while were muted conversations amongst the elders.

Out of the corner of his eye Stivs caught sight of something casual yet innocuous. A hand had briefly touched the back of one of the other Elders. Stivs watched them file out, interspersed with assistants. He prayed that the Elder would turn round. They were at the door and, for a split second Stivs saw her face in profile. She said something before turning back, once again anonymous in the throng.

"Empsar—"

"Walk with me!" Empsar Con Dwig closed off the rest of Stivs' sentence.

Stivs checked himself, knowing that the right time would present itself for his findings.

The empsar walked out into the sunlight, tilting his head to enjoy the full effect of the warming sun on his face.

Stivs walked two paces behind and one to the left and was amused to hear the empsar humming a workman's tune. He did not see Con Pwas and Con Fras in an alcove's shadows watching them leave the council buildings.

By the time the empsar turned and entered a building, he was finishing his fourth rendition of the workman's tune.

Stivs looked up and saw they were at a museum. Without even thinking of asking a question for fear of a rebuke, he followed the empsar in. His first breath inside the old building was full of dust. He stifled a cross between a cough and a sneeze with eyes bulging as he held everything in.

With eyes watering, he coughed as quietly as he could, attempting to clear his throat and restore normal breathing.

Without turning, the empsar ceased his humming.

"Why are the old gods not idolised anymore?"

"Umm…" Stivs wracked his brain thinking back to his school days. "So we become self-reliant?" he offered.

"In what way?"

"Over our destiny and choices," Stivs said with more conviction as his memory was fully functioning once more.

"Is that a good thing?"

"Uh…" Stivs was non-plussed. He hadn't thought of that before. "Good for learning I suppose."

"Mmm. Anything else?"

"Being self-responsible?"

"That's good." The empsar beamed at him. "Responsible for what?"

"Our own emotions?"

The empsar continued to smile.

"Who's there?" a voice cackled from the shadows of a large, beautifully sculpted figure of the old God of War.

"Master of Selection, it is I Con Dwig your follower, accompanied by my trusted follower," Empsar Con Dwig said winking at Stivs.

"Con Dwig, ya young aps! What are you doing here in the company of all those who should be forgotten?" The ancient silvery figure of the master of selection appeared out of the dark.

"My trusted follower was about to tell me his report on the council. I appreciate your understanding and comments on such matters."

"Things must not all be as they seem Dwig, for you to consult an old rogue such as myself."

"Not—" The empsar was cut off in mid-protest.

"An old rogue, yes! As my help has not been required in the last three summers. Except of course for looking after the future children of Atlantis. Well?" the master of selection barked at Stivs.

Gulping, Stivs cleared his throat before starting.

"The Council of Elders—"

"Go straight to the heart of the matter," the master of selection ordered.

"Con Pwas and Con Fras."

"Those two? Yes, that fits. Let me see now." The master of selection bowed his head breathing deeply. With a snort, he raised his blind gaze back up. His passive face relaxed as Stivs watched with bated breath.

The master of selection's eyes seemed to expand and shrink in pulses. Glowing bright white he drew Stivs' gaze in deeper.

"Speak, boy."

"Con Pwas, I sensed was displaced in time for some reason and had separated himself," Stivs stammered.

"And Fras?"

"Con Fras was distant and closed herself to my connection when she realised my attention was on her."

Empsar Con Dwig asked for confirmation from the old man.

"By the old gods, he is the empsar's follower alright." He chuckled.

Empsar Con Dwig smiled in appreciation at the compliment.

Stivs flushed with embarrassment at the unsolicited testimonial to his integrity.

"True Pwas is out of time. He has plans and hopes for the future. Fras is his ally. More she is his lustre. Pwas has always admired the smell of spices from different lands. Fras' physical impulses are turning her away from deliberate choices."

"Does Pwas seek to hold the bowl of more spices?" Con Dwig asked, continuing the analogy.

"That future is yet to be chosen. Now leave me to my dust and mice!" The master of selection disappeared into the shadows once more. He left Empsar Con Dwig and Stivs in the Museum of the Old Gods.

Stivs looked around seeking to confirm the master of selection was joking about the mice.

"What does that mean?" Stivs asked.

"Admiring the smell of spices from different lands could mean many things. But I think it means that Con Pwas is not fully at peace with Atlantis. Or admires the direction of other societies."

"What impact does that have?"

"It may have little, or it may be a gathering storm. Whatever it is, Con Fras significantly increases the potential."

"How so?"

"If we assume they have deep feelings for each other, then think about it. What happens in a relationship?"

Stivs gave it some thought. He thought about it from Con Fras' point of view.

"If I was Con Fras, I would want what Con Pwas wanted; to be fulfilled, to be happy and at peace."

"And if Con Pwas wants more than our society offers?"

"But our society is fulfilling!" Stivs exclaimed, incredulous at any other viewpoint. "Our society has developed at each level to look after the mind, body and soul."

"True, yet that still may not fulfil Con Pwas. He may want more."

"Want more what? Peace? Fulfilment? Food? Trade goods?"

"Whatever the desire is, does not matter. It is what he does, if anything, in response to the desire," the empsar said with a sigh. "Con Fras increases the impact of any action considerably."

"What will you do?"

"Commit my focus to peace!" The empsar looked at Stivs with a smile. "I suggest you too, commit to your tasks."

"What about—"

The empsar cut his question off with a wave of the hand.

"Let us not waste any further energy on this matter. Accept it and focus on our own goals."

Empsar Con Dwig waited for Stivs to leave the building first. An interesting experience to highlight both Stivs' awareness and sensitivity. Also witnessing the desired resulting reaction. Return to acceptance of others. Then letting go of the desire to control, he thought, looking at the young man in front of him.

21

Stivs once again felt he had been tested. A situation was brewing and his reaction had been evaluated. He realised with hindsight, that putting his attention on the matter increased its importance, increased it to a ridiculous level.

Later that evening, he slipped easily into a meditative and reflective state. He considered the day.

It may be reflecting my refusal to desire more than I have, he surmised. I was most surprised that the Elder could wish for anything else.

Stivs lay on his bunk with the last weak rays of the sun touching the tips of his toes. He looked away and saw the fading negative image of his toes. The outline of the wooden frame and woven thatch appeared out of the darkness, as his eyesight adjusted.

The young man was transported back in time. He was four years old and his brother was eight. The night before being selected, he sat at the table next to his brother. Both their stomachs were rumbling. Their father had come back from his duties in the archives, his hands covered in ink from his transcribing. He was quiet and lost in thought. Mother had placed a chunk of dried bread, some vegetables, and a slice of salted fish in front of each of them.

His brother eyed the food before piping up. "Can I have a green apple?"

"You will take what you're given! And no argument." Mother scowled at the ungrateful young boy of hers.

Father looked up, at last, woken from his reverie.

"Eat, son. The apples have yet to be harvested."

"But, Father—"

"Don't but me. Eat what's been given and say no more."

Stivs' brother dropped his head and toyed with his food. Stivs, wanting to make his parents happy, devoured the food on his platter. He smacked his lips in appreciation as he had seen his father do on occasion. His father smiled at him.

Stivs realised from his memory that a pattern had taken root from such a young age. Being happy with whatever was available and not going after what he wanted. *Did that affect going after the woman who caught his eye?* He knew he wanted to speak to her. But something had stopped him in the past.

Stivs fell into a peaceful sleep.

It was market day when he awoke. The sounds of stalls being set up early assaulted his ears. Stivs pulled the rough woollen blanket over his head and attempted to restore the peace and calm of sleep. The morning air had yet to warm up with the sun's warmth. Stivs snuggled deeper into his bunk enjoying the comfort of the bed. He was getting the most out of his time before getting up. The duties of the day had to be completed before venturing into the thriving market.

She might be there, he thought excitedly. It had seemed forever since he had last caught sight of the young woman. She had captured his heart without knowing it.

The smell caught the back of his throat. He knew it was the butcher's sector. Scarlet fluids soaked up by the dust and straw under the stalls. The ruddy-faced butcher lopped off what looked like a sheep's leg with one powerful stroke.

The metallic taste of blood on the air assailed him. He rushed past the line of carcasses festooning the stalls and carried on running until he reached less stomach-curdling wares.

A soft mountain of coarse grey wool was piled up skywards and Stivs grinned at the stallholder. Only the eyes and top of the head could be seen above the piles of wool.

Perfume caught his attention. Lifting his head he peered through the crowd, his gaze darting from one individual to another seeking the wearer.

The whiff of flower blossom was out of place in the market and must belong to her. He wanted so much for it to be so.

Stivs shoved through the crowds, letting his nose lead the way. He gritted his teeth as an elbow winded him in the jostling throng. He continued, determined in his quest.

"She must be here," he whispered.

A gap magically appeared before him and Stivs stood staring, his hopes shattering in an instant.

"Dried flowers?" An old woman offered him a bunch of sweet-smelling dried flowers in a grimy outstretched hand.

Dejected, he shook his head and ignored her glare.

Stivs continued passing through the market, not focusing on his direction or whereabouts.

"Watch out!" A shout pierced his gloom.

Before he could react, he felt the splash of water then the sensation of dampness came through his best trousers. The same trousers that had been clean this morning. Looking down, Stivs grunted in resignation. From his crotch down, the beige fabric darkened, evidence of some sort of accident.

Enough was enough he decided and turned abruptly.

In shock, he stared into the loveliest pair of eyes he had ever seen, brown irises with glints of light, which mesmerised Stivs. They appeared as golden jewels to his mind's eye.

"Oh!" Aor from his dreams saw his wet patch.

Stivs coloured up, face burning with embarrassment. "Bucket... water... thrown at me," he stammered.

"Ah." She giggled.

Stivs felt his stomach flip over. Hope flared eternally.

"Garden?" he forced out.

"Garden?" she queried.

"Would you like to walk through the garden?" Stivs managed a full sentence.

"Oh…"

Stivs's heart was in his mouth.

"Yes," Aor said with a smile.

His stomach burst into an emotional delight of butterflies. A grin spread across his face with joy filling his eyes.

"Aor, my name is Stivs," he told her, leading the way.

"You wouldn't believe this, but I think I have dreamed of this meeting," she replied.

Stivs's whole world spun and he lost any sense of himself. It was as if someone had pulled the earth from under him sending him cartwheeling through space. The only thing that kept him from experiencing vertigo was her eyes. Aor was waiting for his mocking and derision.

"Me too," he whispered to her, seeing her relax with relief.

Stivs and Aor walked smiling into the gardens.

22

Gamute stood facing the spine. The smell in the air was that which immediately followed the rain and a breeze raised goosebumps on his forearms. Mother Nature caressed him, gently ruffling his hair.

Looking out towards the Hills of Terzadon, Gamute searched for some sign of his son in vain. There was a figure walking towards the hills. Nothing unusual about that, but what was that glint?

Light flickered, reflecting off something on the person.

Gamute automatically grabbed his golden chain, a symbol of sacred duty entrusted by a member of the Order of the Librarians. A duty is given by a member of the Council of Elders.

"What reason would the council have to send someone out alone into the mountains?"

"Who are we to ask such a question?" Devas answered.

"But it is dangerous out there still, isn't it?"

"Ever since Terzadon gave up its fight against our city it has been peaceful."

"Is sixteen summers long enough?"

"Long enough for them to look to Atena for prosperous lands to conquer.

"Is it safe?"

"As safe as in our city."

"Hmmmph," Gamute grumbled. "What did you come to speak to me about?"

"The last finishing touches have been done before the ceremony." Devas smiled. "It is your honour to inform the council."

Gamute gave a weary grin. Both men were tired from pushing themselves hard at their tasks. He looked at his friend and laid a hand on his shoulder.

"Without your help, Devas, it could not have happened."

"So long as there are no more heights!"

Gamute chuckled. "I promise you that! No more heights on this job!" He winked.

Devas looked at him, startled, before realising his leg was being pulled.

Gamute looked down at the magical view. Sweeping down the nearest inside of the volcano was a blanket of green. The tree line stopped a few paces below his feet. Down in the centre was the sparkling life-giving water. His predecessors had struggled to use this supply of water effectively so they had opted for the much farther away source in the hills. His idea had been realised at last.

"It was worth it, wasn't it?" Devas asked him as they meandered along the tree line to the opposite side.

Gamute looked pained. "For us and the city, yes."

"And the three?" Devas continued.

"I don't know. The families will be cared for hereafter. The three workers are heroes, their deaths unfortunate. I just wish that we had figured out a safer way of digging out the last part of the tunnels." He saw the three dark blurred rectangles through the water down in the basin and shuddered.

"They would have drowned quickly," Devas offered.

"Another three deaths I feel responsible for."

"You weren't the reason for Jonas's death!"

"He was my first son. You don't know what happened!"

"He went sailing and the gods of the sea took him to Neantra."

"You still believe in Neantra? I wish I did. I shouted at Jonas that day he ran away." Tears were at the corners of his eyes. "For all I know, he too drowned, but with my shouting ringing in his ears."

"He will be enjoying the gods' pleasure in Neantra."

"Neantra. How can gods be so kind if they exist? How can they take away my Jonas and Ellie? Why?"

"We are not meant to know their reasons."

"Why not? Would we feel better knowing the purpose of death so young?"

"Do you know how the sun rises every morn and why?" Devas asked simply.

Gamute looked at his friend.

"Let us not debate gods and Neantra," Gamute offered wearily, "for it benefits us not. Let us look to now and the future."

"And the celebration tonight," Devas said grinning.

"Yes, and the vine wine – your favourite!"

"Now, Rats, you know what to do on my signal?"

Rats nodded grinning with pleasure.

Gamute, satisfied, allowed himself a brief glow of warm pleasure.

"Gamute, what about the children?" Devas pointed at the children in the rectangular area around one of the three reservoirs. It was the same reservoir that they were using for the presentation to the empsar.

"Let them be!" Gamute chuckled.

"But…"

"It will be fun!"

Devas looked at him as if his personality had changed. Now that it was complete except for the ceremony and celebration, the tension was draining from him. The happy, confident, and carefree Gamute was returning.

"But…" Devas tried again.

Gamute only winked.

Finally, the Order of the Librarians quietened and the empsar nodded to Gamute.

"Empsar, Elders and people of Atlantis. I, Master Craftsman Voret, by order of the Council of Elders, under the guidance of Empsar Con Dwig, hereby open the new reservoir system Eternity!" Gamute shouted. He waved his arms over his head to the waiting giant Rats who was one hundred paces away.

Rats hauled on the rope on the pulley system at his side. The crowd drew in a breath. His muscles bunched with every heave. An audible click occurred with every pull. Three, four, five, six. A hissing sound could be heard. Then there was a gurgling.

A child screamed. The crowd turned to face the reservoir. Another child yelled in delight.

The pressure shot jets of water up through holes in the structure under the reservoir. The children dodged the spraying water with delight. The crowd laughed. As the reservoir filled, the water trickled out of the drinking fountain followed by much applause.

Empsar Con Dwig, smiling, walked over to the fountain scooped a handful of water up in two hands and tasted it. Smacking his lips he nodded in approval.

The crowd once again fell silent as everyone watched two apostles lift the shining gold chain of duty from around Gamute's bowed head. Stivs brought forward a jewelled staff between the empsar and Gamute.

"The Council of Elders hereby declare your duty complete and bestow upon you this gift. Our everlasting appreciation to you and your team," the empsar intoned.

Stivs passed the beautiful glittering staff into Gamute's hands and stepped away.

Not knowing what else to do, he raised the staff which shone in the sun. Cheering and more applause followed. All the workers roared their approval and soon the vine wine and sweet bread aromas filled the air. The stalls and tables were overfilled, and the celebrations began in earnest.

Passing people were voicing their thanks to Gamute and Devas. It seemed that every worker was slapping their backs in congratulations. Only when they saw Rats coming to do the same did Gamute and Devas lose themselves in the crowds. They dodged in and around the drinking stalls to avoid a thumping from the giant.

When Devas caught up with Gamute later that evening, he was very much worse for wear. Devas, having had one too many cups of vine wine, was rolling on his feet. Grabbing the staff out of Gamute's hands he used it for propping himself up.

"Thank you for your help, Devas," Gamute said thickly for he too had enjoyed his fair share of wine.

"It has been my honour," Devas hiccupped. "You knew what would happen with the overflow vents?"

Gamute laughed. "Yes… well, I guessed. And the pressure didn't last."

They both peered over the base of the reservoir and saw the heat of the day had dried the surface. It was as if the water had never been there.

"Let me get you a drink Master Craftsman with No Duty."

"No duty!" He beamed. "Let me put this gift somewhere before we celebrate in earnest.

By the time Gamute returned from stowing the staff safely away he found his friend slumped under a table. There was a cup on the point of tipping in Devas' outstretched hand.

"I will help you with that," Gamute told the snoring form and tossed back the remaining wine, barely tasting it.

With a heave, he pulled Devas upright and staggered with him. Unsteady from a mixture of plenty of wine and the weight of his friend he wobbled off towards Devas' home, supporting his assistant all the way, just as his friend had supported him over the years.

23

"Aor."

"Yes, Stivs?"

"I cannot sense you." Stivs frowned, picking his words with care. "It confuses me.

"Why?"

"Because I don't feel safe."

"Safe from what?"

"From hurt."

"You expect hurt? You expect me to hurt you?"

"Expect no... it's... it is new for me... I am being completely open... and want to experience this openness with you."

Aor grabbed his hand and placed it over her heart.

"Can you feel that beating?"

"Yes."

"It can only hurt yours if you want it to hurt yours," she said softly.

"Thank you for reminding me."

"Thank you for your openness. I treasure your willingness to be vulnerable."

Stivs smiled, understanding, firming up his mind about her. *Wonderful, a connection at last.* The universe had truly answered his wish.

"Stivs."

"Yes?"

"Promise you will never close your heart to me."

He looked deep into her eyes and saw his own fears reflected. Her vulnerability mirrored his own. Stivs felt the last remaining barriers dissolve with compassion.

"I promise." He placed her hand over his heart. Something in him connected and suddenly it was all apparent. *So obvious now.* He sensed her to the very depths and knew she could sense him. The depth of connection was what he imagined being a raindrop before dropping. Connected to something so much bigger. As a whole yet individual when separate.

Hugging her close Stivs got a whiff of springtime. As beautiful as delicate blossom flowers growing in meadows warmed by the morning sun. She had soft hairs on the side of her face that could not be seen but tickled his lips as they passed by.

He felt her chuckle vibrate the velvet skin of her neck.

She pushed him away.

Stivs saw small rosebuds of colour tinge her cheeks.

"You are very forward for a librarian."

"Being in your company intoxicates me."

"Maybe I should leave you then?"

"Never. A difficult burden to bear but I will suffer it gladly."

They laughed, watching the sun sink over the horizon in a blaze of orange and red. The stars took over peeking through the trickle of clouds high above. Time for the two had sped by. They had developed an understanding of each other. Such an understanding was far beyond what mere words could describe.

Stivs had found out Aor's ancestors were a mixture of craftsmen, librarians and empsars. Her parents were librarians. Aor had not been selected and had grown up assisting her mother in looking after the household.

"I must return," Aor told him.

"I should too.

24

"SO, have you met your future wife?" Empsar Con Dwig asked.

"Yes, Empsar," Stivs answered him happily.

"And how do you feel about being an assistant."

"No different to before I met her."

"What about becoming my replacement?"

"What?" Stivs' eyes widened. "You... you can continue for many summers yet."

"I feel my best years are past," Empsar Con Dwig said heavily.

"No," Stivs almost shouted.

"How do you feel about being my nominated replacement?"

"But I don't want the position."

"Why not?"

"Leading the Council of Elders is your job. I am too young and inexperienced."

"Firstly, a job is not a lifetime role. Secondly, I was asked when I was one summer younger than you. Finally, you have the best awareness and sense of someone ever. It is on par with the master of selection."

"Thank you for the praise." Stivs was embarrassed. "I don't want your job."

"All the more reason for you to take it." The empsar held out his hand. "Now, my mind is made up. There is one thing I want to show you before convening the Elders. Help me to my feet."

Stivs assisted the empsar out of his chair and handed him the gnarled and polished walking stick. Once the empsar was standing he took away his supporting arm.

At the hall used for chanting, Empsar Con Dwig paused.

"Why the chanting, Stivs Lo Empsar?"

Stivs head jerked up at the title. Allowing himself to settle he sensed Con Dwig's amusement at his discomfort.

"Chanting used to raise the energy level of the city," he replied.

"Why raise the energy level?"

"Happiness, lightness, and a sense of peace?"

"Good."

"Empsar, I haven't done a twenty-four-moon duty," Stivs found himself whining.

"Haven't you?"

"No." Stivs reviewed his time spent assisting the empsar. "Not outside the city."

"No matter of importance. Now to the object I wish to show to you." He brushed away any further protest with one waving arm. The empsar strode out, clicking the walking stick on the pathway.

Stivs followed him straight into the museum.

"Empsar Con Dwig and his assistant," the master of selection announced.

"May I introduce Stivs Lo Empsar."

The master of selection laughed.

"Another young empsar. What is Atlantis in for? Come here, boy!"

Immediately obeying the wizened old man's command, Stivs moved forward. He found his arm grabbed firmly by a pale bony hand.

Stivs felt a gentle breeze flow through his energy with a momentary pause over his heart.

"A wise choice, Dwig, even if he was your assistant."

Stivs avoided staring into the blind milky-white eyes of the old man.

"You'll be here for…"

"Yes, the myth tablet."

"Bah! A waste of space and not worth thinking about," the master of selection scoffed.

"Even so," the empsar continued.

"Over here if you must."

The old man used his walking stick only three times on the way through the museum. The building was filled with sculptures, artefacts and tables.

A shiver went down Stivs' spine. *What is happening?* he thought.

"The myth tablet?" he croaked.

"Yes, only the empsars are allowed to read it," Empsar Con Dwig answered.

"But…"

"I know… a myth. But most myths have a grain of truth to them."

"There you go, Dwig!" The master of selection pointed with his walking stick in the general direction of a table. It was covered by a thick cloth.

The empsar removed the cloth with a flourish sending a cloud of grey dust into the air.

Stivs's eyes watered, and he sneezed loudly in the cavernous museum.

Wiping his eyes, he moved closer to the table's edge and saw an ancient-looking slab of rock in front of him.

Mottled with discoloration he could tell it had once been outside for all to see. Rectangular at the top, it was broken at the bottom in an irregular pattern. A piece must have snapped off.

"What happened to the bottom?" he enquired before focusing on what was etched into the thick rock.

"No one knows exactly. A great storm swept Atlantis countless summers ago. So long ago, even before the master of selection was alive."

A snort of derision was the only response.

"Our predecessors saved the remaining part for our eyes alone."

Stivs, emboldened, stepped closer and read the myth.

Lost of family a man is
with no idea of future
Gifted beyond others
Will put into action
Annihilation of our life
Foundations and all

Unless the past can
be forgiven and living
starts anew

Time will be changed
forever
Except for the few

"I could be that boy," Stivs whispered.

Empsar Con Dwig and the master of selection remained quiet.

"But it could mean anyone who has lost a family," Stivs continued.

"Forgiveness about something… what would need to be forgiven?" Stivs glanced up before once again staring at the prophecy.

"What was at the bottom? How much is missing?"

"Focus on the moment with love in your heart, boy," the master of selection commanded before leaving the two of them alone.

"But how can we ignore this?"

"Who is ignoring it?" Empsar Dwig smiled at him.

"But…"

"Feel into it, Stivs Lo Empsar."

Stivs frowned, then with a sigh relaxed. Breathing deeply and slowly he closed his eyes.

"A point of view," Stivs said, surprised.

"What about a point of view?"

"Treat it as a point of view."

"And…?"

"Everyone is entitled to a point of view. It does not necessarily mean it is right or true."

"What makes it true?"

Stivs closed his eyes again, a smile playing on his lips.

"The more attention that is paid to it," Stivs said confidently, opening his eyes. "The more this is heeded the more likely it will come to pass."

"And you doubted my decision on selecting you." Empsar Con Dwig chuckled.

25

Givas watched the water vole at the side of the pool. It seemed unconcerned about being the centre of attention. He saw the droplets of water slide down the fine white whiskers. It paused before vacating the bathing area. Some green slime stuck to its fur as it climbed onto the bank underneath a rocky outcrop. He saw how easily it cleaned itself with a twitch that seemed to start at its rear and finish at the very tip of its nose. Slime and water droplets alike were shrugged off. The vole disappeared into the tall grass edging the corner of the pool.

Thinking about Atlantis as he did frequently, Givas felt excited. With only two moons left of his duty, he would return to the city. *A two-moon vow of silence had to be done before….before what?*

He knew he'd told Dels that he would find a wife and settle down but how?

Diving into the cold water pushed all matters from his mind. He broke the surface gasping for air. The physical shock of the temperature change was invigorating. Givas used an ungainly scrabbling motion to get back to the bank. He was thankful when his feet touched the bottom.

Ignoring the gaze of a bird perched on an overhanging bough he quietly dressed and left the area. Givas arrived back at the cave with not a moment to spare. She was ready to leave.

Tossing him a canvas sack she grabbed the walking stick.

"I don't need to go back immediately after the two moons, do I?" he asked.

"What else would you do?"

"Look after you, of course."

"I don't need to be looked after yet," she growled.

"You're using a walking stick! You are all alone!"

"Thank you for reminding me!" Dels smiled. "Although I enjoy your company, I will not let you alter your destiny so early in your life."

"But it is my choice," he protested.

"Impacting on me. No. Thank you for your concern and compassion but it's unnecessary."

"But..."

"No, your destiny awaits. I look forward to you visiting me with your wife and firstborn."

"Firstborn. How many children will I have?"

"How many do you wish for?"

"Let me think about that."

Dels laughed. "Now, let us go, we have apples to collect before meeting a friend."

"A friend? Who are we meeting?"

Dels waved off any further questions. "Practice your vow of silence, Givas," she commanded.

The solitary tree stood on a rise. It provided shade over windfall festooned grass. Givas began searching through the bruised apples for the most recent windfall seeking the freshest of all the available apples.

"Givas!" She pointed at the apples in the branches. Without a word, he scrambled up the trunk into the centre of the tree. Unable to see the apples due to the profusion of leaves he was baffled for a moment about what to do.

He realised he may be able to shake them down. Grinning he grabbed a branch overhanging Dels. Taking the best purchase, he could, he pulled. No movement. Givas pushed and still no movement. Undeterred he grabbed a thinner but higher branch. He shook it furiously for a moment then stopped and cupped a hand to his ear. Not a shriek or gasp, but only the chuckling of an old woman.

Sliding down the rough bark he landed on his backside, getting up, red-faced with a mixture of frustration and embarrassment.

Dels raised her walking stick in the air casually and tapped the nearest apple. It dropped neatly at his feet. He tried to hide his admiration with a scowl. After a couple of apples had been similarly tapped, he had turned it into a game. For every thwack of the stick, he would attempt to catch the apple in one hand before placing it gently in the sack.

Dels stopped at a dozen, much to the silent protests of a gesticulating Givas.

She nodded at his pointing and smiled.

"Why get more than we need when the tree here will keep them fresh until we need more?"

Givas could not fault her logic.

Givas heard the bleating of the sheep before seeing the flock. With the crisp clear air in the hills, the sound could carry a day's walk.

He glanced at Ex-Empsar Dels covered in a shawl. He could only guess how many summers she had seen. Despite her bringing the walking stick she had barely used it. He remembered his mistake of assuming her frailty.

Admitting that his help wasn't needed changed his perspective on many assumptions. Assumptions which he had made during his experiences over the past twenty-two moons.

If he hadn't been doing work to help her, why had he been doing it?

Learning. The answer popped into his head.

About what? he asked himself.

Focus. Givas reflected on focus. He was positive there was something more to it than that.

Completing tasks gave him a sense of achievement, but what about during the doing? Tasks brought his focus back to the present.

"Givas," she commanded holding out the flint.

Givas grabbed the flint rock and saw the remains of a fire several paces ahead.

Touching the one remaining piece of wood with the toes of his sandal it collapsed in a puff of ash. He stood there dismayed.

"Givas."

He saw her pointing to a small copse through which they had just passed. Givas strolled back the way they had come, on the lookout for firewood.

"Mother? Is that man with you?" Ortva asked.

"A librarian from Atlantis on his last few moons of duty."

"You have not mentioned him before."

"It was not relevant."

"How are the sheep?"

"They are well. They are fattened and keep the grass low and well fertilised."

Ortva laughed.

"You will have twice as much fertiliser."

"Twice as much wool in springtime too," she agreed. "A task Givas is getting used to," she said, smiling at the memory of Givas struggling with both sheep.

"How is the flock?"

"They are well. Muusi has recovered and I have decided to sell her at the next market"

"How is trade going?"

"The usual. All want the finest sheep at the lowest prices. I changed to Loj and for now, we are getting the best of deals,"

"And your wife?"

"She is expecting again."

"Congratulations! How many will that make?"

"This will be our third. It will give her something to focus on rather than me being away. She believes that these hills are filled with dangerous ruffians and Terzadons behind every rock."

They both laughed.

Givas returned that very instant and Ortva nearly jumped out of his skin.

"Don't worry about Givas here, he is practising his vow of silence," Dels said with a smile.

Givas looked at the shepherd and inclined his head in acknowledgement.

"It is my honour to meet you. My name is Ortva and I am the best shepherd in Atlantis." He too inclined his head in reply.

Givas took his pile of wood to the firepit and dropped them unceremoniously. He regretted having agreed to practise his vow of silence.

Whilst preparing the fire, he listened in on the conversation.

"There was a feast I missed recently which my neighbour told me about."

"A feast? What was being celebrated?" Dels enquired politely.

"The opening of the Eternity water system."

"Oh?"

"Yes. It took many summers and much of the city's supplies in building. All repairs had stopped when it was being made. The master stonemason also managed to get extra rations for everyone working on it."

"Important project then."

"By the old gods, it had us all grumbling. Even I was affected. I didn't get my sweet bread for many moons," Ortva grumbled. "But the Eternity will give the city water all year round."

"Wonderful!"

"Amazing. I don't know where Master Stonemason Voret got his idea from, but it was inspired."

"Why?"

"Holes in the hill. Who would have thought of that?"

Givas searched Ortva's face. He watched his body movements and listened for intonations in his speech, searching for any extra information. Having heard his father's name he was instantly sensitised. Still keeping to his vow of silence he was apoplectic with a fury of questions. A battering of opposing emotions roared through him. It left him confused, shocked and speechless. All he could physically do was sit there and listen, rooted to the spot. At last, his sparks caught, and smoke rose in front of him.

Stirring the fruit juice in the bubbling pot he watched the two adults talking. He moved the stirring stick in a circular motion. Looking up he saw Dels. She had her head tilted fractionally to one side. He realised he had made a mistake. The two adults hadn't been talking. Only Ortva had been speaking with Dels answering now and again with one-word answers.

He looked at Ortva and saw the shepherd dry up in conversation. Dels was accepting him completely. Ortva was smiling inanely.

'Two can play at that game.'

Focusing on the old woman he visualised a beam of energy hitting her and connecting both shepherd and woman. Seeing their outlines, their shapes, and them in their entirety as human beings, Givas stared. Accepting them completely and unreservedly he felt the energetic connection increase. Grinning, he appreciated them even more and found his focus somersault. Givas was neither in his mind nor out of it. He had connected completely with the moment and felt their energetic vibration change. He was aware of a rising, lightening of emotions and being in euphoria. Dels had her eyes closed and Ortva had fallen over snoring.

How dare he? Givas thought. The connection instantly dropped.

The energy was now on Dels alone and he grew bored with it. He'd proved he could do it. *So what!* He did what she had done, but with two people. Had she noticed?

The quickening questions evaporated the connection. The euphoria was gone and but he still felt positively happy. He returned his attention to the fire.

"Thank you, Givas. That was wonderful," Dels whispered.

Givas, pleased, sat staring into the flames, lost in time and space. He felt nothing mattered. His consciousness floated, bobbing in invisible eddies in an energetic dimension; a dimension never before ventured into. He must be ready to return to Atlantis soon... surely?

26

"I am here to give a testament to my love for your daughter," Stivs told Devas Pars, father of Aor Pars.

Devas pushed his plate away and belched.

Stivs stifled a smirk and awaited Aor's parents' decision.

"I recognise you, Stivs," Aor's mother said. "I have seen you in the council room. You are an empsar's assistant are you not?"

Stivs looked directly at Con Ro Pars.

"Yes, Con Pars... I am."

"Listen to him, Devas, so formal and so polite." She touched Devas' arm with a finger.

"Remember your pledging of a testament to my parents."

Devas' eyes misted over and he grinned.

"Your parents didn't think much of me!" He chuckled.

"Oh, please, Stivs, you can call me Ro."

Stivs relaxed more, feeling happy. It was much easier than he had anticipated.

"Aor, give your future husband another cupful of vine wine. This is cause for celebration," Devas commanded.

"Any excuse for more vine wine," Ro admonished playfully.

"Oh, Mother."

"Don't oh mother me, darling! Hopefully, your Stivs won't be as partial to vine wine as my Devas is."

"I prefer honey mead," Stivs offered.

"Pah! Not for celebrating you won't."

Aor topped up Stivs' cup.

"To a new union of love!" Devas toasted.

"To a new union of love," everyone repeated.

Tossing back his vine wine Stivs felt his body react in shock to the liquid.

"To a continuing union of love," Devas toasted, wrapping his free arm around his wife and pulling her close.

Aor had just enough time to refill Stivs' cup.

Stivs tossed back the contents once more.

Three or four toasts later, Stivs was feeling decidedly woozy. He hoped that his future father-in-law was running out of toasts to make.

"To... to..." Devas paused, "life, love, and eternity!" He beamed.

Stivs drank another cupful of wine and prayed that it was the last one.

"Come on, darling, leave the children in peace." Ro dragged her husband away, still thinking up toasts. Any excuse to continue drinking.

"What do you think of them?" Aor asked.

"Hic." Stivs concentrated. "I think your father knows how to toast."

"Stivs, I'm serious." She grabbed his arm.

"I'm serious too. Your parents are wonderful. What do you think they make of me?"

"Oh, they know how I feel about you," she said with a smile.

"How is that?" He grabbed her and pulled her onto his lap.

"Stivs," she squealed, acting shocked stood up. "You make me happy! And I think I should make sure you get home safely!"

"I shall be safe. Hic! But thank you, you wonderful, beautiful woman for your offer."

Stivs stood up, only pausing to stop rolling on his feet.

"Are you going to be alright?"

"I will be fine. Thank you." Stivs aimed himself at the door. With much concentration, he reached his goal. Several sideways lurches slowed him down.

Aor stifled a giggle.

"It is not a laughing matter, darling!" Stivs rebuked her, chuckling as he bounced off the doorway and into the alleyway.

"Stivs Lo Empsar and Aor," he mumbled to himself as he staggered his way home. He felt happy and drunk

27

Stivs woke to the shaking of his arm. An apostle looking worried for Stivs' welfare visibly relaxed as Stivs opened an eye.

"Mmmm?" Closing an eye.

His arm now had a possible chance of being dislocated by the violent movements.

"What?" Stivs groaned.

A Council of Elders token was pressed into his palm.

"What … Oh no! Not today!" Blearily, he looked at the summons token. "I hope by the old gods it is worth the effort." Stivs clutched his head with one hand and the side of his cot with another as he raised himself out of bed.

Tentatively he used his fingertips to confirm his head was actually in one piece. Surprisingly, his head was not that bad considering he wasn't used to drinking alcohol. Surprising too as he'd had a large amount forced upon him last night.

A polite cough signified the completion of the apostle's part in his summons.

Stivs noted his clothes lying in a heap at the bottom of the bed. He wondered how he had gotten back and undressed the night before considering he currently had no memory of it.

Leaning over the water bowl he splashed water on his face waking up further in the process. His small beard which had not grown as much as that of the peers of his age covered his chin and barely crept over his mouth. Aor didn't seem to mind as it was part of him. It was quite unique. Anyway, it would be gone soon when he became an empsar.

Stivs twisted his beard gently, forming oiled curls of golden brown on his chin. Opening up the package the apostle had left he took out the purple-coloured shift.

After pulling on his best tunic and breeches he gingerly arranged the shift over his head. It dropped neatly on top without crease or fold.

To his surprise, a librarian was waiting outside his home.

"What is your name?" Stivs asked.

"Bosa Tim Curdu," the young librarian answered quickly. "I was sent here to assist you…"– He looked at the purple shift – "…Lo, Empsar," he finished quickly. "I guess I am your… will be your assistant," Bosa corrected himself.

Stivs breathed in deeply and despite the waning effects of alcohol, he centred himself. He put his full attention on his young assistant.

Bosa was thirteen hands tall, pale-skinned, and looked as though he hadn't been touched by the sun for many months. He had a delicate-looking mien. His dark curly hair framed a chiselled face with a pointed nose.

Sensing Bosa, Stivs felt the youthful vibrant light energy, the lightness he associated with new librarians who had completed the vow of silence.

"Was the time spent in silence easy for you?" he asked.

"Yes. How did you know, Lo Empsar?"

"It was for me too," Stivs admitted. "Do you know what to do today?" he asked Bosa.

"Stand behind you until you are recognised as empsar and walk two steps behind and one to the left?"

"Well done. Apart from that, if I need your help I will ask for it!" Stivs remembered that this was exactly what was said to him all those summers ago by Empsar Con Dwig.

"Let us go!" Stivs gestured for Bosa to walk first. Bosa frowned in confusion.

"Matter of habit," Stivs said in apology before leading the way.

As they neared the chamber of the council voices could be heard. The Elders were talking in overlapping conversations between sessions.

Stivs walked in unannounced and immediately felt he was the centre of attention. Everyone stopped in mid-sentence. The blaze of purple was obvious in the sea of creams and whites of the Elders. Stivs smiled at Con Ro Pars who raised her eyebrows in surprise.

Receiving a supportive and secretive wink from Ex-Empsar Con Dwig, he moved to the centre of the room. His assistant Bosa stayed at the periphery in the shadows.

The hush that had fallen upon his entrance deepened into one of shock before Con Dwig spoke up.

"I, Empsar Con Dwig, hereby support, choose and offer up my old assistant Stivs Postet as lo empsar as my replacement."

The sight of the purple throw had implied his abdication. But the statement still provoked a shocked intake of breath from most of the council.

"He is very young," Con Pras muttered.

"Who will provide clear and steadfast guidance," Con Fras followed immediately covering up Con Pras's possible argument. She gave him a warning glance.

"Are there any statements of denial against my proposal of Stivus Postet to become elder empsar?"

The room was deathly silent.

"Who supports the inclusion of Stivus Postet on council and initiation for empsar?" Empsar Con Dwig asked.

"I support Stivus Postet," Con Pars called out loudly. One by one each Elder called out their agreement. Everyone, including Con Pras and Con Fras.

Stivs was on his knees on the hard floor. He remained in the centre, wondering if anyone could feel the heat from his blushing cheeks.

So, this is it. The universe works in mystical ways. I have become a powerful guiding force. I didn't ever desire to be one, Stivs thought as an apostle placed a gold chain over his head.

The long laborious initiation proceeded with Stivs in shock at how easy things were. His life had changed quickly and dramatically though he was fundamentally the same.

Stivs was brought back to the present moment. He felt the soft fabric of brilliant white robes put into his hands.

Receiving a nod from Con Dwig, Stivs put his arm through one sleeve and then the other. He took time to adjust the robes.

Stivs held his breath as he watched his mentor lift the small cloth mantle from around his neck. Then Con Dwig placed it around

Empsar Con Postet's.

Stivs fingered the material, adjusting it flat and admired the gold thread pattern. The mark of Atlantis.

Empsar Stivs looked around the Council of Elders. Although his view had only moved forward a few steps the impact of the change was colossal.

He knew that Bosa would be focusing the assistant's energies to provide safety around the city. Stivs relaxed into leading the council's first meditation under his guidance.

Concentrating the energy of the Elders into a focused beam, he directed it straight up into the air. High up into a bank of clouds.

Disconnecting their attention from the energy, he released them from the guided focus. This allowed them to return to their bodies. His consciousness watched golden flecks of sparkling energy fall out of the cloud like rain. The energy falling in the shower covered vast distances and spread bright vitality and joyful energy to all that it touched.

Opening his eyes, he saw many smiles of delight on the Council of Elders' faces.

"That was beautiful." Con Dwart was the first to speak.

"Many thanks for leading that." Con Artis concurred.

Empsar Con Stivus Postet, smiling, looked around the room seeing nods of appreciation. His good humour flickered with uncertainty upon noticing the lack of Ex-Empsar Con Dwig.

"Shall we adjourn for our midday meal?" he asked.

Con Hrap stretched, smiled, and stood up. "Excellent idea. I am famished." He placed a hand on his potbelly. "Any longer wait for a meal and I will fade away."

"After food, we shall decide upon Ex-Empsar Dwig's role of retirement," Stivs said before they all departed.

28

I t had been his idea and he was doubly pleased that the council had agreed readily.

"Empsar Con Stivs. Your knowledge and imagination are of great worth," Con Twor acknowledged.

"Ex-Empsar Con Dwig was insightful in nominating you," Con Hrap confirmed.

"Thank you, fellow Elders," Empsar Con Stivs said colouring somewhat. "Shall we invite Ex-Empsar Con Dwig in?" He nodded to the novice at the door.

"Greetings Ex-Empsar Con Dwig," Empsar Con Stivs said, beaming at his mentor.

"Greetings, Empsar and Council of Elders." Dwig half bowed despite his difficulty in doing so.

"We have invited you here to offer you a role of retirement."

"I did not realise I had a choice in the matter." Dwig joked. "So what is it, my friends?"

Empsar Con Stivs noticed a momentary frown on Con Pras's face at Dwig's lapse in protocol.

"Your walking stick first please, Dwig," Con Hrap said. Con Hrap's assistant's arms were out ready for the well-used polished stick.

Stivs stood towering over the stooped figure of his friend and mentor.

"I, Empsar Con Stivus Postet, hereby thank you on behalf of all Atlantis for your service."

"Get on with it… I am an old man." Dwig chuckled.

"The Council of Elders hereby select you for the role of Master of the Big Deep." He nodded at his assistant.

Bosa offered the jewelled Staff of Atlantis to the surprised Dwig.

"We the Council of Elders hereby bestow upon you this gift. And our everlasting appreciation." Stivs, with tears in his eyes and overcome with emotion, broke with tradition and shook Dwig's hand.

"Thank you, friend," he whispered.

Dwig winked. "I accept the role of Master of the Big Deep with honour." Using his staff for the first time he stood straighter and marched out. The click of the golden staff rang through the hall as the Elders gave him a round of applause.

29

"I have been talking with my mother," Aor told him.

"Oh, and what did she say?"

"That you are now the empsar!"

"I am."

"Did you not care to tell me?"

"I did not deem it important."

"Not important? We are engaged and I have found out from my mother that I am marrying the empsar."

"I apologise. I did not think it would affect how we feel for each other."

"I did not say that."

"What are you saying then?"

"If it's important to you then it is important to me."

"It was not important to me at first. I was selected. Circumstances occurred beyond my control. Now I am empsar."

"Now you are empsar." Aor looked at Stivs seeing the same calmness, the same naivety, and the same happiness.

Stivs placed her hand on his chest.

"This heart is open to you, and I remain joyful in your presence regardless of being empsar, my love." He kissed her gently on the lips.

"Empsar Postet!" Aor burned up with a confusion of passion and embarrassment at the public sign of affection.

"Yes, Aor?" He chuckled throatily.

"You are to shame me before the ceremony?"

"If only I could change tradition." Stivs' eyes filled with desire.

"You are not to alter society for your desire alone."

Aor was reddening in response.

Stivs cupped his hands in the water of the fountain and threw it above her head, showering Aor with cool water.

"Cool down, young Empsar!" She gave him a playful shove.

Stivs tottered, losing balance and fell backwards into the water with a splash.

Empsar Con Stivus Postet stood up. With water dripping, he stretched out his hand in an unspoken request for assistance.

Aor grabbed his hand, pulling to aid him out of the water. She shrieked loudly as he dragged her into the water after him.

"Stivs," she complained laughing.

"There, now our ardour is tamed for the moment."

30

G ivas stood at the pile of rocks reflecting.
"You lived a full life, Ua. I wonder where you are now."
He placed one last rock on the pile gently. Twelve summers he'd had her company.

Dels was waiting for him when he returned, sitting cross-legged, still supple despite her age.

He prodded the fire with a stick, sending a flurry of flickering ash into the sky. The heat brought a tightness to his face before he turned away and sat facing Dels.

"I have decided on your return to Atlantis."

"Great! When do I go?"

"In twelve months."

"Another summer? What can you teach me in addition to all that I have learnt already?"

"It is not for me to teach anymore. It is for you to learn."

"I don't understand."

"Completion for you is internal and only you will know what to learn."

"What?"

"Your journey is now integrating yourself so you are free to be present."

"Free to be present?"

"Totally." Dels closed her eyes signifying the conversation was over.

Closing his eyes, Givas breathed deeply, centring himself. He felt the urge to go back to Atlantis now. Patience, he told himself.

Givas felt angry. The anger flared up inside blossoming from the spark into a sudden blaze. Opening his eyes he glared at the serene Dels. She must have sensed his attention because she opened her eyes. She smiled at him with compassion.

His temper ebbed and he paused. In that pause, Givas accepted and admitted his darkest emotions. Breathing down through them he became aware of a sadness. More than basic sadness – it was grief. He felt the emotion expand within him washing through him in waves.

A vision of his mother floated in his mind making Givas sob out loud. Jonah in a boat, smiling, waved at him through the tears. Givas raised an arm before realising the vision was only in his mind.

Getting up, he staggered away from the fire. He attempted to free himself from the overpowering feelings. Running blindly, the emotions followed him closely. They were glued to him and would not let him rest. Branches whipped his legs as he rushed through the undergrowth. A bush tugged at his shorts as he staggered past. A gap in the vegetation opened up, releasing him to the waterfall and pool.

Givas stepped into the shower of water, wanting to flush the emotions out. Head bowed, the cold water shocked him. It physically roused him from his internal turmoil.

"Why me?" he screamed out.

The enveloping water silenced any reply as the crest of emotion passed.

Sitting on a rock with hair plastered on his skull, he removed his tunic. A gentle breeze dried his skin tenderly.

With his tunic fluttering on a tree branch, Givas settled in the aftermath of his emotional outpouring. His sobbing, for the moment, was gone. Feeling drained he sat alone surrounded by the beautiful setting. A blood-red sun glowed reassuringly. Its last attempts of the day to warm him comfortingly.

The stars were out when Givas moved. Goosebumps spread up his body as he grabbed his now dry tunic. Having no idea of how long he had been there he ambled back to the fireside in no rush. A quiet calmness had replaced his impatience. His return to the present had

126

begun.

Givas felt her attention and was filled with irritation. Stewing in the feelings got under his skin. He took his candle out into the night.

The sky was reassuringly lit with the brightest of stars. Lying back on the grass he looked up at the abundance of twinkling lights.

What could be up there?

Givas accepted how small he was in comparison, yet not insignificant.

The irritation came back in full flood.

"They don't want me! Then I won't go back," he ranted. "But I want to see Goras and Hennie. Seeing others my own age would be good too."

The stars kept their own counsel.

"What do I have to do though?" Givas plucked a blade of grass and focused on it.

He saw the uneven edge against the light of the candle. Looking out into the darkness, the shape of the blade of grass stayed with him. The orange and blue lights in his eyes took their time to fade. The smell of candle wax stuck in his gullet, reminding him of the time spent alone on the bunk in the order. He threw it away petulantly. The flame snuffed out instantly as it flew through the air leaving Givas alone in the dark.

31

Empsar Con Stivus Postet adjusted his tunic for the umpteenth time.

"You look fine," his father told him.

"But am I good enough?"

"What?"

"I said, am I good enough for her?"

"Is she good enough for you empsar and all!"

"I love her too much to care," Stivs admitted. He saw his father looking back at him.

"Yes, I know. That is all that matters." He brushed more imaginary dust from his clothes.

The crisp clean whiteness of his best robes would blind someone if they had been cleaned anymore. His hair was oiled and slicked back away from his face and ears leaving his handsome open features for all to see.

His father, not one for expressing emotions freely, had a tear in his eye.

"Father."

"Yes, Stivus?"

"Thank you."

"My pleasure." His father hugged him fiercely before shoving him away.

Stivs knew that was enough sentimental display between them. Time to go, the ex-empsar was waiting.

She was breathtakingly beautiful. The pale blue robes set off the brown of her eyes. With no hood on the matrimonial robes, her hair too was pulled back. It was laboriously tied with numerous matching blue ribbons.

Stivs' heart flipped as he stood beside her, refraining from staring into her eyes for the moment. He nodded to Ex-Empsar Con Dwig to start proceedings.

"Aor and Stivus turn and face each other," Ex-Empsar Con Dwig commanded.

Stivs felt himself swimming in joyous emotions as he looked at his soon-to-be wife. Aor looked overjoyed at the moment too. Her skin had been dusted to appear even whiter than its pale shade and her lips had been artfully stained with scarlet berry juice.

Time lost meaning as words washed over them. Everything was slow yet speeding forwards until they both felt the tug of hair as they were tied to each other.

Stivs looked at the red ribbon connecting their hair in one long braid. He felt his mother's approval on his back. He had spent so much time the night before on his hair braiding deliberations.

He saw Aor's mother holding back tears of joy with the protective arm of Devas around her shoulders.

Aor had an eyebrow raised at him in question. Stivs winked at her.

"Let it be known that Aor and Stivus are now husband and wife for now and evermore."

The small group of family applauded and at last Stivs and Aor embraced fully. They kissed tenderly amidst much cheering and applause.

Devas slapped his back in fierce approval and shoved an overfull cup of wine into his hand.

"Thank you, Father," Stivs said thickly.

"Less of the father. Devas, call me Devas." He let Stivs go, looking around for another refill of his cup.

"Ah, your father." Devas went off, leaving him alone with his wife and her mother.

"Have I told you how beautiful you are?"

"Yes, and today I will not get bored of hearing it." Aor's eyes sparkled.

"Is beauty a natural trait in your family? For your mother is almost as pretty as you."

"Empsar Con Postet your head is befuddled with vine wine."

Aor's mother blushed and smiled at the same time.

Stivs was led away from the loud ribaldry by his wife.

"Stivs."

"Yes?" Stivs saw his father and mother being hugged by Devas.

"Stivus!"

Stivs looked at her. "Yes, my love?"

"Will this feeling last forever?"

"I know not, but I hope so. I feel our love will outlast time itself."

Any other sentiments were stifled as Aor kissed him fully on the lips.

Seeing her pupils expand with desire, he knew instinctively that it was time to leave the proceedings, leaving the celebrations to those who enjoyed the vine wine more.

Putting his wife over his shoulder he carried her away to his new quarters.

On reaching the room, he found his assistant had carried out his instructions to perfection.

Enough candles were lit without it being a fire hazard. Myriad flower blossoms were scattered around the large bed, scenting the air with a delicate perfume. Some of the softest sheepskin rugs blanketed the bed all combed straight and soft. A platter of mixed sweet breads and fruits lay next to a jug of the finest vine wine.

"Oh, darling, you thought of everything." Aor began crying.

"What is it? What is wrong?" Stivs was concerned.

"Nothing... everything is..."

"What?"

"Perfect." Sitting on the bed, her confidence was gone. "I don't know if I will be as good as you hoped," Aor cried.

"Please do not think of it." He grabbed her shoulders and looked deeply into her eyes. "We will learn about each other naturally. The rest will follow one step at a time."

Stivs untied their hair from the ceremonial binding and put a quieting finger on her lips.

"Shhhh... for ease of movement nothing less."

Nervously, Aor untied her robes and Stivs gently pushed them off her shoulders.

His look of delighted awe, at last convinced her, and she smiled as her fears finally evaporated.

32

"You are expecting, Aor?" Aor's mother Con Pars asked seeing the healthy glow on her face." Aor demurred. "You are, I sense it, Aor." Con Pars was definite.

"It is what we have been trying for." Aor smiled, happiness blossoming across her features.

"I am so pleased." Mother embraced daughter and tears of delight were shed by both.

Devas looked at Stivs with respect. "Will you decide on a name soon?"

"I haven't even thought that far ahead." Stivs paused. "Any suggestions?"

Devas smiled. "Darling," he shouted over his shoulder. "We have been asked for suggestions on the name of our daughter's firstborn."

"Twoa," Aor started.

"Fera," her mother continued.

"Tupe," Aor replied.

"Lolu." Her mother was warming up.

Devas gave Stivus a wink. The names came thick and fast.

"Deva." Devas raised an eyebrow. "Stivus" Aor countered.

Aoli, Lia, Horee, Grea, Givas, Horus and Sulur Were all brought up for consideration.

The evening flowed into the night with Devas ensuring the cups were full of wine. Stivus, now used to his wife's father and his thirst, had devised a slow sipping tactic to ensure a clear head.

"So it is settled then." He eventually brought the conversation to a close.

"Yes," the two women agreed.

"Jora Devas Stivus Postet, if it is a boy," Aor confirmed.

"Jamu Heles Ang Postet, if it is a girl," her mother acceded.

"Jamu Heles Ang Postet," Stivus rolled the names across his tongue as if tasting each name.

"Darling Heles Ang?" Devas enquired.

"My mother's and your mother's names."

"I know, that is why I asked," he grumbled. Stivs looked at Aor.

"Oh, Father! They will love the child as if it is their own." She pressed a hand against her flat belly marvelling at the possibility of a child.

"It may give them some common ground," Devas said looking at Stivs. "They did not like our marriage." He placed a hand on his wife's shoulder patting her gently.

"My mother thinks you enjoy vine wine too much." Con Pars defended her mother.

"And my mother thinks your mother thinks she has the ear of the old gods."

"And you fathers?" Stivs asked grinning.

"They should be empsars the way they avoid arguments." Devas and his wife smiled at each other.

"One will want Jamu Ang Heles Postet and the other will want Jamu Heles Ang Postet." Aor rolled her eyes.

"And if we have a boy?" Stivs put his hand on top of Aor's.

Devas looked to his wife, the one who knew most about such things. She shook her head once.

Aor grew in size rapidly, much to Stivs' delight. Being the empsar's wife, Aor had her own assistant. An assistant who gave Aor time to relax and be pampered daily.

Stivs would come back from his empsar duties and dote over his pregnant wife.

"Stivus, I cannot relax anymore."

"But, darling, you are carrying a child and you should rest."

"I may be pregnant, but I have been relaxing all day whilst Kuri has been doing all my tasks." Aor waved at Kuri who was leaving at the end of her working day. Kuri smiled and scurried away like a frightened mouse.

"Let me feel our son."

"I will let you feel our daughter." Aor gently raised her tunic above the bulge.

"Daughter? You and your mother are convinced, aren't you? Who would have thought, the empsar's wife not believing his judgement." Stivs lay his head against her belly.

"I trust my husband in all matters apart from that of my own body." She smiled fondly, with her hand resting on the back of his head.

"Was that a kick?" Stivs was in awe of the miracle of new life underneath him.

"She moved, yes."

"Empsar?"

Stivs returned from his reverie. He had been thinking about Aor again.

"Empsar Con Stivus?"

"Yes?"

"Will you lead us in our meditation?"

"Yes… yes, of course." Stivs focused on the task at hand. Breathing in deeply he centred himself before beginning.

Choosing his favourite, Stivs got the order to expand their focus, filling land, sea, and air with loving peace. This time though was different. Either he felt different, or something was holding him back. He put the sensation to one side and concentrated fully again on the task at hand.

Allowing the Elders back in their own time, he opened his eyes and watched their reactions returning from their journey. Most were appearing dazed as usual and most were feeling a total loving peace flowing through them. A couple were the same as if nothing special occurred.

Stivs attempted to hide his irritation and almost managed to do so except for a pursing of his lips.

The rest of the day was the continuation of decision making on more mundane matters than peace. *Or was it the fulfilment of peace that their decisions were being made for?* It was always a question to confuse Stivs. Like the question of which came first the chickens or the eggs.

Stivs looked out across the waters of the volcanic basin. A light breeze ruffled the water, the surface ripples breaking up the glassy reflection of the sky. The grey-blue dulled with tiny wavelets, giving it a consistent texture.

"You have an interesting situation," Dwig offered.

"Yes." Stivs dropped his gaze. "A beautiful wife... a child on the way... and yet I sense something. A shift perhaps."

"I advise you to take no action until that something becomes more clear."

"I know, I know. I feel there is no purpose. There has been peace in our city for many summers. The young boy of the myth has gone."

"Now, Empsar Postet," Dwig remonstrated. "Do not label the... I suppose he will be a young man now. Labelling him is creating the possibility of the event occurring."

"But I cannot ignore the myth."

"Indeed, you should not."

"But—"

"But nothing! Accept the possibility and then create what you want to happen."

Stivs saw the determination in his mentor's gaze.

The line in Dwig's hand tugged sharply.

Both men's focus was drawn to the water. Fish ran the line out of Dwig's hands only to be hauled in hand over hand. Three times the fish ran. As Dwig allowed the line to snake over his palms and through his fingers on each run it brought up red welts.

Finally, the fish tired and Dwig wound in his line for the final time. They both saw the flash of scales as it neared the surface.

Dwig held the line taut as it writhed and flicked its tail in its vain attempts for freedom. With a heave, it was landed and jerked spasmodically on top of the sack gasping with air.

Stivs watched Dwig smack the fish once. It lay still; alive no longer.

"I do not like them to suffer much."

Stivs nodded in agreement, still somewhat shocked by the speed of its demise.

"So, what do you want to happen?"

"I want peace to expand and everyone to feel the love that I feel inside," he said beaming.

"Indeed!" Dwig nodded. "Keep that intention and trust."

"Trust what?"

"Trust your actions, thoughts and words for they will bring your attention to life."

Stivs watched Dwig prop himself upright by the use of the golden walking stick – the Staff of Atlantis. In this instance, it was being made use of and not merely a token of love and affection but a useful tool.

He grabbed the sack with the fish inside it and offered it to the old man. Dwig sighed "Thank you. I find bending down easy. It is the getting back up that is the difficult part." He subconsciously rubbed the small of his back.

Stivs offered a hand of support and was waved away.

"Let us return and on the way, you can tell me what you are going to do."

Stivs threw the bag of fish over his shoulder. Walking slowly alongside Dwig, he matched the old man's pace.

33

He felt her attention and smiled broadly at her.
"Why do you smile so?"
"Because I choose to."
"Are you happy?"
"I am what I am. I am both happy and sad. I focus on smiling and I connect with happiness. I accept the sadness is there too. I can be sad if I choose."

Dels nodded.

Givas continued. "Happiness, sadness, good, bad, left, right, right, wrong. They are all judgements. If I focus on being one... of achieving one it is the same as stating I am its opposite. If I choose to be happy, I smile and I focus on the feelings of happiness. I realise now that I am in control of my life." He raised his head and looked her straight in the eyes.

"Thank you for keeping me here. You were perceptive of my needs and what was best."

Dels merely nodded with an enigmatic smile on her lips.

"Curious, letting go of the need to be anything but me was more difficult than focus and attention."

The light from the fire cast tall shadows all around. Givas waved his bare hand through the flames in a slow arc. He brought it back and, glancing at his palm, he made a sound to confirm his thought. His hand was unhurt and as healthy as his other. The skin was unblemished from the obvious heat of the fire.

With his other hand, he threw another branch into the flames. Sparks soaring skyward took his gaze to the stars.

"They are beautiful, are they not?" Dels whispered as she too stared into the heavens.

"They remind me of us," Givas stated.

"How so?"

"Each Atlantean is bright, fiery and a beacon for others around to see. Surrounded by others alike can light the way."

"The way?"

Givas pondered before answering.

"A good point," he acceded. "Lighting up. Illuminating because it is so. The way is not a physical journey or traversing space or time but enlightenment. Personal illumination!" Givas grinned. "It does not matter where I am, I shine brightly."

Dels smiled.

Givas stood and moved over in front of her. He put his hands on her shoulders and stooped down kissing her on each cheek.

"I will go to sleep now. My return to Atlantis starts tomorrow," he said with finality. It was at that moment he realised he was a man… a grown man.

The journey back was unusual for Givas for although it was through land which he had travelled before, it was still new to him.

A bird of prey hovered in the distance and Givas slowed his pace to watch. He felt the silence in the morning light. The bird dived instantly out of sight.

Breathing in deeply he extended his awareness. He sensed the bird getting a vicelike grip with its talons before flying off to some rocky outcrop. No emotion but pure basic instinct.

Givas felt so alive and connected to everything. All the animals he passed were aware of him too and he sent pulses of calm to them.

The sun warmed his back and as he turned with the natural swing of the hills his left cheek began to redden. His travelling cloak, already dusty, was keeping him overly warm. He was relieved to take it off at the site he had selected to sleep that night. It was the same site as he, the two soldiers and Ua had stayed so many moons ago.

Knowing what was needed he had collected wood in the run-up to the campsite and had an armful to get going.

He settled down after a repast of heated vegetables and a honey-covered mix of nuts and berries. Givas contemplated his new adventure with a cup of fruit juice, courtesy of Dels.

Stars kept him company and nothing bothered him. Nothing except a dream-filled sleep.

An image of Dels filled his mind. She wore a red cloak fixed with one button at the breast. For some reason, this excited Givas, and Dels changed into an alluring young woman. The face. He couldn't focus on her face. The cloak opened to reveal delights in womanly form. The image faded and he felt utter loss. Desolation and feelings of sadness made him whimper in his dream-filled sleep.

He was surrounded by thirteen people. There was a feeling of sadness and he wanted them not to be angry. Givas felt the need to placate and justify. Then there was anger. More colours spiralled and swam through his mind. Then sleep took him deeper into its peaceful stillness.

Waking bleary-eyed in the morning Givas felt irritable. Further dreams had plagued his mind leaving him out of focus and needing quiet.

A trilling songbird called to its mate and its vibrancy and joy cut through his brain like a knife.

"Sing somewhere else," Givas complained, scowling.

The bird on a branch paused, looking at the man with beady eyes before continuing in full vibrato.

"That's good, ignore my needs!"

Givas took some food from his sack and forced himself to eat. He was eating without pleasure, barely noticing flavours and textures, and only when he had a lapful of crumbs did he realise he had finished.

Grabbing the crumbs, he flung them away in disgust.

Gathering up his belongings, he rearranged his clothes. Only then did he realise the bird had stopped singing.

"Small mercies."

Looking around he saw the bird pecking away at the crumbs, still eyeing him warily.

"Enjoy!" And at last, a smile cracked across his stony countenance.

"Oh, what a horrible life!" he shouted, exaggerating his grouchiness. Givas smiled at the absurdity.

Starting the next stage of his journey, he wished the bird joy and long life with love. He passed underneath the branch it was perched on. In reply, it trilled once more, even louder this time; obviously, it had enjoyed its hearty breakfast. It had enjoyed it more than Givas.

Givas reached the trail to Atlantis. It was a well-worn path used by sheep, shepherds, traders, and travellers alike leading the way home. He saw no one. Just as well as Givas was lost in thought.

His mind was buzzing with unanswered questions. Fantasies about the future and furtive fears that never appeared fully formed. But they continued to lurk around the edges of his thoughts.

He tightened his grip on his sack, pulling it higher up his shoulder, improved his balance and marched determinedly onwards.

Too soon he was walking along the spine seeing the outer walls of the city grow in size as he got closer.

"Who goes there?" a soldier shouted down.

"Givas the librarian."

"Where have you been librarian?"

"I have finished my training with Ex-Empsar Dels of the hills."

The soldier must have signalled to his comrades, as the next moment the gate opened. The soldier allowed Givas entry to Atlantis.

"Is this usual, questioning visitors?" Givas enquired.

"No. It is not usual." The guard eyed him warily.

"I am curious that is all. I have been away from home for many moons."

"You won't know then?" The soldier looked around to ensure nobody was within earshot.

"Know what?"

"There are rumours of the rising of Terzondals"

"I didn't know that. Are there supposed to be many?"

"Not so many Terzondals, but I have heard the Grekas have joined them too."

"The Grekas, eh?" Givas had no idea what or who the Grekas were.

"Fierce warriors with hearts of bears." With that, the soldier made a sign to the old gods before remembering Givas was a librarian.

Givas had no further opportunity of getting gossip. The guard had moved off, avoiding any more indiscretions in front of librarians.

Centring himself he allowed his mind to settle and all doubts to dissipate.

Taking the longer route via the volcano, he felt the heat of the sun drawing moisture from all around. The spine he walked on was often bare rock. Only a few clumps of wild grass were growing in the shadows of the many nooks and crannies. He avoided the wild grass, for it was sharp enough to slice his flesh open.

Givas stumbled upon reaching the summit of the edge of the crater as it was so sudden. Looking down he saw the sky reflecting off the water. He adopted his meditative state and expanded his awareness down into the massive basin of the volcano.

He was aware of the swaying of the treetops in a light breeze, the sheltered feel within the basin despite its size. Givas felt the ripple of wavelets brought on by puffs of wind and his awareness went into the water where he noticed the fish in the warmth, darting, cruising and some lazing in the shallows. A life force caught his attention. He realised it was a man.

Coming quickly back to his physical body he stretched and yawned then blinked several times before his vision was restored to its previous clarity.

Making his way down the inside of the crater he occasionally grabbed trees for support. With every touch, he felt the texture of the bark and perceived the strength flowing up from the roots. The life force of each tree was tempered with the flexibility of the branches.

Not once did he stumble and he coughed politely before approaching the man. The man was old, that was for certain. His silvery-white hair was in disarray from the touch of the breeze across the water.

"Do you enjoy fishing, young man?"

"Empsar." Givas recognised him instantly. "Please forgive my intrusion."

Con Dwig waved his hand. "Ex-Empsar nowadays."

Givas felt the attention of the old man flicker over him and spark with curiosity.

"Do I know you, young man? You seem vaguely familiar."

"My name is Givas. Givas Voret."

"Ah, I seem to remember a young boy with a much-loved dog. How is… Ua is it?"

"I am amazed you remember me, Empsar. My dog… well she ran after her last rabbit some moons ago."

"I am sorry to hear it. So, what brings you here?"

"I have finished my out-of-city duty. My learning has finished. Or should I say my learning has changed?"

Con Dwig smiled. "Sit with me fishing for a while. I rarely get visited." Con Dwig saw his indecision. "I insist."

He patted a nearby rock as a seat.

"So who has replaced you as empsar?"

"My ex-assistant Empsar Con Stivus Postet."

"I have yet to meet him."

Con Dwig nodded.

"How many fish have you caught?"

"Today?"

Givas nodded.

"Today I am still to catch a fish. Here, hold my pole for a while and allow an old man to rest."

Givas took the fishing pole and closed his eyes. He expanded his awareness down the pole, the string and through the water until he reached the bait.

Two small fish were nipping small chunks out of the bait and swimming away quickly. Either they were frightened, or they sensed the threat that a bigger bite would pose.

"What do you feel?" the old man asked, bringing him to awareness instantly.

"Two small tiddlers nibbling your bait."

"Bah, I seem to be doing them a service by providing a free meal. It should be the other way about."

Givas grinned.

"How is Atlantis now?"

"Atlantis is much the same. Full of opportunity for change and yet still the same."

"I heard about a possible Terzondal uprising. Is it true?"

"There are always rumours circulating. Some people worry and some people fear peace. A possible Terzondal uprising? That is one possibility for the future."

"You do not seem to be concerned, Ex-Empsar."

"Many other possibilities could occur too. Should I worry about them too and become upset about what-ifs or focus on what is happening now? You do not need to answer that do you?"

Givas was sheepish.

"Of course not. What did Dels teach you about focus and attention?"

"What? How did you know... how did you know I have been taught about focus and attention?"

"Focus and attention!"

"Umm... focus is powerful. Attention is control."

"And?"

"Whatever I focus on grows bigger. My attention puts energy into the constant flow of creation."

"Ah, wonderful. I recognise the influence of Dels."

"There is something I wanted to ask you." Givas gulped. "Why did I get sent away earlier than everyone else in my class? Did I do something wrong?" Tears welled up in Givas' eyes unexpectedly.

"It was the best moment for you to go."

The fishing pole jerked in Givas' hands.

"Quick, don't let it get away," Con Dwig said excitedly.

Givas pulled the pole back quickly bringing with it an empty line. The hook sparkled completely bare on the end of the string.

"Ha! You are as good a fisherman as I am."

Givas laughed.

"So why did I go early?"

"Apart from being the best opportunity for you back then, there was concern about you being the one of the myth," Con Dwig answered candidly.

"What does the myth say?"

"It says that someone who has lost family will be the reason for the destruction of the way of life."

Givas was stunned into silence. The blame fell on his shoulders. Part of him thought about the death of his mother; the part that he had always asked if it was his fault.

He was in turmoil. Once again he felt powerless in the face of outside forces.

"Someone who has lost family, eh? Could be any of us."

Givas looked at Con Dwig, wanting to scream, It wasn't me! It's not my fault!' Instead, he breathed and just experienced the turmoil.

"And the myth will only become fact if it is paid heed to." Givas returned to the present hearing the logic in Con Dwig's rationale.

"But the myth already exists, doesn't it?"

"Yes."

"That means much has been put towards it coming true already."

Con Dwig had no answer.

34

S tivs wrung his hands. He stood up then decided against it and sat back down again. He rubbed his eyes then massaged the bridge of his nose. The lack of sleep affected him deeply. Stivs was like a dog with one persistent flea. Unable to sit still and unable to relieve the stress.

"Aor had been fine until two nights ago," he told Devas.

Devas only looked at him, knowing it already.

"We were laughing." Stivs pondered. "Is it because we were too happy?"

"Empsar!" Devas' voice sliced through his train of thought.

"You are right, Devas." Stivs quietened down. His spirits lifted briefly when his assistant returned with a tray of food and drink.

"Empsar, you must nourish your body." Concern was etched across the young man's face.

"I will have time for nourishment when I know my wife and child are well," he growled.

Standing abruptly, he paced over to the door of the sleeping quarters. He felt the surge of pain and fear blooming from the centre of the room.

He could not see his wife, for the view was barred by a swarm of nurses. Aor's mother gently led him back out of the room and into the fresh air. Despite the heat of the noonday sun, he felt it noticeably cooler and fresher outdoors.

"We will call you if there is any need for you, Empsar." She battled her anguish. "Stivs, there is nothing you can do to help."

"But I am empsar," he said lamely.

"I know, Empsar, but still."

He was left outside.

The ones with knowledge told him that there are sometimes problem births. He had asked what was to be expected and they refused to tell him.

Stivs knew he was not his peaceful self. He surprised even himself when he found himself being dragged out of the room shouting. Aor was whimpering in pain. He had heard her.

The sounds broke his heart and tore through his soul.

His love and unborn baby were in physical peril and he was unable to change anything.

"Maybe you should meditate, Empsar?" his assistant offered.

Stivs glared at him.

"Don't you know what is happening in there?"

Bosa flinched at the anger and retreated to safety.

"Empsar," Devas warned again.

Stivs dropped his head in shame.

The men outside sensed it first. Then recognised the silence. They held their breath waiting. Waiting for that cry… the first cry of a new life.

Nothing.

Silence.

The silence shattered what was left of him and shredded his soul.

A tear slipped from Stivs' eyes and dropped off his chin. Jaws tightened in anger and blocked out all other emotions.

Devas' shoulders slumped for he too knew deep down what had just happened.

Con Ro Pars stood at the doorway; her face was a mask of utter grief. Blood covered her clothes and hands.

"My child?" Stivs croaked.

A shake of the head.

"Aor?"

A slower shake of the head.

As Devas held his wife, Empsar Stivus Postet collapsed onto the bench. His perfect life had shattered about him. His reality ripped from under him leaving him reeling in waves of grief and anger. Blackness filled that which was once pure light.

Chanting reverberated through the library buildings. The tone was a constant reminder of death. Stivs sensed the energy of the Council of Elders gently attempting to lighten him. He appreciated their intentions but was still unwilling to let go of his pain, his companion in the darkest hours. It followed the death of his wife and unborn child Jamu Heles Ang Postet.

35

S tivs had found love and completion with Aor. Her passing could never be fully accepted. Stivs did not want to experience loneliness. Cherishing the suffering blocked it out. It also blocked the sound of chanting from heightening his feelings.

Anger fuelled his determination to stay in grief. His black robes billowed about him in the wind as he stood on the top of the eastern harbour wall.

Stivs was unaware of the crowd's sadness, tears and sobs. The empsar's wife had been well-liked in the brief time since the wedding. *Eight moons. That was all it had been.* Stivs clenched his jaws in frustration.

"Eight moons for the love of the old gods,." he railed.

Those nearest to him looked up in concern.

His eyes watched the small boat float out on the tide but his mind was elsewhere. Another boat and another loved one left him.

Stivs did not see the wave upon wave of flaming arrows hit the craft setting it alight.

Stivs came back to the present, seeing flames reach for the sky. The crowd went silent as if on an unspoken command.

Stivs glanced around seeing his own grief reflected in the faces of so many others.

Con Ro Pars, the mother of his beloved, was letting go of her daughter with grace. Tears trickled from the corners of her eyes in silence.

Devas Pars, the father and grounded strength of the family was grieving too. Anguish filled his face but perhaps he was the closest to letting go. He stood straight, with a protective arm draped loosely around his wife's shoulders. Stivs was both jealous and happy for them. For they had the love he hadn't any more.

His parents had had a long partnership, lasting until the death of his mother. He had noticed his father accept growing old from then on. A walking stick came first, and then his father's lifestyle got smaller and smaller. It reduced until he was confined to bed.

The death of his father the previous summer was perhaps easier to accept. At that time he was riding on the waves of love and joy of being newly married.

"Empsar, it is time," Bosa whispered, interrupting his mental meanderings.

"Yes, it is indeed."

The silence was an unseen pressure on Stivs. He sorely wanted to shout and scream. The dominant part of him kept him quiet and externally calm. He felt sympathy from everyone, and anger bloomed inside. The anger burned from the ashes of the barely started marriage he had had. Stivs' face was impassive.

The protocol was broken with a hand resting on his arm. Con Ro Pars was reaching out to him in sorrow. He acknowledged her with only a nod before moving on. Stivs broke from the flanking crowds, and it took all his self-control to prevent him from bursting into a sprint.

Only Bosa, his assistant, followed him. Even then, Empsar Stivus Postet was relieved to leave him behind at the door to his now empty living quarters.

A single flower in a vase caught his eye. Its significance was not lost on him and he lifted it and admired its beauty as it lay in his palm. The fragility of the flower was countered by the strength of the stem.

Lying on the bed on his side, he traced the outlines of the petals with a finger. His mind took flight from his anguished state and escaped through exhaustion and sleep.

Stivs awoke still craving the comforting blanket of sleep. His heart was closed and he felt blank. Usually, his heightened awareness connected him with the vibrant life force. Today was different. Today was a grey day. Splashing his face with water he forgot about shaving. The water was cool but not cold enough to bring him out of his stupor.

Today was not a day for his morning stretches either.

Bosa was surprised to see him but said nothing, which Stivs was grateful for.

Stivs walked in a measured way to the sanctum. He gave not a word nor sign to his assistant and desired no response.

Sitting in his place, he closed his eyes and settled, his breathing regular and relaxed. He was aware of the councillors filling up the room and their shocked reaction to his presence. Their surprise was quickly followed by total silence.

Empsar Stivs Postet opened his eyes, smiled and closed them again. "Let us go on a journey."

He felt their energy join him and he guided them straight up into the sky. No preamble, just direction and intention. Twice he paused and allowed the group to catch up. There was no emotion, only movement.

Sensing nothingness, he paused, confused. The nothingness was dark with foreboding. Stivs was aware of returning quickly. It was far quicker than he wanted. Fear coursed through his over-sensitised mind. His energy shrank and Stivs lost connection with the group. In an energetic freefall, he had just enough sense to focus on his physical form. Thankfully this is what he returned to.

He opened his eyes to tears. Only his assistant noticed the hand movement brushing them away.

Many of the Council of Elders took their time opening their eyes. Stivs noted with annoyance the two who were alert the quickest; the same two he did not want to have noticed anything unusual.

He was about to say something, but she caught his eye and motioned to wait for the whole group's energetic return.

Stivs bristled in anticipation. He decided to grasp the situation before he lost control.

"Councillors... friends," Stivs corrected himself humbly. "It appears I have still some to learn in dealing with grief and the darker emotions. I hope you found the journey to be of value despite the speed and duration," Stivs said, looking at the two councillors directly, challenging them to argue.

After a moment, they dropped their gaze and retreated from the brink of confrontation.

"I suggest we all look inwards. We can contemplate integration of all our emotions, self-beliefs and desires." Empsar Stivus Postet stood.

"Good day!"

Many of the Elders stood, surprised at the early conclusion of the session. Others rejoiced, ready to seize the opportunity of an early finish.

Stivs strode out of the sanctum, his sandals slapping the slabs and his robes billowing around him. Rubbing his chin subconsciously, he suddenly remembered his unshaven appearance. He remembered the reason for it too.

With a frown, he knew he had to let go. He had to release the dark emotions for the safety and benefit of all Atlantis. Stivs had to let go of the darkness of grief. He had to let go and the sooner the better.

36

G ivas waited now. Although he'd enjoyed his time with Con
Dwig he could hold off his return no longer. Or so he
thought. Waiting outside the sanctum, he felt the heat of the
day wane. Under the shadow of the high roof, he kept cool.

The Querks began chanting once more, no joy to their tone as if
the city was subdued. He sensed a sadness wafting through the
alleyways. A sadness that was out of control. It moved yet was
persistent.

"What has happened?" he whispered, tears welling up in his own
eyes as he connected with the emotion.

An assistant appeared, passing him without a word. The assistant
pushed open the door and stepped into the chambers.

The guarding librarian glanced at Givas.

Standing up slowly, Givas stretched his arms above his head and
yawned. Out of the corner of his eye, he saw the librarian put his hand
to his mouth covering a yawn.

"A slow day?" Givas said pleasantly; seeing a nod and a smile he
continued. "Chamber busy?"

A shake of the head.

"Is the empsar in there now?"

Another shake of the head.

"And yet I am still required to wait."

Suddenly the door opened and the room emptied. Elders followed by their assistants; Givas counted twenty-four in all. A moment later one remaining assistant came out, features set in a frown.

"Assistant?"

Bosa looked up.

"I am Givas, complete from out-of-city duty and returned to start my silence."

"Not today."

Givas sensed the flickering of irritation blossom and fade quickly.

"I apologise. I shall wait here for a more opportune time." Givas sat down with his back to the wall, crossing his legs as he did so. Closing his eyes he settled on one breath and expanded his awareness outwards.

He sensed the surprise in the assistant and mild confusion. The guarding librarian was curious too about what was being played out.

Givas felt the waft of air as the assistant disappointingly left. Centring himself he allowed his attention to dissipate. He did not even notice the guarding librarian leave his post for the day.

Well after dusk, Givas opened his eyes and then gingerly stood. He had to massage the muscles in his legs and arms in an attempt to stimulate his blood flow.

Wandering through Atlantis he sensed the hubbub quietening. The air was full of a variety of pleasant moments. He could smell intriguing spices from across the sea. Frying fish, mutton stew and sweet bread aromas also tantalised his tastebuds. They and others frustrated his already growling stomach.

Without realising, Givas found he'd walked right to his old room. It was empty but not vacant. A pile of possessions were at the end of the small cot. Givas realised how much he had grown.

Wandering past the line of aps rooms he heard another Querks' session filling the air with sound. The pitch was higher than before and more appealing.

As the vibration receded, Givas turned a corner and almost fell over someone.

"Watch out, ruffian," a querulous voice ordered.

"Ruffian?"

The old man raised a cane at Givas and as he did his hood slipped back to reveal a shock of silvery-white hair. The bluish white of the blind eyes took Givas back through time.

"I sense a change in you, boy."

Givas smiled.

"You are still as wise and aware."

"That may be, young man. Give me your arm."

Givas was glad to at last be listened to. He told him all about his many-moon duty, only being subjected to the occasional question. Although he supported the old man with an arm, he was the one being guided through the city unerringly.

"Where are we going, Master?" Givas enquired.

"For some food, young man. For some food, of course. I could hear your stomach imitating a herd of charging elephants."

"What are elephants?"

"Oh my! What did they teach you as an aps? Anything about life outside the city?"

"It seems not."

They arrived at a door to a house inset amongst a hodgepodge of buildings. Through the doorway, Givas caught a whiff of mouth-watering stew. His stomach growled as a reminder of his growing hunger.

"Is this your house?"

"Does that matter?"

A shriek of joy was followed by a scampering child as others became aware of the arrival. Givas was amazed at the change. The gruff old man had turned into a lovable, doting grandparent with a toddler climbing over him.

"Petr. You are a strong lion cub."

"What is a lion cub?" Givas asked.

The master of selection raised his eyebrows.

"Grandpapa. You have brought a guest. How wonderful!" The mother of the family beamed at Givas. She quickly disappeared through to the kitchen for more preparations.

Petr, the little boy or lion cub, looked up at Givas wide-eyed with a small finger stuck in his mouth. Givas focused on the boy, appreciating him for just being. He felt the connection of energy. It was joy. Pure joy. Smiling at Petr he saw the shyness and momentary indecision. Givas reached out his hand and Petr gripped his thumb in a baby vice.

"Hah! He likes you," the master of selection stated.

Petr pulled Givas, who followed willingly. He was dragged into another room which was dominated by a large wooden table. Around the table sat ten chairs. A young woman was arranging another setting. She looked up and flushed with embarrassment.

"Petr, what are you doing?" she hissed at the boy.

"I came happily." Givas smiled at her.

She looked at him.

"My name is Givas. I have just returned from out of the city."

"My name is Ukre, Con Grote is my great-great-great-grandpapa."

"Who?"

"The master of selection."

"Oh." Givas thought for a moment. "Great, great, great grandfather?"

Ukre nodded, then shrugged. "He is very old, but don't tell him he is too old."

"Boy," Con Grote yelled from the other room. "Leave my little girl Ukre alone."

"I am not a little girl," Ukre yelled back.

Givas smiled, seeing her face animated. A small frown of irritation and puckered lips made her look even lovelier to him.

"Boy, come here!"

Givas looked deep into the eyes of Ukre and felt an instant connection. She was tall for an Atlantean woman, almost as tall as he was. Her curly brown hair framed her face. The candlelight accentuated her pretty features. Her eyes were a sandy brown changing to an alluring green. Givas was momentarily mesmerised.

"Givas!"

The sudden use of his name shocked him out of his stupor. Ukre covered her smile with her hand.

Givas backed out of the room, bumping into the wall, and turning finally to face the old man.

"Mmmph!" he snorted. "Cast a spell over you already, eh?" He was pointing with his cane to a blackened fireplace.

"How are your fire-making skills?"

The woman, who Givas guessed was Ukre's mother, was at the entrance from the kitchen.

"Grandpa, you haven't got our guest doing work have you?"

"He can earn his keep." The master gesticulated at the fireplace again.

Givas, amused, began snapping twigs into hearth-size lengths.

"That's it! Build layers. Layers work."

Givas, smiling, built up a heap of twigs, and small and large logs until the master of selection was satisfied. Despite the old man's blind eyes his perception and sensory acuity amazed Givas.

Before he could be chastised further, Givas took out his flints. He deftly struck some sparks into the pile of wood shavings and dried grass.

"One strike, eh?"

Givas guessed the old man was as close to being impressed as he could be.

"Young man, Grandpapa," the woman called before shouting. "Food is ready."

"Later for me!" The master waved over his shoulder before inching closer to the flames. "Givas, go get some of the food Atrum has made before it has all gone."

Three men appeared from nowhere: a sun-wizened mature man, who Givas guessed to be Ukre's father and husband of Atrum, and two young men about the same age as Givas also sat at the table. They were deeply tanned and broader in the chest and both were grabbing bread or vine wine.

Seeing a chance to be closer to Ukre, Givas followed Atrum to the kitchen. He offered his services to carry through a platter or two.

"Toas, Sude, look at our guest helping with the food!"

Atrum handed a platter heaped with sizzling meat to Givas. His eyes tracked Ukre's movements in the background.

A polite cough returned his attention just as the heat began burning his hands. It was close to being unbearable.

Toas and Sude glowered at him as he entered the dining room. They were ravenous and helped themselves, filling their plates.

"That's fine, Givas!" Atrum pointed at an empty chair beside Sude. "Grandpapa," she yelled through to the other room.

To Givas' delight, Ukre sat opposite him and he restrained himself from staring at her all the time. Givas politely waited for all to sit before helping himself. There was a wide selection of food on the various serving dishes.

The master of selection – Utek as he is known to a few and Grandpapa to those around him – sat down whilst Toas and Sude grabbed a spoon each.

Utek coughed and Givas noticed the spoons obediently go back down.

"Our guest will say a word of thanks."

Givas gulped in shock. Toas and Sude, father and son, grinned. Seeing a supportive smile and nod from Ukre he relaxed. Closing his eyes he breathed in and out.

"May we be grateful for this delightful meal. May we appreciate the care and effort put into creating such."

"Well said," Utek confirmed. "Let us eat!"

Givas saw Ukre smiling at him, and he happily began to eat.

"So, Sude, where were you working today?" Toas asked.

"I was tasked with the repair of the south harbour." He looked over at Givas. "What do you do, Gipas?"

"Givas." Ukre corrected him on his behalf.

"I have returned to the city to find out," Givas replied.

"Are you a trader then?" Derision crept into Sude's voice.

He felt all eyes on him now watching him for a reply.

"I learn," he said simply.

"You learn!" Sude was scornful. "About what?"

Givas paused for thought. What do I learn about? he asked himself.

"I learn about myself."

Sude frowned, not understanding.

Utek thumped a hand on the table. "Excellent answer, Givas. The best thing I did was send you to Dels," Utek said, beaming.

Everyone except Sude and Petr was looking at him in a different light. Sude scowled, feeling outmanoeuvred somehow and being out of the attention.

Petr was too busy filling his mouth with an oversized piece of bread to notice.

"Dels… isn't she the woman of the hills?" Atrum enquired.

"I did stay in the hills," Givas agreed.

"Did you see any lions?" Ukre asked, already amazed.

"No."

"Elephants?" Petr demanded

"No."

"I am sure he saw lots of other interesting things instead," Atrum concluded.

"Does that mean you are a librarian?" Sude asked with contempt.

"Not until after my vow of silence is finished."

"Will that be difficult?" Ukre asked.

Givas felt her looking deep into his soul. "It depends on who I am with." He smiled back at her.

"Librarians are very important," Atrum stated.

Sude was intent on his food and only grunted. Toas was non-committal, saying nothing to upset his great, great grandfather or the guest. Nor did he say anything to incite anything more from Sude.

"As important as repairing the harbour wall?" Sude challenged.

"More… possibly… where would the harbour be without the knowledge of how it is structured in the first place?" Ukre reasoned.

Knowing he was outnumbered, Sude became overly interested in his plate of food.

"I think the harbour wall is more important," Givas reasoned. "For your work will last for many more summers than anything I have done up until now."

Sude looked across at Givas confused. His competition had turned into an ally. The room went quiet, waiting for his response.

"True," Sude said grinning. "But wait until you become the most famous librarian," he joked.

Givas nodded. *How close to the truth Sude's joke had been.*

"Fame? Fame?" Con Grote hobbled in, hand already outstretched for a vacant chair – his chair. "Fame is unimportant in this life. Helping make a difference to the city, to another person, is what matters."

Atrum shovelled some food onto a plate for Con Grote.

"Did you hear that the Dance of Light Festival is next half-moon?" Atrum asked no one in particular.

Givas noticed Ukre's eyes flash with interest. "Has it been delayed?" he asked.

"Yes, of course, you wouldn't know. The empsar has been mourning the loss of his wife and unborn child in childbirth. The council delayed it to mark respect for his grief."

"Will there be dancing, my darling wife?" Toas asked with a grin.

"Don't you go getting any ideas, husband! I remember last time and the results," she said, patting her son Petr's head as he sat on the chair beside her, trying but failing miserably to hide her joy.

Givas looked at Ukre and saw her excitement at the prospect of dancing.

"Will you be going to the festival?" he asked her.

"I have yet to be invited."

"Would you like to go to the festival with me?"

"Yes, but won't you be in your vow of silence?"

"Who needs to talk, sis?" Sude nudged her laughing.

"Sude," Atrum said sharply.

"He speaks true, wife." Toas smiled. "When I first danced with you, I was speechless."

As everyone carried on with their meals, Givas was given one quick nod from Ukre. Then she focused on what was on her plate. She turned a delightful rose colour as she blushed.

After the meal, Givas had been pressed to sleep in a spare bunk. Rather than going into some temporary accommodation, he was sharing with Sude.

Sude had grumbled a little but had fallen immediately asleep and was now snoring loudly. Givas lay there quietly thinking in the darkness. Remembering Ukre, Con Grote and the mother – Atrum. It was all a mix of thoughts, memories and feelings. Atrum was a caring mother who reminded him of his lack of memories of his own Con Grote. Only one Con Grote. Givas had known no one like him. 'Ukre!' Givas thought with a smile. A connection he hoped could grow into something beautiful.

With pleasant thoughts floating about his mind, he drifted off to sleep.

The dream was lucid and full of feelings. His father stood facing him, horror etched across his face. Givas sensed the question, What have I done? The vision wavered but remained. He saw tears in his father's eyes. There was a look of sheer remorse, so much so that Givas felt true sorrow. So much compassion went far beyond their father-son relationship. The shimmering continued and then his father disappeared. Clouds swirled around Givas.

He was floating in the sky and there was something wrong beneath him. A bright orange line was moving through the streets of Atlantis and houses burst into flames. The strength of fear Givas sensed was so intense that even in a dream he recoiled.

Flying over the spine he saw what appeared to be an army. A large army. Not in the same colours as Atlantis and in different clothes too.

Givas awoke in the early light slick with sweat, his pumping heart and adrenaline making him fidgety. He dressed soundlessly and crept out of the house without a word to anyone. Not that anyone was up and about.

Walking out into the dawn, quietness blanketed the city. The air, yet to be warmed by the sun, brought up goosebumps. Givas strolled aimlessly trying to shift his emotions. He checked himself momentarily and asked what he was running from.

Feelings.

He was trying to evade feelings. *What would Dels have told me?*

You cannot outrun yourself.

Givas sat down in the middle of the street and closed his eyes. The fear was there: hot, oily, and almost overpowering. With difficulty, he sat still and acknowledged the fear. It lessened. Sensing outwards Givas realised it only went as far as his own energy. He felt it for what it was – a feeling. That thought did it. The fear disappeared instantly.

Smiling ruefully, he opened his eyes and glimpsed a look of concern and curiosity on the face of a passer-by.

Returning to the house he was just in time to sit down opposite Ukre for breakfast. Givas and Ukre kept on catching each other's eyes and smiling at each other throughout the meal.

The men – Toas and Sude – were eating a thick gruel with a large, sweet bread as if there was no tomorrow. Toas finished first, belched, and shoved the bowl away only to be copied by Sude moments later.

"Work," Toas said simply.

"Bye, dear!"

A quick peck on the cheek then they were gone.

The old man had yet to make an appearance and Petr tugged at Givas' sleeve.

"Hello!" Givas put his attention fully on the boy.

He appreciated the child, just as he was. Appreciated he may have been naughty. He appreciated him for being good. He appreciated him when sleeping and when noisy. He even appreciated him crying. He felt the energetic connection solidify into the strongest he had ever been aware of.

Givas smiled at Petr. Petr grinned, let go of the sleeve and ran about the room warbling with delight.

"What did you say to him?" asked Atrum.

"Nothing at all!" Givas grinning, stood up and helped her take the dishes to where Ukre was cleaning them.

"What are your plans today, Givas?" Atrum asked.

"To find out when my period of silence begins… and hopefully begin it."

Ukre looked up and straight into him. Givas smiled and openly accepted her gaze. Seemingly satisfied, she returned to her duties.

"Mama?"

"Yes, Ukre?"

"Will you help me with my dress for the Dance of the Light Festival?"

Givas smiled at Ukre, nodded once then left the kitchen area. He knew the rest of the conversation would lose him in details of sizes, shapes, colours and trims.

"Boy," the old man commanded.

"Yes?"

"I will walk you to the council."

"I will get your stick." Givas grabbed the staff that was leaning against the wall and placed it in the open palm.

Walking through the streets some passers-by acknowledged the ex-empsar. Others avoided the experience of being stared at by those bluish-white penetrating blind eyes. Givas enjoyed the feeling of helping and yet somehow being protected.

"Did you learn of the art of appreciation from Dels?"

Givas looked at Con Grote. "The art of appreciation, no! I was instructed to appreciate objects as tasks."

"Oh."

"Why do you ask?"

"I sensed your connection with Petr."

"You said the word art?"

"Is there a way of appreciating?"

"If there is, you do it very well."

"Oh," Givas said, pausing for thought. "Is there a way I can do it better?"

"That is a good question to ask yourself."

Givas was about to ask another question but Con Grote waved it away.

"Appreciate the sounds of Atlantis and tell me what you sense."

Givas dubiously closed his eyes. He was completely reliant on the blind man's unerring sense of direction. Seeing it to believe it was one thing, but experiencing it without visual confirmation took some getting used to.

Breathing deeply, Givas settled and allowed his awareness to expand. Washing over buildings, his senses gave him perceptions of women going about their tasks. Expanding out further, he realised there was a large open square with what seemed to be a queue of people. All sorts of emotions could be picked up. There was a mixture of fear, excitement, happiness and something deeper... love.

"Well?" demanded Con Grote, interrupting his perceptions and jerking him back to the connection of the guiding hand on his arm.

"I sense women finishing off tasks in their homes."

"And?"

"A long line of people in the marketplace."

"What about them?"

"Lots of emotions along the whole line."

"Good, they are waiting already."

Givas realised what the line was for.

"They are waiting to be selected, aren't they?" he asked, already knowing the answer.

"Yes, after I speak with the council."

Givas sank into quietness, not wanting any further details from the master of selection. He was realising he had been in Atlantis for over a day and yet he hadn't thought much of his father until now.

"It was best for you," Con Grote said gently.

"What?"

"You being selected. It was best for you. I saw two futures at the time that I still recall clearly. Highly unusual for me to remember for so long after, but I do. One was full of anger, outrage and spite, the other well… you tell me how different it is!"

Givas gave his full consideration before answering.

"I felt secure. I have had everything I needed except…" Tears quickly filled his eyes.

"It needs to be said, boy!"

"Love!" Givas sobbed. Tears streamed down his face, blinding him, and he held on to Con Grote's hand with his free one. His other was on the arm supporting the old man.

They walked on, Con Grote silent as the sorrow and self-pity bubbled from the depths of Givas' soul.

By the time they had reached the chambers, Givas was in the tranquil aftermath. Recovering from his emotional outpouring he was not his alert self.

Con Grote nodded to the silent librarian guarding the entrance. The librarian opened the large wooden door for entry.

Before Givas knew what was happening he had entered the chambers, Givas's hand still clamped on his arm providing support.

A few irritated looks fell on Givas and yet to him it no longer mattered.

"We greet the master of selection and his companion," the empsar stated.

"I have come for the order of commencement for selection." Con Grote bobbed his head once in his minimalistic way of obeisance.

"Your companion?"

"My companion has finished his out-of-city duty. I ask the council to pledge his support to me whilst he undergoes his vow of silence."

Givas started at this turn of events but felt a hand on his arm kept him from reacting further.

"What is the name of your companion"

"Givas Voret who has finished duty with Ex-Con Dels."

All the councillors went silent, looking to the empsar for their lead.

"Let him take a breath of fresh air and some sunshine whilst we give this request our undivided attention."

Con Grote lifted his hand off Givas' arm.

"It may be of benefit to you also, Master of Selection," the empsar politely ordered.

Givas moved around quickly and pulled Con Grote out of the chambers.

"What has just happened?"

"I asked for you to be tasked to help me during your vow of silence."

"Yes. I understand that." Givas was still catching up. "Why did they not answer immediately?"

"You tell me!"

"What?"

"Feel into it and find the answer!"

"Hmmph!" Givas looked at Con Grote who stared blankly back. Settling down with a few deep breaths he closed his eyes and expanded his awareness.

"Fear."

"Yes."

"Fear of the past... fear of me? Fear of the future... something deeper... pain... heartache... sorrow... loss."

Givas opened his eyes and wiped a tear away from each eye.

"So?"

"Is my future still being dictated by the past?" whined Givas.

"Do you have something to resolve or forgive in the past?"

"No. Nothing. I have yet to see my father, that is all."

"Oh?"

37

Empsar Con Stivus looked out across the water feeling a gust of wind breathe gently across his face.

The early morning light had yet to brighten the whole of the crater and the eastern side was ominously dark and foreboding.

Alone with his thoughts, he stood ankle-deep in the shallows. The shock of the cold water kept him from returning to the despair that kept resurfacing.

Sitting on a rock he felt the warmth and watched, detached, as water dripped from his sandalled feet now dangling over the water.

His thoughts once again returned to his dearly departed. Remorse brought tears instantly. Sinking into his emotions, the tears slid unnoticed down his cheeks.

"It's peaceful at this time, isn't it?"

Stivs saw Ex-Con Dwig out of the corner of his eye. He nodded, not trusting his voice.

"You have let her go, haven't you?" Ex-Con Dwig asked softly.

Stivs nodded in agreement, feeling the last remaining pieces of heartache lift.

"Just in time too," he croaked.

"Oh?"

"That young boy has returned as a man."

"What young boy?"

"The one mentioned in the myth."

"Who decided for certain he is the one of the myth?"

Stivs grunted. "Oh, he is the one alright. I can feel it." Stivs did not feel Ex-Con Dwig's alarmed stare.

"And what is this young man doing now?"

"Awaiting my... our decision on whether he assists the master of selection during his vow of silence."

"What will you choose?"

"Oh... I suppose we will grant the request. Nothing else springs to mind for him to do. After all, he won't be able to do much wrong helping the master of selection."

"Mmm."

Empsar Con Stivus got up and began moving back in the direction of the chambers up the steep path.

"Thank you for your counsel," he said matter-of-factly over his shoulder, again unaware of Ex-Empsar Dwig's reaction.

Back in the chamber, Empsar Con Stivus settled in his chair. He allowed his fellow Elders to quieten before speaking.

"I propose we approve the master of selection's request."

"What if he is the man of the myth?"

"Who are we to decide he is the one of the myth?" Empsar Con Stivus replied.

"Yes. If we treat him unfairly it may provoke a situation," another Elder added.

A few heads nodded in agreement.

"Anyone opposing this request?" Empsar Con Stivus asked.

The room was quiet.

The empsar nodded to the apprentice librarian at the door.

The master of selection and the young man were allowed back into the chamber.

"We greet the master of selection and companion Givas Voret."

"We thank you for your time, Empsar, and that of the council." Ex-Con Grote replied.

"You have a large group to assess from, master of selection."

"I have seen none larger."

"Ensure quality prevails as with previous selections." Empsar Stivus nodded, then remembered Ex-Con Grote was blind. "Your request has been granted." He again nodded to the apprentice at the door and the young man, Givas, guided the master of selection out of the chamber.

"Why does Ex-Con Grote want that young man to help him?" Con Hrap asked nobody in particular.

"Has he ever had an assistant before?" another asked.

Empsar Stivus listened objectively, not getting drawn into the conversation.

"He may even have mellowed."

"That was just because he was asking for a change," opined another.

"For the man of the myth, he is quiet."

"Possibly hiding his true colours. What do you say, Empsar?"

"Feel into it, friends, and sense his intent."

Empsar Stivus was already bored with the subject but did not want it to show. Being a young empsar, he was still wary of the councillors' abilities and intentions.

"Now to the next matter." Stivus' assistant placed a scroll in front of him.

"Ah… yes. The master stonemason is reducing his workforce. The repair of the harbour walls is on target with his previous proposal."

"How much of a reduction?" Con Hrap queried.

"Two hundred labourers, generally unskilled."

"Much in numbers," another stated.

"Suggestions, friends?" Empsar Stivus asked.

A moment of reflection-filled silence followed.

"A wood cutting expedition in the Big Deep?" offered one.

"A hunting expedition west of the Hills of Terzondal?"

"What about an increase in the numbers of the city's garrison?" offered Empsar Con Stivus.

The room went deathly quiet.

"Empsar, that would be a sizeable increase."

"The outlying villages may sense or assume our feeling of insecurity if we do so, Empsar," Con Pras suggested.

Empsar Con Stivus Postet looked at Con Pras with the full force of his attention. Nobody moved, but they were all watching Stivs.

"Would we be insecure about increasing our security? Or more likely to be prudent and wise in the current situation, Con Pras?"

"What situation, Empsar?" Con Fras asked.

Empsar Con Stivus eyed Con Fras with the same intensity he had looked upon Con Pras. Neither she nor her lover seemed fazed by his attention. Were they expecting this or surprised?

"If this young man is the man of the myth would it not help our defences to have stronger security?" he said at last.

Murmurs of agreement. Empsar Con Stivus eyed Con Pras, waiting. After a few seconds, Con Pras shrugged indifferently. Empsar Con Stivus, although satisfied, yearned for something more substantial. He increased his awareness and was surprised to sense real indifference in Con Pras.

"Are we agreed as a council to move the workforce to begin garrison training?"

"Yes!"

"Yes!"

"Yes!"

"Yes!"

"Yes!"

"Yes!"

"Yes!"

"Yes!"

"Yes!"

"Yes!"

"Yes!" Con Fras agreed readily.

"Yes!" Con Pras confirmed.

Empsar Con Stivus continued with administering basic logistics. The matter of security soon faded into the background with the monotony of scroll upon scroll of decision making.

After the council had broken up for the day and he had dismissed Bosa, Stivs sat in the chamber alone.

A flickering candle caught his eye as it was on the brink of extinguishing. The wick was floating in molten wax. Stivs watched tendrils of pale smoke drift up the ceiling. It drew his eyes up to the symbols of Atlantis.

Mind, Body and Soul.

They were all around him – reminders. Reminders to reconnect with the peace and flowing natural life force within each and every one in Atlantis.

"How am I supposed to fulfil my highest calling with the sorrow I have endured?" The candles flickered noncommittally.

He got up and one by one doused each candle with his thumb and forefinger, feeling no pain nor heat.

"Is it increasing willpower or letting go completely?" Again, no verbal answer. Stivs looked again at the symbol of Atlantis and saw the triangle within the circle. The corners of it were the turning points. *A turning point.* He smiled to himself and extinguished the last candle. A turning point indeed. A time to change direction, move on and still be connected to what once was, he thought happily.

He left the dust motes to float in the slivers of dusk's light in the chamber. The empsar went out into the evening, ready once more to face the memories of his empty accommodation.

A purple flower was resting on the sill of his window when he arrived. He knew it was left by Con Ro Pars, a token of her love and compassion. He left it there and entered into a mix of memories. Walking slowly into the room he felt the past assail his senses. The perfume of his late wife was everywhere. Objects that were gifts of love to each other filled the room and all Stivs felt was the emptiness. His tears had been shed.

Stivs knew he couldn't have done anything different to save his wife. But he had an opportunity to save Atlantis. Somehow, he would save Atlantis.

38

Givas saw her and sensed he knew her. She was an apprentice too. She looked up and saw him. A tentative smile. It was Sua, Givas realised, grinning and desperately wanting to laugh and shout to her.

Sua did not recognise him at first, then for a moment flashed him a smile that sent him soaring.

Givas put a finger to his lips and then touched his chest. She understood and did the same before adding two fingers.

Sua only had two days left of her vow of silence.

Walking towards her, he saw she had grown more beautiful than the pretty girl he could remember. Of course, he had changed over the summers also. No longer a gawky youth.

Givas caught himself about to break the vow of silence that he'd pledged to his advocate to the council. The master of selection, although solemn during the event, had a sparkle in his eyes, throughout. Givas was expecting some witty remark at every opportunity. He looked around, double-checking they were alone. The memory of Kors came to mind.

Sua held up two fingers, nodded, then turned and walked away, turning and waving every so often.

Givas felt happy – truly happy. He walked over to the room used for assessment. The queue of people at the front was subdued and docile. He felt a strong desire from some. It seemed to be an honour to be selected or have your child selected. Pausing briefly at the door he nodded to the other novice. He was a classmate who was also undergoing a vow of silence. He couldn't remember his name, even after three summers…

'Stult… that was it.'

Givas nodded to Stult and walked into the assessment room. The master of selection had a hand on the head of a child and held the boy's hand with his other.

"Does this boy ever eat fish?" Con Grote asked.

The father shook his head embarrassed.

Givas waved at the man, pointed to his eyes then at Con Grote and shook his head.

"No, master," the man said finally.

"And yet... I am still undecided!" Givas raised his eyebrows in surprise.

"What about the boy's mother?"

"She is tending her mother who will soon depart this land."

"See you tomorrow!" Con Grote patted the boy's head and smiled with warmth.

Givas picked up a scroll and made a note. He sensed some confusion in Con Grote, so placed a hand on the old man's arm.

"Ah, Givas, I know. I am getting old that is all."

A young girl was brought in with her mother. The girl was wide-eyed and curious.

"What is your name? No, wait, let me guess... Clar?"

"Yes," she shouted delightedly.

"Breathe in slowly and close your eyes, child." The master of selection sensed into the child. Givas paused and also felt into her sensing innocence and happiness.

"Givas, she is clear is she not?"

Givas tapped his sandal once.

"Mmmm. A butcher's daughter. Her transition was fraught with family learning. She can be of greater good there. Mmm." Con Grote placed a hand over her heart and a hand on her head.

"Not this summer," he announced at last.

Givas saw the mother frown. The child ran to her mother.

"I told you, Momma. I want to be a butcher like Papa!" The mother couldn't stay disappointed any longer.

"Let us go and tell him the good news then."

Givas was kept busy with scrolls and the infrequent request for a second opinion. After some time when the sun was at its highest, he took a break and ventured out to the fountain to freshen up.

"I hoped I would find you," a voice from his past whispered.

Givas turned sharply to see a hooded figure with a golden walking stick.

"Who are you?"

The stranger pushed back his hood to reveal his suntanned and well-lined face.

"Father!" The word escaped before he could stop himself. His legs buckled and he would have fallen had it not been for his father's strong arms.

"Givas, my son. I can see your mother in you. Your eyes are just as hers were."

Tears were spilling as Givas battled with overpowering sorrow.

"My son. She would be proud of you so," Gamute husked.

Givas' face melted as tears rolled freely down his face dripping onto his robes.

"Are you in your vow of silence?"

One quick nod.

"Please forgive me for sending you away." Givas' father was close to losing control too. He coughed and settled somewhat. "It was what your mother dreamed of; you being a librarian. Of being someone important. Of someone who helps others!"

The words poured out of his father, tumbling and falling fast, having been stored up for so long. Givas let them wash over him. Some words he was surprised to hear, others flowed past his mind as he felt the feeling of security return. That feeling of returning to the safety of his family expanded within his soul.

He felt like a little boy again, cocooned within his father's protective arms. Feeling safe from the big world.

"You do forgive me, son?" His father was weeping.

Givas came out of his dream world with eyes dried and a lightness to his being.

Placing a hand on Gamute's shoulder he nodded slowly and deliberately.

Givas felt the change within him. The security from within now. The purpose and his destiny were now certain.

His father seemed a spent force, the vitality diminished somewhat.

Givas picked up the staff and admired the craftwork.

"A gift from the council for my work. But what about you? You have grown so tall. And a librarian at that!"

Givas smiled at his father, appreciating him for all that he was.

"My son is a librarian. We can talk after your vow is completed?"

Givas nodded once, peace emanating from him.

"That will be wonderful."

His father raised a hand and then stopped himself from patting his grown son's head. Instead, he clapped him on the shoulder as he would any other grown man.

"Until then, Librarian."

Walking away Givas felt an increased depth of sensation from all that his awareness flickered over. The line of children and families, although reduced, was still impressive in length.

"You have met your father then," Con Grote stated matter-of-factly.

Givas smiled serenely and tapped his foot once.

"Good, now let us continue." Con Grote carried on as if nothing much had happened.

Givas was not asked for any more opinions. It was as if the master of selection knew that he had met his father. Givas knew that he needed time to integrate his recent experience completely in peace.

Givas occasionally sensed a child that Con Grote had selected for the order. Catching a glimmer of the future in his mind, Givas was amazed at his new increased insight. He also found that the decisions Con Grote made were without error.

"Good, eh?" Con Grote chuckled.

He was occasionally surprised by the old man's perception. It was a pleasant feeling now. A sense of inclusion and connection to something greater than the two of them.

Givas felt part of some big plan in which he was only beginning to understand his part, had been chosen for him to play.

That evening, Givas felt the need for solitude and wandered the streets after the meal. Walking soundlessly along the alleyways he came out at one of the harbours.

Shimmering with reflected light, Givas lost himself gazing into the depths of the sea. He felt light and heavy, happy and sad, but most importantly, more complete and at ease within himself, than ever before.

A feather floated down in front of him. A sign from above? Looking up he saw no bird. But he did see the darkening sky colouring from sky blue across into the star-spangled jet black. He pulled his hood up to prevent any loss of body heat as the temperature dropped then meandered along the streets, back to the Grote family home.

Con Grote was sitting in front of a roaring fire.

"You've done well today, young man!"

Givas recoiled at the open praise, taking time for it to sink in.

Ukre was standing by the doorway looking at him. He returned her gaze and was surprised when she cocked her head in question. She knew something was different for him too.

Givas glanced away feeling guilty.

Why should I feel guilty? What have I done to feel guilty about? An image of Sua briefly returned to mind. He blushed in embarrassment, confused and guilty.

Attracted to two women, what should I do?

"She recognises you have changed today." Con Grote said

Givas breathed out with relief. He went to his bed totally at ease with the snoring now but not so much at ease with his mind having thoughts fly about at the speed of light.

Fear spread through his body. What am I afraid of? Givas thought.

Loss. The word popped into his mind and he felt emotion course through his veins. His fingers gripped the old blanket that was covering him tightly. The smell of flowers that the women used to clean the blanket rose. Then it was overpowered by the constant dust.

Givas tasted metallic fear. His legs were energised with adrenaline but he refused to move. With eyes screwed up tight and blanket up to his face, he recoiled with the panic rising from the depths.

Stop! His mind screamed and was followed by a brief surcease.

Expanding his awareness, he tentatively felt the fear. Curiously the more he opened up to it the weaker it became. He put his arms by his sides and relaxed into it.

A hazy image of a woman appeared in his mind. He couldn't see her properly, but he knew who it was. His mother.

Tears rolled down his cheeks leaving a damp trail past his ears before soaking his cushion.

Waking early, Givas felt more settled than ever before. He grabbed a sweet bread to fill his growling stomach and set off in search of the stables.

He could smell the cleansing sea and tune into the powerful ebb and flow of the mass of water. Then, getting nearer the odour of the horse, used straw, the dusty perfume of the hay and the snickering of horses took him back in time.

Butterflies were dancing in his belly. He revelled in anticipation of seeing Hennie and the master stabler once more.

Just as before he left, the stables were being tended and tidied early in the morning. The sun still to rise from the eastern horizon enabled Givas to approach in shadow.

He allowed himself a polite cough despite the vow of silence. The master stabler had a face on him, suggesting he disliked morning interruptions.

"Yes, Librarian… Givas, is that you?"

The master stabler grabbed him in his sweaty embrace and Givas was aware of the smell of leather. The stabler's odour all mixed in with the vibrant and thrilling tang of horse aroma reminded him of his time there.

"Givas, how are you? Boy, you've grown these past summers."

Givas could do nothing but shake his head and place fingers in front of his mouth.

"Ah… they got you to do the vow of silence! That'll be easy for you."

Givas was held at arm's length by the master stabler.

"You've changed, boy… you've changed, Givas." He realised he was looking at a young man. "Let us see, Hennie!"

Givas went first, sensing the palpable strength of the horse. She must have been used for Atlantis Garrison or for dragging timber or blocks of stone.

Hennie had her ears back listening to the two men walking over to her. She raised her head from the fodder and sniffed Givas' outstretched hand.

The horse must have recognised him as Givas was nuzzled strongly. He placed his hands on both sides of Hennie's neck and pushed his face into the mane. The coarse hairs tickled his face as he automatically sensed her energy.

As with other animals, Hennie's was a deep but constant vibration and sensation. Unlike humans, there was no flickering or changing.

She bucked her head playfully, snickering for him to get on top.

Givas looked excitedly at the master stabler.

"Go on… bring her back before the morning meal."

Without needing another chance, Givas vaulted on top of Hennie and grabbed the reins.

The master stabler opened the gate and Hennie took Givas for a ride.

39

Empsar Con Stivus looked out across the water as the slow lapping of the water at his feet gentled him.

"You have done what?" Con Dwig asked in surprise.

"We have… I have moved two hundred workers on to garrison training. They were no longer needed for any maintenance of the harbour."

"Are they needed on garrison strength?"

"Well, they could be. The rumours of Terzondals… the myth." Stivs knew he was justifying himself.

"Basing decisions on rumours and the myth may be reinforcing the potential of them occurring." Con Dwig said softly.

"I knew you would be like this. I couldn't help save my wife but I will do all in my power to save Atlantis."

"Stivs."

"Empsar Con Stivus Postet to you Ex-Con Dwig." Empsar Stivus forced the statement out. He felt cornered. He didn't intend to be arrogant, but, the line had been drawn.

Ex-Con Dwig bowed his head in polite acknowledgement and said no more.

Empsar Stivus moved back out of the water and made a pretence about taking time to dry his feet. The silence widened between them, and he felt desolation creep through his bones. His confidant, friend and tutor was gone.

Slowly he pulled his hood over his head and walked back up the slope. The silence turned his stomach as he walked away. Part of him screamed on the inside to reach out with a token gesture. His stride shortened as the gradient increased before he had to fully focus on the path.

Ex-Con Dwig remained sitting on the rock gazing out across the water. A fish floated up in front. He gazed idly at it not seeing what was in front of him. The fish slowly revolved in the water, finishing belly up. Ex-Con Dwig raised his eyebrows. Grabbing his normal wooden walking stick he cajoled the dead fish to the shore.

With slow determination, he bent down to inspect it.

Touching the fish with a finger, he almost missed the difference between this fish and all the others.

This fish was warm. The eyes were whitened as if they had been partially cooked. Stunned, he just stared at it. Then, dazed, he looked out across the water. Seeing nothing out of place he dipped his toe in the water.

It was warm, but then again he was in the shallows. Carefully he went in deeper. The water was up to his knees. Deeper still, up to his waist. A couple more steps. He lost his balance.

Sputtering he thrashed the water. He lost his walking stick and saw it floating out of reach. He managed to propel himself towards the bank. Warm water surrounded him. It was alien. It shouldn't all be warm, he shouted inside his head.

Something is wrong!

After some struggle, his foot touched the ground. He moved towards shore. His other foot touched down. Clawing the water out of his way he walked back to the rock.

Ex-Con Dwig coughed up some water. He felt horrified. It sapped him of conscious thought. His breathing slowed gradually. The sun-warmed rock helped dry his robes.

"What could be happening?" He asked no one.

He saw the dead fish and toyed with the idea of taking it as evidence. He saw his walking stick float out towards the deepest parts of the lake and he knew it was impossible.

All his strength and energies would be needed in getting up the slope without his stick. He would have to inform the council. He would have to speak with Empsar Con Stivus Postet.

40

Sude's heart had leapt when he found out he was being moved on to garrison training. Many moons of chipping away at rocks to get them just right in size and shape had gotten boring. There may be excitement ahead.

If the council had put so many of them onto security, maybe, just maybe they were expecting something. Possibly battles.

He shifted his leather band in his right palm before hefting the weight of his spear. Grabbing the balance point as they had all been shown came quite naturally to him.

"Well done, Grote!"

"Is it a Terzondal uprising?"

"Keep quiet and focus." The instructor moved along the line.

Sude pointed his spear at an imaginary foe and stabbed the air.

His father chuckled and slapped his shoulder with one free hand.

"Leave some enemies for me, son."

Sude grinned.

"Shield!" A small rectangular board with a hand strap was passed to him. Another instructor watched, as once again Sude handled the shield.

"Hmmph." The instructor was not as impressed.

"Past life warrior, were you, Sude?"

Sude shrugged. "Natural… that's all," he said noncommittally. His mind was already racing, imagining battles where he was the hero and victor. Visualising killing, maiming and despatching enemy forces.

"The Grote army shall take them on." His father broke up his reverie.

"Silence," an instructor hissed, pointing at the huge halls of Atlantis. "Enemies could be listening to every word we say," he whispered forcefully.

Sude and his father lapsed into quietness. Sude, more from determination to be right. He wanted so much to be recognised as the best trainee soldier out of the two hundred here today.

He looked around. His father in his fighting leather jerkin didn't seem to care. Past him, he could see a few more including Almac, the man who'd lost two fingers from a falling stone. Sude clenched his spear and shield tighter.

Glancing around the other way he saw a young boy, maybe thirteen years old, look at him fearfully. His helmet was far too big for him and was slipping over his eyes. He tried to push it back up and clinked himself with the corner of his shield.

Sude couldn't help but smirk.

"Terzondals? We're against the Terzondals?" he whispered to Sude.

"Yes. Bloodthirsty ignorants the lot of them," Sude told him.

"Ignorants?"

"Yes, they are still believers in the old gods." Sude grinned. "We will teach them a lesson or two about the might of the Atlantean army."

"How many Terzondals are there?" the boy asked.

"Many scores of hundreds." Sude estimated with his one day's experience, feeling confident from the day of garrison training.

"How many Atlanteans on security?"

"We are now up to four hundred. I heard them say that. The training master it was," Sude's father confirmed.

The young boy looked at the wall and gulped. His helmet once again slipped over his face. This time he was slower to push it back up.

Sude saw a figure he thought he recognised. It was the apprentice librarian with the hood up.

"Father, isn't that Givas?" Sude asked. As if Givas heard he looked around and raised a hand in recognition.

Sude raised his shield in acknowledgement.

"You know him?" the young boy asked.

"Yes. He helps our grandfather, and stays at our house."

The young boy breathed in sharply, looking from Sude to the figure of Givas walking away.

"Why?" Sude saw the boy's reaction.

"He is the one of the myth," the boy whispered.

As if the whole line of men heard, they all went still.

"Givas… nah. You're joking."

"It is. My father's brother pointed him out to me yesterday." He nodded furiously.

Sude looked at him. "Are you sure it's him?"

He looked at Givas, now a distant figure. "Our grandfather would know," he said, not so confidently as before.

"It's him. It's the man of the myth!" he said, this time so loudly the line did hear.

Sude looked around, seeing they were being watched and listened to by everyone.

"I am sure you are mistaken. My grandfather is the master of selection and would not have invited the man of the myth in. Ha, far from it," Sude continued in a whisper. "Shhhh, boy, you will get us in trouble."

41

Ex-Con Dwig arrived at the chamber's entrance and waited to be invited in. His robes were stained with grass and mud. After his difficult climb without the walking stick, he struggled. He had, in his haste, slipped and fallen several times. Blood was on one knuckle that he had scraped in one of his tumbles.

He was forced to wait for some time. Ex-Con Dwig allowed himself to settle as much as he could. But the fear of what was happening to the waters did not allow him peace.

Finally, the apprentice opened the door for him and nodded for him to enter.

"We greet Ex-Con Dwig. By the old gods what has happened. Have you been attacked?" Empsar Stivus Postet asked, shocked at his old friend's attire.

"I am unharmed but have upsetting news to tell." Ex-Con Dwig saw the empsar blush, probably thinking it was a personal attack.

"It is about Big Deep."

"Oh?" The empsar sounded relieved.

"I fear something terrible is about to happen."

"What happened? You look as though you have been rolling on the ground?" Con Ro Pars asked.

Con Dwig looked down at his muddied robes. The once creamy white fabric was stained with patches of green. It had been muddied from his slipping and sliding on his journey back. He wiped his bloodied knuckle on his left sleeve adding more colour.

"I misplaced my walking stick. I recommend not leaving the Big Deep without one." He cracked a small grin. "Something is happening within the lake," he said slowly.

"A dead fish floated past. I believe it was cooked within the depths of the lake."

"Has this happened before?" Empsar Stivus asked his colleagues.

The Elders thought back, remembering into the depths of time. One by one the Elders shook their heads.

"Has any more work been done on the channels?" another asked.

Ex-Con Dwig slowly shook his head.

"Cooked you say?" the empsar asked.

"Yes. I felt the change. I swam into the lake and felt the warmth. It was hot."

"Could you have incorrectly perceived it?" The empsar pressed.

"The water is usually cold. The shallows are usually pleasantly refreshing to the feet."

All the council's eyes were drawn to the damp of Ex-Con Dwig's robe and his feet.

"And it was hot?"

"Yes, Empsar."

"Will that affect the aqueduct system?" another asked.

"Apart from warming the water… no. As long as we don't find dead fish floating in our aqueducts," said another.

"Can you ensure no dead fish go into the channels?" Empsar Stivus asked.

"That is more a matter for the master stonemason, Empsar."

"Yes… yes… you are quite right." Empsar Stivus spoke to Bosa over his shoulder. "Summon the master stonemason."

"How many fish did you see?"

"One."

"Will there be more dead?"

"I hope not, Empsar."

"Thank you for your report. Is there anything you need?"

"No, Empsar." Ex-Con Dwig was tired physically and drained emotionally. He knew that something was being overlooked, but every time he thought it was close, it evaded him.

"Yes, Ex-Con Dwig?" Empsar Stivus noticed his indecision.

"I feel something is amiss."

"Can you explain?"

"It eludes me for the moment, Empsar." Ex-Con Dwig nodded to the empsar and the tables of councillors.

What was it? What is this feeling? he asked himself. Ex-Con Dwig went in search of the one person he knew could help – Con Grote master of selection.

He found him in the selection room. Ex-Con Dwig was not surprised to see Givas assisting with the scrolls.

"My friend, you are fearful. What is it?" Con Grote asked, already aware of his presence and sensing his energy.

"I found a fish cooked dead in the lake. The water was or is that hot!"

"A dead fish is not what you are fearful of, is it?

Ex-Con Dwig felt the full attention of Con Grote and Givas. Breathing in deeply he relaxed into his feelings.

"I felt the heat of the water. It was unusual. Disturbingly so!"

"And?"

"And … the power. The energy needed to heat the water in the lake is vast. Stronger than the sun. I sense something momentous."

"What say you, Givas?" Con Grote demanded.

Givas looked in surprise at Con Grote. He motioned to Ex-Con Dwig's mouth and shook his head.

"Your words are needed now more than the purpose of the vow of silence." Ex-Con Dwig instructed him.

Givas breathed out surprised and relieved at the break in tradition.

"I know not what you ask of me," he said at last.

"Feel into it, boy," Con Grote ordered.

Ex-Con Dwig watched the young man relax, close his eyes and settle.

"I sense turmoil, more than emotions. A shake-up. Massive power."

"And?" Con Grote didn't let him stop.

"I remember a dream where there was fire running through Atlantis. It feels connected."

"Givas has connected and has told us the future!" Con Grote stated. "What say you, Dwig?"

"My friend, I cannot take this to the council and Empsar Stivus Postet."

"Why not?"

"For one, he has broken his vow of silence."

"It matters not when the lives of all Atlantis are concerned."

"More importantly, the empsar believes Givas is the man of the myth."

"Bah," Con Grote growled. "Does young Stivus not connect anymore?" He asked no one in particular.

"Since his wife died giving birth he has changed. He has lost his family."

"A man who has lost his family," Givas reiterated.

"What did you say, boy?" Con Grote demanded.

"A man who has lost his family."

Ex-Con Dwig breathed out in surprise as if punched in the gut.

"A man who has lost his family. How did we not see it?"

"We have all overlooked it," Con Grote countered.

"What?" Givas was lost.

"The empsar could be the one of the myth."

"And given his recent experience, he would not contemplate the possibility. He is fixated on you being the one."

"What can we do?" Givas asked.

"Nothing but wait." Ex-Con Dwig said, deflated.

"The lake is boiling, there may be fire flowing and burning Atlantis soon and we can do nothing."

Ex-Con Dwig saw the passion in the young man's expression.

"What do you suggest?"

"Leave Atlantis. Leave the city."

"The empsar would not accept that nor allow it."

"The empsar? We are talking about the survival of Atlantis. Survival of everyone!"

Ex-Con Dwig saw the frustration growing in Givas.

"We understand, Givas." He raised a hand to quell the young man's urge to express his outrage.

"We will do what we can do," he told him.

"Guide me home, Givas," Con Grote ordered.

"Connect with the empsar's higher self, Dwig. Let us do that until there is a change in viewpoint."

"Con Grote we—" Givas was cut off with a wave of the hand.

"Givas. We know the consequences or possible consequences. Focus on now. Beyond that, your vow of silence will do you well. Remember you can change reality by a change in your beliefs. It is quicker than forcing someone to accept your version of reality," Con Grote said softly.

Givas lapsed into silence. Guiding Con Grote through the city he kept to a speed that the old man could cope with. The lightness of the man's grip on his arm tightened when he put on too much speed. He felt he was leading. *What was different?* Givas smiled to himself. He had at last truly trusted what he felt and what he dreamed. Givas felt the courage grow within him. A sureness filled him. Self-confidence grew from within his belly. He lifted his hand and felt his back straighten. His shoulders moved back easing his back muscles. Breathing in deeply he connected naturally and easily in the silence.

"Welcome back, Givas," Con Grote told him.

Givas mentally thanked him. Reaching the front door to the house he smelt the evening meal. For once he allowed himself to savour the moment, the aromas and his hunger. Givas could barely believe it was enjoyable to feel hungry. Up until now, he had wanted immediate satisfaction regardless of the long term.

Sitting down at the table, he was quiet among the hubbub of family life. The mother chatted to the daughter. She occasionally badgered her sons or husband for some account of their day.

Givas picked up a piece of bread and sniffed it. This caught Ukre's attention. She stopped to watch him with curiosity. He took a small bite, closing his eyes in rapture. The texture was a mixture of crusty, crisp shell and soft melting, fluffy bread. The lightness teased his tastebuds. Buttery velvet rolled along his tongue providing sensation after sensation.

Dipping the bread into his bowl of stew he felt the added weight. He could perceive the aromas of lamb and assorted vegetables in a rich, thick gravy. The heat made his tongue recoil instinctively before it searched out the new tasks once more. Blowing on it to cool it down he still had his eyes closed. He sensed the two boys' attention on him and heard a lull in the conversation.

Mouthful by mouthful he savoured the food with delight and patience. Each moment opened up new experiences of flavour and texture.

"That's what I like to see." Atrum broke his reverie. "You lot take mealtimes as a competition as to who can finish the fastest."

The heads of three men bowed slower this time to their bowls.

Givas nodded to them and focused once again on his meal. Atrum wanted to refill his bowl with more stew, but Givas opted for a fresh bright and shiny apple. His tastebuds once again became overjoyed with sensations. His senses went wild in the most basic of experiences.

Con Grote cleared his throat. "Two nights into his vow of silence has heightened his senses already."

Atrum frowned, momentarily taking it as a slight and the men looked up, perking up in mood. Petr seemed oblivious to all and Givas watched him avidly tucking into his smaller portion of food.

It's amazing the awareness and focus of a child, he thought in wonderment.

Petr looked up and grinned. Of course, being a direct descendant, he would never go in front of the master of selection. The male side of the Grote family would never be allowed to apply for librarian selection. The order had put that in place upon Con Grote's appointment as master of selection.

No favouritism and also no animosity. A rule that was protection for all.

42

Ex-Con Dwig freed his consciousness from his body and let it soar into the universe. He intended to connect with Empsar Stivus. Within moments he faced the empsar in his mind's eye.

I greet thee, Empsar, for the benefit of all.

No response.

The image of the empsar flickered.

I send respect and love for the benefit of all.

Still no response.

The welfare of Atlantis is in your hands and I ask thee to move to safety.

The city is safe from Terzondals, responded the empsar.

There is great peril from the lake. We have seen fire and destruction.

The city is safe.

The image of the empsar faded from view.

Ex-Con Dwig opened his eyes and found tears trickling down his face.

Looking out across the lake he watched in fear and awe as steam rose from the surface. The master stonemason had put some sort of grille over the channel entrance. But that problem was the least of the city's worries now. Ex-Con Dwig wiped his tears with the back of his hand. The pile of dead fish lay at his feet. The fish he had spent much effort in retrieving from the surface of the lake. More effort was spent on not falling into the hot water than actually moving the fish.

Wiping the perspiration from his brow he picked up his replacement walking stick and trudged slowly up the path, stopping frequently to catch his breath.

Old age and a steep climb do not go together, he thought, regretting his increasing infirmities.

Getting to the top of the treeline, he looked down at the basin and swayed with shock.

There was a red glow from the centre of the lake. A constant glow. The mirage of heatwaves could not obscure it.

Panic seized him. He turned and moved as quickly as he could. The walking stick bounced off a stone. It hit the earth. Ex-Con Dwig moved. Again the stick moved forward. Up to the top.

I must get back, he implored himself.

Breathing quickly. Adrenaline pumping. Sweaty palms as the replacement walking stick slipped in his grip. It went back down. It found a hole. It was quick.

Ex-Con Dwig saw what was happening but was too slow to react.

The old man leant on the support that was no longer there. Bouncing off a rock his head glanced off the side. Blackness reached out and dragged him into unconsciousness.

43

C on Grote felt panic. It arose in his belly in a burst of flames and then went out just as quickly.

"Givas!"

"Yes, Master?" Givas rushed to his side.

"What do you sense?"

"What?"

"What do you sense? Feel into it now." Con Grote allowed his feelings to settle, not reacting to them unduly. Confirmation is required, he told himself.

"I feel the massive power is getting closer. It will happen soon."

"Get the children together! Take them to the far side of the spine to the far city gates."

"But…"

"Do it, boy! Now is the time to act. I release you from your vow of silence. As the master of selection, Ex-Empsar Con Grote, I free thee from your vow and pronounce you full librarian." He felt the shock in the boy. "Now, go, boy, go!"

Givas left the room and stepped into the bright daylight. The children were all sitting in the sun. They stopped chattering as soon as he stood in front of them.

"Do you like adventures?" he asked with a smile.

"Yes!" they all shouted together.

"You didn't say it loud enough. The master of selection is getting hard of hearing," Givas said, grinning to himself, hoping Con Grote would take it in good humour.

"Yes!" they all shouted together, much louder this time.

"Would you like to visit the far wall?" Givas looked at them.

"Yes!" they all shouted.

"Now, you all have to hold hands behind me. Who wants to hold my hand?"

There was a scampering and jostling behind Givas as he turned his back showing the way.

He felt a small hand clutching his. Looking around he was pleased and surprised to see a chain of a score of children all holding hands. Givas expanded his awareness and energy to envelop the whole group.

He thought about the long journey, realising the difficulty the youngest children would have.

"Guess where we are going first?"

"Where?" they shouted in unison.

"The stables." Givas smiled hearing them gabbling and chattering to each other about horses.

He sent out a pulse of energy to Dels and felt her friendly aura. She was still strong and comforting.

He called out to Goras as he got close.

"Master Stabler? Have you got the contraption still?"

"Givas!!" A delighted yell. "What happened with your vow?"

"I have been released from the vow of silence."

Goras saw the children. "Are you a teacher now?"

Givas spoke softly and quickly to Goras to ensure the children did not hear them.

"I sense massive fire and destruction will be running through the city." Givas looked back at the waiting children.

"Will you help me save these children and some of your horses?"

Goras looked deep into his eyes.

"I have felt something brewing," he said at last. "But could not understand what. Give me a moment and we will leave in style."

"Who wants to go on a horse?"

Every child screamed and put their hands up at once. Some put both hands up. Givas smiled. He must have learnt a thing or two from his teacher about handling groups of children.

Within moments, Goras brought out two horses. Then he rushed back into the stables.

The children thought this was funny and laughed. Givas smiled and automatically gentled the two horses. Their ears were pricked up and flicking occasionally hearing the children chattering. He rubbed the coat of the horse nearest the children and then noticed Hennie was the other horse. She whickered in recognition. He ruffled her mane, feeling the warmth of the beast through the fine coat.

Goras brought out a wooden platform. He proceeded to sort out the buckles and fasteners of the horses' halters.

Moments later he brought out another two horses and another platform.

Finally, Goras finished. Wiping the perspiration off his brow he looked at the group of children and scratched his chin.

"How about eight children on each platform and one child on each horse?"

Goras began counting the children.

"A score," Givas said simply.

"Good." He stood in front of a little girl. "Would you like to sit on Hennie? She is a very happy horse."

The little girl nodded unable to say a word.

Lifting her out of the group he plopped her lightly onto Hennie's back and watched as she grabbed the mane.

"That's good. Keep hold of the mane and you won't fall off."

Goras turned and before even asking again all the hands shot up eagerly.

Givas and Goras placed another three children onto the backs of the remaining horses.

"Put the rest of them on the platforms. I will be back soon."

Givas watched Goras again disappear into the buildings. He returned his focus to the task at hand.

One by one, he placed all the eager children onto the platforms. He only had to recount twice due to their wriggling about with enthusiasm.

Just as he placed the last boy onto the second platform, Goras returned with several full canvas bags.

He threw one to Givas.

"We may need these." Goras fastened his bags onto the platforms and Givas hoisted his over his shoulder.

"Shall we go?"

"Yes!" the children shouted, laughing delightedly.

Goras led the procession as Givas watched over the children. He saw them reach out and pat the horses' rumps as he had done. His mind returned to his vision of the burning city.

"Pass by the school," Givas shouted to Goras.

Goras nodded, pulling the reins of the leading horses as and when they needed direction.

Givas saw Hort look up from his scrolls, the curiosity evident on his face.

"An unusual way to bring the new class to me."

"We are on a journey to the safety of the hills," Givas told him. "A massive force is boiling from within the lake and…." Givas walked to Hort so he was out of earshot of the chattering children. "I saw a vision of Atlantis burning." Hort started in shock, then had a realisation.

"I knew this day would come. I must get to the class." He looked at the apparatus that carried the children.

"Just as well they can walk. No room up there."

"Catch us up! We are on the way out of the far city gates."

"I will tell Pos who has the other class. He has a horrible limp. He will hold us back," Hort complained.

"Tell him to get in a fishing boat." Givas placed a hand on his old teacher's shoulder.

"Master Teacher, be quick and strong for your children."

He saw the resolve in the man's eyes and felt him straighten up with vigour.

"We will see you soon. If you get a chance bring some food and water bags but do not delay. Time is short."

Givas nodded to Goras and again took his place at the rear of the horses.

They increased the speed to a bumping, jostling pace. The children were delighted and even more excited. Givas smiled, glad they were ignorant of the impending disaster.

44

Ex-Con Dwig came to, feeling hot and uncomfortable. He tenderly touched his head. The stickiness of congealing blood from his brow coated his fingertips.

A moan of pain escaped his lips as he moved. He saw the offending rock and steam beyond. The view of the lake was now replaced by a giant wall of steam clouds.

"No," he croaked, eyes wild in panic.

Scrabbling on his hands and knees he found his walking stick. Propping himself up, he managed to stand up on his feet. A wave of dizziness almost took him back to unconsciousness. White knuckles gripped his cane as he held on for support.

He got to the brow of the crater's edge and saw the city before him. "Help!"

Staggering down the path he went.

"Help!" Nobody could hear him croak.

He slipped. The walking stick went flying. As he instinctively put his arms out, he felt one break as he hit the ground. Pain shot through him.

"Help," he moaned before the darkness took him.

Nobody heard him. Nobody saw him. His attempt to warn them had failed.

45

Empsar Stivus felt a weariness. So much to deal with, he thought.

"Empsar," Con Ro Pars said loudly from across the room.

"What?"

"Do you sense something?"

"What?"

"Something... I do not know what it is, but I feel we need to leave." Her eyes were wide and her face pale.

"What say you, Elders?"

A few nodded quickly. Fidgeting in their seats. Empsar Con Stivus saw another Elder's face twitching with a tic. Most were looking to him for a decision.

He closed his eyes and felt his stomach expand with deep breathing. It took several breaths before he managed to sink into the calmness.

Run! A word popped into his mind unbidden. Stivus opened his eyes. Con Ro Pars was looking directly at him, her fingers at her mouth.

He closed his eyes. *She sent me that word. But why?*

FLEE! Another unbidden word.

Ignoring it, he went deeper. Expanding his awareness he floated through the emotions of the others. A mixture of fear, defiance and boredom. Moving out further through the house and home he felt no panic, nothing untoward. Just before returning something caught his attention. One adult he sensed and some children.

The aps! He knew instinctively.

"Guards!" he screamed. "Guards, somebody is taking the children! Guards!"

Two guards burst in. The apprentice behind the door was sent flying.

"Empsar? What is it?" The first guard looked around the room.

"Guards. Someone is taking the children away from school. Stop them!"

The guards ran out shouting for their colleagues.

"I sensed it!." He looked around the Elders feeling so alone. No one to trust.

Empsar Con Stivus stood up. His chair went over. Bosa stepped back out of his way. With his robes billowing, he strode out of the chambers with his assistant following in his wake.

By the time he reached the school, the place was deserted.

Fear curdled in his stomach. "Have I been too slow to save them Bosa?" he whined.

"Empsar, that way!" Bosa pointed.

Children's screams could be heard coming from the harbour area.

Empsar Con Stivus ran. He ran with fear flooding his veins with adrenaline. Heart pounding. His breath rasped. He was out of shape. He knew it. Bosa easily kept pace at his shoulder.

Two guards had pinned a man on the ground. Four others surrounded the screaming children.

"I am a teacher," the man protested.

The children shrieked not knowing what was happening.

Empsar Con Stivus could barely think.

"Let him up."

A wizened old man got to his feet, half lifted by the guards and half supported by his own two legs.

"Your name?" the empsar demanded.

"Teacher Pos, Empsar."

"Bow to the empsar," a soldier hissed.

"Apologies, Empsar." Pos awkwardly bent attempting a bow. "Since having a turn the last moon I have great difficulty moving."

Empsar saw the left side of the man. All his facial muscles were relaxed. The effect was disturbing. A lopsided face with a drooping arm and twitching leg.

"Teacher. Where are you taking these children?"

"Empsar... don't you know?"

"Know what?" he shouted angrily.

"Disaster is upon us. I am taking these children to safety. He waved to the six children now cowering behind the soldiers.

"Disaster? What disaster?"

"Master Hort told me. Don't you know?"

"He told you what?"

"Disaster is upon us. Flee! Run! He told me to get to safety." Pos smacked his left side with his good arm. "I could not take all the children!" He was crying. "My own body is not good enough to save my children!"

Empsar Con Stivus looked at the children. There were only six of them.

"Where are the others?"

"Master Teacher Hort has them following Librarian Voret." Pos sobbed. "I am too slow to leave by land!"

Empsar Con Stivus turned in consternation. "Bosa! Why do I know that name – Voret?" He wracked his brain.

"Voret… Givas Voret. Is that the librarian under the vow of silence? The one tasked with assisting the master of selection?"

Twelve other Elders arrived from the chambers all shouting and asking questions.

The empsar held his hands up. They quietened miraculously.

"It seems Librarian Voret the man of the myth has taken children out of the city," he shouted.

They all began questioning again.

"Silence!" Hands held aloft. "Guards, lead me to the master of selection's house."

The soldiers unceremoniously dropped the teacher to the ground. They marched off down the alleyway with Empsar Con Stivus following. He in turn was trailed by a group of chattering Elders, closely followed by a handful of assistants.

Bosa helped the teacher up off the ground.

"Teacher, is this all the children that are remaining?"

"Yes… all that's left of my class," he moaned.

"Come let us get a boat."

Teacher Pos looked at the assistant in disbelief.

"What?"

"I sense we need to escape and save the last few children, don't you?" Bosa smiled.

One more look at the assistant. "Children to me. Let us go on an adventure in a boat."

They yelled in delight.

The door swung open easily, creaking ominously. The empsar walked in alone. The smell of burning made him cautious. Walking into the kitchen he found the source of the smell. A pot was smoking untended over a cooking fire. The contents were blackened and sizzling.

"Gone," he whispered. Slowly he turned. With the adrenaline gone his limbs were weary and heavy. He wearily walked through the other rooms. Clean plates were strewn across the table and a couple of chairs were overturned.

He found the group of Elders and assistants peering in as he got to the doorway.

"They have all gone… in a hurry, it seems. The family did not eat their meal before leaving." He bowed his head in failure.

Empsar Con Stivus had lost the aps children, the master of selection and family, and his own family.

Walking back to the chambers they saw no one. Quietness.

"What do you sense, Bosa?" Empsar Con Stivus asked.

He looked around. "Bosa?" Eyes widening he looked at the group following him and felt tendrils of fear grip him.

"Bosa?" he whispered.

"Empsar?"

He looked up seeing Con Ro Pars a pace away.

"Yes?"

"I sense an ominous power. It is unsettling."

"Yes, I feel it too," added another.

"What can it be?"

"The lake?"

"Yes, remember Ex-Con Dwig?"

"Where is he now?"

"Let us hear his report."

"Guards," Empsar Con Stivs shouted.

"Empsar?" They appeared at his side.

"Find Ex-Con Dwig. He is probably at the lake. Bring him back to the chambers to present his report."

"The lake?" They exchanged worried glances.

"Yes, the lake! Carry him back if you have to! It's urgent."

They ran off in the direction of the southern path.

"Empsar, I feel we should evacuate the city."

"Evacuate? Why?"

"The lake. I sense a terrible event is about to happen."

Empsar Con Stivus saw his colleagues were frayed at the edges. He felt their collective fear. Some were on the verge of panicking,

"We must wait for the report of Ex-Con Dwig," he told them firmly.

"But…"

Empsar Con Stivus saw the conflict within Con Ro Pars: duty and personal safety.

"If…" he began slowly, "any of you have a greater desire to leave than to do your duty as Elder of Atlantis you may go."

Several faces looked relieved.

He turned and walked into the chambers not daring to see if any stayed with him.

Closing his eyes, he sat down in his chair attempting to settle himself.

He heard chair legs scraping on the floor.

I am not alone, he realised with relief.

The walls began shaking. The ground trembled. Screams outside. A beam fell onto the table. Dust billowed everywhere.

"Empsar," Con Pras shouted. "We must leave! Now!"

"Con Pras?" the empsar got up shocked.

"Empsar, now!"

Empsar Con Stivus felt his arm being pulled and he went willingly. Loud rumblings continued.

Con Pras and Con Fras stood at the entrance. Empsar Con Stivus looked at them confused.

"I thought you two would be the first to go," he said softly.

"Why?"

"I thought you were wanting to join the Terzondals."

"No… never!" Con Pras was dismayed.

"We sent a peace envoy, Empsar, as is our duty." Con Fras told him.

Two soldiers returned gasping for air. They carried a body. The nearest one handed him a gnarled wooden walking stick. He knew it was Dwig before seeing the old man's white face.

"We found the body on this side of the path to the lake."

"No report then, Empsar," Con Pras said bleakly.

"Evacuate the city," he said grimly. "Let us hope I am not too late," Empsar Con Stivus whispered.

As if the lake had heard him silence descended.

The city's inhabitants appeared at their doorways. People screamed adding to the confusion. People streamed out into the streets carrying their most valuable possessions.

"Soldier," Empsar Con Stivus commanded. "South sector to the south harbour. Get everyone out on anything at all that floats."

Con Pras and Con Fras were the only remaining Elders that followed the empsar. He seemed in no hurry to get to the harbour himself. He was mesmerised. He watched Atlanteans run past him, some with overflowing canvas sacks and some with babes in arms.

Warm rain began falling. Looking up he was amazed to see a vast cloud billowing from the volcano.

His two colleagues had had enough. Grabbing an arm each they marched him as fast as possible towards safety.

46

Givas looked back and saw the steam obliterating any view of the crater. Then there was the trembling earth. Goras had also looked back. Givas shook his head and put a finger to his lips. The children had not seen the communication between the adults. Most of them were dozing under canopies that Goras had set up. The four children hadn't minded moving from their lonely seats on the horses to the platforms.

He just hoped that Con Grote had gotten his family in time to escape the city. Givas closed his mind to any thoughts of Ukre's fate other than safety. He schooled himself to close his heart to the suffering and anguish spewing from the city.

Givas sensed the eruption before it happened. The enormous force pushed through from below what was once a freshwater lake. He remained determined. He was completely focused on the Hills of Terzondal and was ignoring the devastation occurring behind him. That was the past.

When they met the sentries at the far gate the soldiers were full of questions.

"Master Librarian, what is happening?" A young soldier recognised the robes.

"The ground has poured forth fire from within the lake."

He saw the soldier pale.

"People are fleeing Atlantis by foot, horse or by the sea."

"Did you happen to see my parents? The family name of Ercu."

"We did not have a chance to speak with anyone. Which area of the city do they live in?"

"Near the harbour. South harbour."

"They would have been well placed to leave by the sea then."
An older soldier looked at Givas with piercing eyes.

"Givas?"

"Toc Strevs?"

The veteran soldier who had escorted him into the hills gave him a bear hug.

"It is good to see you."

"It is good to be seen," Givas said. He was delighted at seeing the veteran soldier again.

"No longer a junior librarian I see." Strevs eyed his white robes and the natural authority Givas now held.

"We have come from the city." He motioned to the heads peeping out from the edges of the canvas. They disappeared with giggles. "To them, it is an adventure still." Givas smiled.

"There may be stragglers, others who have left the city by this route. Can you send them on to us to the place in the hills?"

"You are leaving the city?"

"I fear the city will be no longer. Mighty forces have burst forth to shower it with fire." Givas remembered his vision all too vividly.

"Toc Stu…" Strevs was momentarily downcast. His determination returned with a tightening of his mouth. "We will hold our position for two more days, then we must check for survivors and see what is left of our city."

"Good!"

"But you will have an escort of a hundred men for your safety."

"One hundred? Have you enough?"

"Since the transfer of two hundred from the harbour workings, we have more than enough." He turned and shouted.

"Toc Strevs, take Abeb garrison out of training. They are now on permanent duty for the protection and escort of this group." Toc Hootas breathed deeply.

"I look forward to seeing you before the next full moon." Givas bowed his head formally.

"I bid you a safe journey, Junior Empsar." The words hung in the air.

Toc Strevs bowed low and stepped backwards. He turned and left Givas in bewilderment.

"Goras, how are our provisions?" he called refocusing on his task.

"Junior Empsar, we have enough for our journey into the hills after we refill our water bladders." Goras grinned before giving a mocking bow.

"Junior Empsar?" Givas rolled it around his mouth as if tasting the title as a fine wine. He rubbed his chin thoughtfully. *May need to shave my whiskers now.*

Not only did they manage to refill the water bladders, but they also managed to get some extra provisions. They found dried and salted meats. Not that the children would eat them, but it would serve for Goras and Givas. Or junior empsar indeed! Givas thought wryly.

Givas saw the mixture of men who made up their sentry. Although he had no experience, bar his time with Toc Strevs and Stu, he sensed the eagerness of the men. They seemed keen to be doing something other than practising.

Two faces in the group caught his eye.

Toas and Sude

He breathed in deeply, not allowing himself to think of the possible death of Ukre.

"Givas?" Sude shouted moving towards the front of the group.

"Sude."

"What is happening?"

Givas looked at Sude, Toas and the others. One hundred soldiers in all.

"We are the first ones to leave Atlantis," he shouted. He held up his hands to stop the barrage of questions.

"Others are leaving the city by this route and by the sea." Givas paused, letting that sink in. "Our duty for our family, for our loved ones and for the children is to persevere." He pointed at the clouds that could be seen enshrouding the city. The black billowing clouds were hiding the fire. They prevented anyone from seeing what must be horrifying devastation below.

"We must now protect the aps." They stared at him goggle-eyed.

"For our loved ones, for our families, for ATLANTIS!" he roared.

Goras shouted, "FOR ATLANTIS!"

A hundred men and boys shouted, "For ATLANTIS!"

47

The pressures deep beneath the lake had been building and building. As with any pressure, it sought a weak point. Finally finding one, the lava was forced up into the lake. It evaporated the water into scalding steam instantly.

The pressure was not satisfied and continued its jettison.

Lava shot up through the fissure, filling the crater with molten rock. As if it knew, it found the three channels that had been dug by men. The lava followed the escaping water out along the aqueduct system. Unchecked, it poured over the stonework of the unsuspecting buildings and streets below. Anything wooden burned. The burning wood sent flames leaping high, which in turn exacerbated the effects of the lava.

Some buildings provided enough of a barrier to divert the flow elsewhere. But the lava kept moving, engulfing anything it could in its path.

The elderly and infirm were swept up by the river of death, burning to cinders.

The force of the pressure cracked open the fissure sending tremors out a great distance. The lava quickly filled the crater and spilt over the ridges, burning anything in its way. Smothering stone buildings, it devoured the city until finally reaching the flat ground. It slowed to a stop at the harbour's edge, turning the sea angry, hissing into the air.

Con Grote sat atop the bundled fishing net, feeling the sea breeze on his face. Breathing in the fresh sea air he felt excitement at the freedom bestowed upon him so late in life.

His family were subdued at his feet in the bows of the boat, Atrum, cuddling Petr protecting him from seeing any horrors besetting the city.

"What about Givas? What about Toas and Sude?" she asked.

"Toas and Sude will be safe," her father told her. "Remember they are on garrison training up at the far gates."

"Givas?" Ukre whispered tears at the corners of her eyes.

"Feel the connection, child," Con Grote told her.

"But, Great-Grandpa, I don't know how."

"Remember what I taught you. Picture him in your mind's eye," he said simply.

She closed her eyes obediently.

"Breathe into your stomach, child."

Ukre's chest rose and then her stomach inflated.

"Feel the connection. Remember his eyes, his nose, and his mouth. Feel his energy."

"Oh!" Ukre opened her eyes. She was smiling.

"He's alive, isn't he?"

"Oh, Great-Grandpa, I managed it! He is alive. He may be with Toas and Sude too!"

Con Grote relaxed. *The boy has done well getting the new intake that distance.*

"Con Grote?" Con Ro Pars interrupted his thoughts.

"Yes?"

"I am Con Ro Pars."

"I sense you are upset. What is it, child?"

"The empsar, the other Elders, I fear for their safety."

"Mmm."

"Do you sense them?" Con Ro Pars grasped his hand. "You have the strongest awareness of everyone here. Please tell me."

"I sense many people. But no… not them." Con Grote held her hand feeling the depths of her sadness.

"Who is with you?"

"My husband Devas and Gamute Voret."

"Inform Gamute Voret he should be proud of his son this day. For it is he who has saved the aps."

Forgetting he was blind she nodded and moved to the front of the boat through the crowded deck. All the time the boat rose and fell on the peaks and troughs of the growing waves.

"Ukre."

"Yes, Great-Grandpa?"

"How many boats can you see?"

Ukre looked back towards the harbour. "I... I cannot make them out... there are many sails."

"Petr."

"Yes, Grandpapa?" The young boy struggled out of his mother's grasp.

"Stand up here." Con Grote patted the netting beside him.

"It smells."

"Yes, what does it smell of?"

"Fish."

"Good boy. Now get up here and count the boats."

"Be careful, Petr," Atrum warned seeing him clamber up the rough ropes of the fishing nets. He put an arm around his grandpapa's neck and she relaxed.

"Now how many boats do you see?"

"One... two... three... four... six... nine... seven."

Ukre and Con Grote smiled. Con Grote raised a finger for every count the boy called out.

"Seven boats! Any rafts?"

"What is a raff, Grandpapa?"

"It is like a boat but it has no sail."

Petr squinted.

"One... two." He beamed at his grandpapa. "There are two rafts."

"Seven boats and two rafts. I hope there are more from the eastern and western harbours."

Sensing the remains of the city, he knew the devastation was complete. Thousands of summers of Atlantis life were destroyed in one day.

He could sense everyone's attention on the black clouds enshrouding what was once Atlantis. There was a sombre silence on the boat only broken by the slapping of the waves on the bow.

48

Empsar Con Stivus stumbled and fell. Cons Pras and Fras stopped to lift him back up. He gasped as a bolt of lightning shot up from his ankle.

"A walking stick?" he gasped.

Con Pras shot into the nearest house coming out a moment later shaking his head. He sprinted down into the market. Empsar Con Stivus saw him scratch his head, and then rip a piece of wood off of the nearest stall.

Empsar Con Stivus spent precious seconds getting to his feet. He propped himself up with the wooden plank under his arm. The pain was still there. He saw the looks on the faces of the only Elders who stayed with him, the same Elders he had believed to be traitors.

"Go," he told them.

"But..." Con Pras tried.

"Leave me and save yourselves." He pointed south. "The southern harbour is the farthest point from the mountain."

"May the old gods protect you," Con Fras said, kissing him on the cheek.

Empsar Con Stivus laughed. Con Pras and Fras ran southwards leaving him alone. He hobbled into the nearest building.

The Museum of the Old Gods.

"Anyone here?" he shouted, not expecting an answer.

Dust swirled in the air behind him as he moved between the old statues. Their benign countenances made him feel surprisingly calm. "Just you and I left in this wonderful place," he told them. Bumping into a table, he looked down, saw the rough blanket, and knew what was under it.

He pulled it back with one hand and looked at the mottled rock. He ran a fingertip over the etched letters closing his eyes as he did so.

"Who is the person of the myth?"

The image of his dead wife and stillborn child flashed into his mind.

"No," he wailed, falling to the floor.

A tremor shook the very earth itself showering Stivs with dust.

"It can't be me!"

The statues swayed with the movement. One crashed into another, setting off a chain reaction. The last one tipped over.

Stivs saw it coming. He rolled over to one side. Pain zipped through all his nerves as his ankle moved. Blackness came and he gratefully passed out. The statue's head landed squarely on the table smashing the tablet to pieces. The table broke in half. A cloud of dust burst into the air, settling moments later in the quiet aftermath. A dust blanket covered the prone form of the last Empsar of Atlantis.

Stivs came round. He could smell fire. Blinking back dust and grime he saw a red and orange snake creep through the doorway. Its slow stealth was ominous as it slithered into the museum. Stivus scrambled up onto the fallen statue, ignoring the pain this time with a surge of adrenaline. A wooden post was swallowed by the hungry snake, bursting into flames within seconds.

He crawled up a statue that was on top of his. Seeking a higher vantage point, he took his time so he would not touch anything with his injured foot.

The lava covered the museum floor. Silence, except for the cracking stones shattering with heat. The table that had supported the tablet was consumed by the intense heat.

Stivs trembled on top of the highest statue. Perspiration beaded his brow and his tunic was sticking to his back.

Closing his eyes he accepted his fate. Breathing deeply, he felt the warm air fill his chest and let his consciousness soar out of his body. Floating far beyond anywhere he had previously visited, he felt the tranquillity and wonder of being truly connected. The darkness lit up with stars. Some part of his mind realised he was in the heavens.

49

"Petr, come down from there," Atrum shouted. The boy moved quickly pulling his grandpapa down off the nets too.

The waves had increased wood creaking as the boat rode the waves. A large roller pounded the bow, spraying the occupants. The wind whipped the sails, snapping them back and forth on the single mast.

"Everybody hold on," the fisherman yelled.

Ukre, Atrum, Petr and Con Grote huddled at the back. Everyone slid back and forth on the deck as the waves lifted the boat, crashing it back down into the troughs.

"From the cooking pot into the fire," whispered Atrum.

"Give me a hand girl." The fisherman was struggling with the ropes.

Ukre jumped up, helping untie the sails. A wind grabbed the sail snapping it fully.

The sailor screamed as the rope sliced off one of his fingers. The sail, no longer held in place, floated off with the wind, disappearing over the crest of a wave behind them.

"Take the tiller." He held his hand above his head.

Atrum pulled the man down amongst them. He wrapped a cloth tightly around the injured hand, stemming the flow of blood.

"Thank you."

"Shhhh." She reassured him, talking to him as she would gentle her son.

"It'll be alright. Shhhh… you will see… just relax there." Smoothing the man's hair, she realised he was no older than Toas.

"Ah, Frig." She looked at her husband. "He is only a boy!" Her features softened with her mothering instinct. Petr came to her side watching the sailor. Soon the young sailor's eyes were lowering. The adrenaline and tension drained out of him, leaving only the exhaustion.

Atrum looked up at her daughter, still steering the boat. She smiled at her. Her daughter was so good in a crisis.

"But where are we sailing?"

Gamute Voret looked out into the greyness where the skyline touched

209

the sea. It had taken no time for the squall to disorient them. The storm had reduced any chance of seeing land.

"Is the sailor awake?" he called to the back of the boat.

The woman checked and shook her head.

Sitting in the aft of the boat he had been soaked by the waves breaking over the boat spraying them all.

Gamute knew little of seafaring and even less about what was out there. For all he knew there were monsters in the deep. They could be angry having been woken up by the storm and hungry for his flesh.

He had been put at ease by Devas' wife telling him his son was safe and proud that Givas had saved many of the aps. He hated to think what he would have felt if Givas had not escaped in time.

If I can survive this, then I can rebuild the relationship with my son, he thought.

Another large wave broke over the boat sweeping them all back into the bows. Squeals from the youngsters and groans came from the older generation. Any talk was interrupted by the chattering of teeth.

"We are not done yet," he roared. He grabbed a bucket and scooped out the water that was pouring in. Other passengers followed his lead using their bare hands.

A clap of thunder sounded. It deafened them all. A flash of light blinded them.

They continued struggling to throw the water out of the boat. Everybody apart from the youngest was doing their bit. Ukre continued steering the boat. She steered but to where?

The fisherman came to and was disorientated. He searched the greyness for any indication of land.

The greyness turned into darkness as their efforts slowed. As the darkness set in they were all exhausted. They huddled together in small groups and shared space in exchange for body heat. For those who were the most exhausted sleep took them despite the water's constant pounding against the wood.

Dawn brought more grey light. Gamute sensed something was different. His mind was still shaken from the previous day's ordeal. He stepped to the front of the boat and realised something was missing. There were no waves.

"We are not moving," he croaked.

Some people began stirring whilst others just opened their eyes.

He looked down into the waters. A grey mist lay above the sea. Too thick to see far. Bending over to the water's surface he peered down into the depths and saw something green. There were slime-covered rocks.

"Rocks! I see rocks," he choked. "We must be near land!"

Devas appeared beside him with bleary eyes.

"What?"

Gamute laughed. "Land," he shouted.

Gamute climbed over the edge despite the cold. Devas threw him the bowline.

"If you are going into the water use that, will you?"

Gamute flashed a weary smile. "Certainly."

The other passengers pressed behind Devas and watched. Gamute lowered himself into the water. Sinking sideways he went completely under before coming back up gasping and spluttering.

Standing up he found the water was only waist deep.

Using the depth as a guide he ventured in one direction and then another until he found the depth decreasing.

Gamute stepped gingerly forward. Using small steps, he went slow and steady until he found the shallows.

"It is shallow here!"

A splash and a tug on the rope followed.

"What?"

"Where are you? Ahh… there you are." Devas followed the rope to him.

Together they found land at the very extremity of the rope's length.

"We've found land!" they yelled. "Follow the rope."

One by one, they splashed into the water, helping each other when needed until all twenty-three of them were lined up on the rocky beach.

Con Grote grasped Gamute's hand. "There are other people nearby," Con Grote whispered. "They don't know of our arrival yet."

Gamute looked at Devas who looked back at him.

"Where is the fisherman?" he whispered forcefully.

The fisherman was pushed forward. He was shivering and worse for wear.

The shock of losing a finger was replaced by the pain in the damaged nerves.

"What is your name?"

"Potr."

"Do you know anything about this land, Potr?" Devas asked him.

"I don't know. We could be anywhere."

"Think! If we had gone straight for most of the time from your original heading, where might we be?"

"Well, there is land south-east of Atlantis. But I have never been there."

"Do you know if it has a similar rocky shore to this one?" Gamute pressed.

"It could be. It is difficult to say for certain."

"What do you know of it?"

"There are savages there... man-eating savages, I heard. They are likely to eat each other when hungry I was told once."

"What do you think, Master of Selection?"

"I sense them. They are peaceful enough. But they have yet to see us."

"Are there many? Can we get past them to shelter?"

"We can try," Con Grote suggested.

Con Grote the blind ex-master of selection led the fully sighted group into the mist. They had all linked hands so as not to become separated.

"It is beginning to clear," someone whispered.

"Hush!"

The sun could be seen as a yellow blur above. Images of huts could be glimpsed through the lightening greyness.

"We'd better stop here," Con Grote said quietly. "Gather round."

The mist evaporated quickly. It was then that they realised their predicament.

The Atlanteans were stood on a rock slab with a large black soot mark in the centre.

"We are standing where they make a fire," Devas hissed angrily.

Surrounding them were dozens of straw huts. Con Grote must have led them directly to the centre of the village.

A savage could be seen. He stopped and looked at them, puzzled at the sudden appearance of strangers.

He let out a howl and stomped the ground with alternating feet. Soon he was joined by what appeared to be the whole tribe. They were all howling and stamping their bare feet on the ground.

They ringed the strangers in their howling and stamping ritual.

As if on cue, and without any discernible signal they all stopped. The tallest savage stepped forwards. His hair was a bushy mane, his clothes tatters of leather and leaves. Animal bones were protruding through either side of his nostrils. The man had numerous black markings across his tanned bare chest and arms.

The man raised a stick, pointed at the strangers, and yelled unintelligibly.

The group of Atlanteans were dumbstruck. Everyone was immobile except Con Grote. He walked towards the leader of the savages and pushed back his hood. The man saw the shimmering silver hair and blue-white eyes. He shrieked in horror and threw himself down on the ground, pressing his face into the earth.

Within moments all the villagers followed suit and were face down ringing the Atlanteans.

Con Grote walked to the village leader and said something that the rest of the Atlanteans did not understand.

The village leader looked up fearfully and saw Con Grote smiling at him. Con Grote tapped both shoulders of the village leader with his walking stick.

To everyone else's relief, the village leader got up and danced round in front of the ring of prostrate villagers. All the while he was chanting, gurgling and laughing in a language that only the villagers knew, except for Master of Selection Con Grote.

50

Givas looked at the soldiers. They were fresh-faced and the whites of their eyes shone, showing good health.

That is one thing I didn't have to worry about, Givas thought.

They were in their defensive tunics, thick coarse shirts covered by ceramic tiles that glinted in the sun. Toc Strevs was wearing a tunic that was covered in bright green tiles signifying his leadership and seniority. Toc Hootas, his deputy, was the leader of the security forces. His tunic was covered in pale blue tiles. On their heads was the Atlantis helmet, a carved wooden dome with a finger of wood running down from the forehead to the tip of the nose.

Givas doubted its ability to protect the face, but he realised they were not expecting trouble. Despite the destruction of their city, they were still at peace with the Terzadons.

Givas dusted down his robe. He used his fingers to comb his hair away from his face. *A junior empsar must look good.* He smiled to himself.

"What are you grinning at?" Goras gruffed.

"Myself."

"Mmmph. We have been ready but what about our protection?"

"They will soon be ready, Master Stabler." Givas grinned. "Have you seen the oxen that are transporting their possessions?"

Goras's eyes lit up and he went off in search of the fabulous work beasts.

"What are you doing, Empsar?" an angelic-faced girl asked as she peeked out from her shaded seat.

"I am relaxing my eyelids."

"Oh, Jac, Putr and Stuc are doing that too," she said with boredom.

Givas opened one eye. "What is your name?"

"Pata."

"Pata, are you not tired in this heat?"

"No, are you?"

"No, but I may be tonight."

"Why sleep now and not tonight?"

"To look after you, Ja, Putr, Stuc and the others tonight."

"Will you be looking after the soders too?"

Givas smiled at her pronunciation. "No Pata. The soldiers will be looking after us from this point on."

Goras came back smiling.

"Givas... I mean, Empsar. Those beasts are wonderful. They may not be as fast as my beauties." He patted Hennie's nose as she searched his hands for a tasty treat. "But the amount of heavy equipment they can pull is impressive."

"Do they have the same contraptions that you have?" Givas motioned towards the two platforms.

"No I used the oxen panniers."

Toc Hootas arrived.

"Junior Empsar, we are ready." He inclined his head.

"Let us move then into the future."

Toc Strevs touched his chest in salute as Givas passed through the tall outer gates of Atlantis. Givas nodded back with a tear in his eyes.

The column moved through and out into the grassy lowlands that preceded the Hills of Terzadon.

The soldiers formed up to flank the children with Givas and Goras leading the way.

"We could have waited until morning," Goras offered.

"We could have. But this way we will start our new lives sooner."

"Our new lives," Goras repeated tiredly. "Starting again at my age."

"I understand, Goras, my dear friend. Would you enjoy looking after the oxen and the horses when we get there?"

"Now you are talking, Empsar." Goras smiled and chivvied the horses to go faster.

"Hold on," a soldier called out, gesticulating behind them.

"What now?" Goras grumbled.

Givas walked down the length of the soldiers with Toc Hootas right beside him.

The older class of aps had just arrived. Master Teacher Hort was talking to Toc Strevs. He had been pointing through the gate.

"Master Teacher." Givas walked across to him smiling.

"Givas. It was horrible. Atlantis has been destroyed."

"How many children did you bring?"

"Fourteen. Pos took the other six. He took them to the harbour."

Givas closed his eyes and expanded his attention, searching for the energies of the children.

"They are far away," Givas murmured. "They are alive."

"Thank the old gods." Hort realised he'd misspoken. "Sorry, Librarian."

"Junior Empsar," Toc Hootas butted in.

"Oh. I am sorry, Junior Empsar," Hort stammered.

"Master Teacher Hort. Meet Toc Hootas. He is the leader of our security.

The two old men nodded to each other sizing each other up in the process.

"How are the children?"

"They are in shock. I could not stop them from seeing the black clouds over the city. We were lucky to get out alive." Hort looked at Givas. "Thank you, Junior Empsar. If it wasn't for you we wouldn't have escaped."

"Do you think they are ready to go on?" Givas pressed him.

"They need to move forward so that they are not thinking too much about the past."

Givas nodded.

"If they are tired, can they go on the animals?" Givas asked Toc Hootas.

"We may be able to fit three or four of them on each of the oxen." Toc Hootas smiled. "The soldiers will have fun looking after them."

Toc Hootas was right. And so was Hort.

The children were excited at having a seat on the back of an animal. Their minds were taken off the smoke-covered city they had left behind.

"I will stay with them," Hort offered.

Toc Hootas handed him a water bladder.

Hort looked into the soldier's eyes. "Thank you."

With a nod, Toc Hootas and Givas left him as they walked to the front of the procession. At the head of the now larger contingent, they moved off towards the hills.

Givas called a halt to the entourage. He was about to prepare a fire in the dusk's light when Toc Hootas called a handful of soldiers to do it in half the time.

With Goras checking all the animals were tethered and watered, Hort looked after the children. He ensured all of them had some food before curling up in one tight mass of children in front of the fire.

Givas sat cross-legged facing the sunset in a meditative pose.

For once he could not mentally settle straight away. He took extra time to allow fearful thoughts and worries to lift. Once his mind stilled, he spread his awareness out into the hills and reconnected with Dels. Her energy pulsed with surprise and pleasure. Having made their presence known to her, Givas expanded his awareness out over the ruined city and the sea.

A fierce storm brought up feelings of fear and anxiety in one direction, whilst another was sadness and depression. The third direction his attention went was the strongest. He sensed Master of Selection Con Grote.

Pleased that he'd located a friend, he brought himself back to the fireplace and the warmth.

Blinking, he said, "What do we do, Master Teacher?"

"Start again," Hort told him steadfastly.

Givas looked at him before exhaling audibly and nodded slowly.

"Catch, Junior Empsar!" Goras threw him a thick horse blanket which reminded Givas of Hennie.

"Thanks, Master Stabler." Givas smiled back at his friend.

Staring into the fire he watched the flashes of blue and green amid the lurid orange and warming reds.

The smoke reminded him of the shepherd and Dels. Wiggling his toes, he felt the comforting warmth and weight of the horse blanket.

The sky draped clouds over the treasure of the skies, leaving only a few glittering diamonds to catch the eye.

Givas settled back, his head in the crook of his arm. Snores from Goras only added to the feeling of security.

Guilt sprang from nowhere and overpowered any conscious

thought. He was childlike in its grip.

"Why didn't I die?" he whispered to the sky. "Why am I always running from death and destruction?"

Tears trickled down his face. Givas was barely aware of the cold wet streaks that were all the more pronounced on his cheek nearest the fire. With no emotional defences remaining, he could only experience the sensations unconditionally.

Birdsong woke Givas from his slumber. The glowing remains of the fire winked at him from amongst the whites and tired greys of ash and embers.

Breathing deeply, he enjoyed the acrid taste of smoke hitting the back of his throat. The stillness of the camp gave rise to his feeling of excitement at the newness of it all.

Atlantis would never be forgotten. But a new direction was being offered. It was an opportunity to expand further. From a society shut off that hoarded its knowledge and experiences, they had a whole new world at their feet.

Givas sat up smiling. The emotions of the previous night were completely forgotten.

"Junior Empsar." Toc Hootas broke into his reverie.

"Yes?"

"How far are we going into these hills?"

"See that peak there?" Givas pointed it out. "Beyond that is a valley between three hills that is fed by two streams. It has plenty of green grass for grazing for all the animals and more."

"Is that ground good for growing?" Toc Hootas' eyes lit up with interest.

"The soil is good enough for the mass of wild berries it has. So for farming, it should be ideal. Why do you ask?"

"My father was a farmer. He taught me always to have seeds and grain for planting just in case." He showed Givas a bulging bag that had been tied around one shoulder.

"I am pleased for you," Givas said glancing at the size of their encampment. "You may have plenty of requests for your meal and flour."

"I have been thinking about that too," he said smiling. "Then it came to me last night. The north slopes of the spine may not have been touched by the fires."

"In our security force are there any farm labourers?"

"I am sure many of them will know the ways of the crops." Toc Hootas grinned.

"When we settle in the valley with two streams a group of knowledgeable workers should go out to harvest what remains."

"It would be my honour to lead the venture if it pleases you, Junior Empsar."

"Your idea has merit and once we arrive you will make the arrangements," Givas told him with a nod and a smile. "But for now, ensure our entourage has a hearty breakfast."

Toc Hootas bowed again before rousing his new lieutenants.

Goras yawned loudly. "Junior Empsar, when did you become so wise in dealing with men older than you?"

"Master Stabler, is it wise or common sense? Either way, if it pleases someone to carry out their ideas, then it must be better to encourage the best results for the completion of that idea surely?"

Goras nodded.

"How are your animals, Goras?"

"Oh, Givas... they are magnificent. I thought the horses were wonderful. But these beasts have such strength and fortitude. It will be my pleasure tending to them and learning more about them when we arrive at our destination."

"Hopefully by this very evening." Givas again saw the size of their group. "Then again probably late tomorrow evening."

The party moved slowly and steadfastly nearer their objective. The peaks of the hills appeared no closer throughout the day with the slow pace of the oxen.

The children were given more freedom, and, as the air was cooler they ran about, laughing and screaming as they hid and chased each other amongst the soldier's legs.

The soldiers took it all in good spirit. One or two of the soldiers joined in before quickly tiring with the weight of the packs on their backs.

Givas was pleased that despite what Atlantis had experienced, everyone seemed in good humour. Many of them were full of excitement at the prospect of a new beginning.

As the sun rose in the sky, conversations became muted and sporadic and then stopped entirely. The sun was at its most fierce when at its highest point and it was then that nobody spoke.

The clink of harnesses and the swishing of horses' tails lulled the children into docility. They had all returned to safety under the canopies.

Walking dreamlike alongside the horses, Givas gave Goras a wan smile. They trudged along feeling the sun directly above their heads. The air was an invisible force keeping their objective ever distant.

Only Toc Hootas seemed unaffected as he went down the lines of men, forcing them to drink their water.

"Junior Empsar." Givas was given a water bladder.

Givas pointed at the children. "Aps first!" That was all he could say.

"Lead by example," Toc Hootas ordered.

Givas saw the determination in Toc Hootas' expression.

Relenting, Givas uncorked the water bladder and took a swig. He smacked his lips despite the tepid taste.

"Thanks, Toc."

Toc Hootas only nodded. Then he turned to Goras and Hort and ensured they drank some water too.

Despite the adults showing the way, some children still rejected the water. Constant cajoling in the heat only increased tempers and Givas noticed the growing concern of the soldiers.

"Do you know the song of the sun?" he asked Toc Hootas.

The soldier grinned and in full baritone began singing the marching song. His lieutenants followed suit. The new soldiers added their voices and soon everyone was either singing or humming along.

They reached the gentle slopes in good humour considering the dwindling water levels. As they moved up the slopes the air cooled and when Givas looked back towards Atlantis he could only see a heat haze masking the view.

He relaxed when walking and attempted to connect with Dels. A fleeting contact only added to his desire for haste.

"Toc Hootas," he called over.

"Empsar?"

"What say you, about splitting the group and moving on quicker?"

The soldier looked at the position of the sun, then the peaks of the hills that were getting closer.

"Empsar, I understand your desire to complete this journey quickly but keeping the group together benefits morale and attitude. Safety in numbers will secure both the children and livestock."

"Toc Hootas, your counsel is wise. We shall continue together, and I will accept this pace."

Goras shouted out. "Junior Empsar, are you finding our company boring?" He laughed.

Several heads poked out from under the canvas. They were interested in the exchange.

"Master Stabler, why would I ever want to be parted from your friendly banter?"

"So why do you want to hurry?"

"Mmmm, a good question indeed. There is no need for haste, surrounded by friends as we are."

The following morning the last of the dried meats were devoured before they finished the last leg of the journey.

The children did not need the canopied platforms, so ran about the column. They were ignorant of the adults and their tired states.

"Empsar… Empsar, there is an old lady over there!" The girl pointed out a dot on the horizon. "Is she who we are looking for?"

"Well done, Pata. You have the eyes of a sea eagle! That is Grandmamma Dels." Givas told the young girl. "She will want to know all your names."

Upon hearing this, the children raced off towards the barely discernible figure in the distance.

Toc Hootas sprinted over. "Empsar, they are not safe! We should bring them back."

"Toc Hootas." Givas smiled widely. "Can you feel it? Can you feel the safety?"

The soldier looked at the now distant children. He shook his head slowly as if getting rid of an ant in his ear.

"Empsar, it feels… it feels like we are… home." Toc Hootas was surprised. "Safe!"

Empsar Givas Postet grinned. "Enjoy the feeling before you go back for the grain." He winked at the soldier.

As the horses brought the children into the valley with Hort looking around for confirmation, Givas remembered Dels asking that question.

"How many children?"

She would probably not be surprised with his return so soon. But, she may raise an eyebrow at bringing twenty children.

The horses pulled up and Givas left Goras in charge of releasing them from their platforms. Givas strode purposefully up to the old woman of the hills and the children parted like a wave.

Kissing her on the forehead he grinned at her surprise.

"Mother Dels, may I introduce you to the last aps of Atlantis. We have come here to start a new life."

Dels did raise an eyebrow and waited patiently.

"I have changed somewhat since we last saw each other. I am now... Junior Empsar Givas Postet." He knelt on one knee with his head low in penitence.

"I see you, Empsar Givas Postet. Welcome home." Tears of joy were in her eyes.

Goras clasped Hort's shoulder. "He was schooled by you wasn't he?"

"Yes... although I think I may have learnt more from his openness and love than he learnt from me," Hort said honestly.

"Come now! I have a surprise." Goras lifted a bulging sack from the back of the second platform. It clinked loudly and Goras became even more careful in his handling of it.

The corked vine wine urns were peeking out when he loosened the drawstring.

Hort gasped. "You had this all the time?"

"It would have been a waste two nights ago. Even last night. This stuff is for celebrating!"

"What are we celebrating?"

"How about the future?"

Hort paused and looked around at the green valley with its two life-giving mountain streams. The soldiers had dispersed into outlying defensive positions which left the two friends alone.

Somehow the master teacher appeared younger. Goras eyed him sceptically. After the horror, the excitement, and the slow journey the master teacher seemed rejuvenated.

Hort looked at Goras and they both grinned. Goras was the first to laugh. Deep belly laughs rippled up his torso and burst out into the sky. Hort quickly followed suit.

Tears were rolling down their smiling faces even before they opened the first urn.

Givas looked across at Dels who was gently stroking the hair on Pata's head. The young girl lay by her side and the old woman was surrounded by sleeping children.

"Atlantis is no more, Mother," he said softly.

"Yes." That was all she said.

"I am a junior empsar now."

"Yes."

"What shall I do?"

"What needs to be done."

Givas knew not whether it was a question or a command.

"Yes… whatever needs to be done."

The junior empsar prodded the fire until sparks floated into the sky. Givas watched them soar into the night until all he could see were the coloured memory imprints on his vision.

"So much to do," he told himself grinning. "No rush is necessary."

Givas pulled the heavy horse blanket up to his chin. The familiar snoring of the master teacher had a soporific effect on him, the sound banishing all the feelings of loneliness he'd ever had.

Givas could now look forward to an enjoyable exciting future. A future in which he had some choice in the matter.

He closed his eyes deliberately allowing his body to relax into the present moment.

After all, he reasoned, it is a gift, isn't it?

51

S ua had huddled with the children, quietening them down during the evening. She saw Pos devastated by the destruction of the city and was concerned by the state of his mind.

"Teacher... tell us a story."

He glanced around the group barely registering them all.

"AT was the son of a shepherd. His father, grandpapa and great-grandpapa had been shepherds too. He was not interested in becoming a shepherd. At the age of fifteen summers, he had set off with all his belongings in a sack over his shoulder."

The children listened with their eyes wide and sitting up. They were already enthralled.

"AT walked through the hills and mountains eating cheese his mother had packed him. He also picked fruit wherever he found it growing. He drank water from the stream he followed.

"At night he heard animals howling but AT was not afraid. He sat close to his fire knowing the sounds came from animals scared of fire.

"But one night he heard different sounds. They were sounds of talking and whispering.

"So, curious, AT grabbed a branch from his fire and used it as a torch.

"He found a family cowering amongst the rocks. The father of the family was out hunting for food. The family were starving. The mother was looking after her baby, while the oldest daughter, almost as old as AT tried to make a fire."

"Was it a cold and wet night? She would have struggled then" one child asked.

Pos smiled at the child. "Of course. They were glad to see AT and even happier when he lit the fire with his torch. The father returned in the morning with two rabbits.

"Over roasted rabbits, the family told AT of land that was fertile enough to grow food. A land surrounded by seas full of fish.

AT looked at the girl who smiled and nodded at him."

"Did she like him?" a young girl asked.

"Yes, and he liked her," another boy stated.

"So AT went with the family to the land where food grows aplenty and the seas are full of fish."

"Then what happened?" asked another child.

"Well AT liked LAN very much so they married each other and many summers later they had a baby called TIS."

"Oh!" a young girl said.

"That's not your best story," a boy reasoned. "How did they catch the rabbits?"

"Where did AT, LAN and TIS live?" Pos asked.

"ATLANTIS!" The children shouted delightedly.

Sua saw many of the adults look around. Everyone's mood had lightened.

Quietness resumed with only the gentle lapping of the water on the boat disturbing the silence.

"Where are we going?" she asked the sailor.

"The nearest land that has a port."

"What is it called?"

"Corse."

"What is it like there?"

"Much like Atlantis, I think."

Sua hoped he was right and prayed that everyone had managed to escape the city in time before the river of fire.

"Will we ever see any of them again?" she asked Pos.

He shrugged his shoulders not wanting to voice his fears.

"Atlantis is no more. We shall never be back," the sailor told her mournfully.

"What will we do?" she whispered, downcast. "What can we do?"

Afterword

The Atlantis: Order of the Librarians is a work of fiction and was inspired by the story of the utopian society written about by Plato around 360 BC. All the characters in this book are fictitious. They have been created by the mind of Irwin Glenn. Any similarity to real persons, living or dead, is coincidental and not intended by the author.

In the writing of this story the author has taken the liberty to quote:

"The past is history,
the future is a mystery,
now is a gift
that is why it is called the present."

While there is a variation of this quotation by Bill Keane and it may appear in Winnie the Pooh by author A.A. Milne, the original quotation is attributed to American author and historian Alice Morse Earle (1851–1911) in Sun Dials And Roses of Yesterday. 1902.

Thank you for reading *Atlantis: Order of the Librarians*. I hope you liked it. If you have a moment, I would be grateful if you could leave a quick review online. Honest reviews are very much appreciated and are useful to other readers.

Another story based on Atlantis is coming soon!

Atlantis: Storm at Sea

Master Shipbuilder Marcu Foleh has built the first-ever two-masted ship for Atlantis. Only he knows every individual length of timber and only he knows what the ship can handle. Unfortunately, Marcu has never sailed a boat in his life.

With a skeleton crew, his oldest friend to sail the ship, and a Councillor of Atlantis and his assistant to witness the event they undertake the sea trials.

When the councillor insists on going farther than planned events take a turn for the worse.

Who will survive the ensuing chaos amidst humiliation, murder, revenge, and the fight for survival?

Other books in the Atlantis series are out now

Atlantis: The Council of Twelve

After the fall of Atlantis, survivors journey to the site of the rising sun.

With the city gone, can the Atlantis civilisation continue under the guidance of new leader Empsar Givas Voret?

The Atlanteans may have escaped from the rivers of fire but their journey has just begun.

The Council of Twelve is the second in the Atlantis-based trilogy featuring Givas Voret.

Atlantis: The New City

After fleeing Atlantis, the survivors have settled near a disease-ridden, fire-ravaged city – one that is already occupied.

Now, two distinct civilisations must learn to live together side by side.

Who will dominate and who will thrive?

What will happen when they discover that some Atlantean children have special powers?

The New City is the third in the thought-provoking trilogy featuring Givas Voret.

Visit www.irwinglenn.co.uk and sign up for the newsletter to hear about the release date of the next in the series.

Follow on Facebook
https://www.facebook.com/IrwinGlennauthor

Printed in Great Britain
by Amazon